Preface

I expect you will do it anyway but I beg you not to read this. If you choose to do so I absolve myself of any responsibility. I am not the author of this tale. The manuscript I found in a single "doctored" volume of a set of encyclopaedias bought in a Manchester antique shop. I won't name the shop; in fact I had to rename many of the names and places I encountered in the text, for, as I am sure you are beginning to glean, this is a true story. I knew Professor Peralis by repute. She was, I hope *is*, a remarkable lady. Her disappearance in 198- caused a minor sensation in certain esoteric circles.

You might ask why I took the trouble to have this published. I cannot answer you; except to say that I didn't sleep for a long while after reading it and the nights are lonely. If you choose unwisely to do so I suspect your nights may be as sleepless as mine.

If it were possible to share loneliness we would.

If you read this we could share nothing else.

*I slept with faith and found a corpse in my arms on awakening;
I drank and danced all night with doubt
and found her a virgin in the morning.*
Aleister Crowley

THE DEATH TABLEAU

Craig Herbertson

black horse books
February 2015

First Edition
published February 2015
by
black horse books

The Death Tableau
© Craig Herbertson
All rights reserved.

ISBN 978-1-326-18236-6

Contents

Chapter		Page
1	The Giant	9
2	Ka	24
3	The Bubble Gum Cards	37
4	It Begins	55
5	The Theosophist	77
6	North	88
7	Book Dealing	102
8	Words	116
9	The Garden	137
10	The Body	148
11	Killing	156
12	Kennedy	164
13	Snow	172
14	Ghosts	177
15	The Indian Spell	184
16	Old Friends	192
17	The Maze	199
18	The Karmic Wheel	205
19	Lifted	211
20	The Black Room	219
21	Butterflies	231
22	The Fairy Tale	241
23	The End Of All Tales	249
24	Footfalls	257
25	Stairway	262
26	The Final Conflict	270
27	The Bubble Gum Card	278

Chapter 1
The Giant

THE WITLESS GIANT sat in the waiting room of my office while Kennedy and I peered at him through the two-way mirror.

Looking at his vacant face, I had no idea that this empty being would not only change my perception of life, but would change my perception of realms of reality beyond life. If I *had* known, I would have run without looking back. In happy ignorance I watched, pondering whether he was a fake or part of an elaborate joke. As I did a small spider raced over the blank of his brow unremarked. An actor might have betrayed some tiny sense that the spider was there; the giant remained in a state of apparent catatonia.

"He's not a tramp," said Kennedy. I peered again at his cheap grey suit. It was shabby and ill fitting; indubitably chosen by someone else. So it was with the rest of his clothes; a grubby nylon shirt barely concealed the contours of his immense torso. Huge feet sported plastic shoes, crammed on to large sockless feet. His neck was bare, perhaps because the institutions he frequented might be wary of attempted suicide. On his head, a battered trilby shielded his upper face. Under the shadow of its rim a faint smile lingered on his lips.

There the giant sat like a big child, patiently waiting for an adult command. You might say, "Fetch me an apple from the shops". He would go without a murmur. But his indifference to the spider betrayed a lack of commitment to human purposes.

"He looks like a tramp to me," I said finally. My examination over, I sat down on the Lancashire ladder-back chair, some whim had inspired me to bring to the office kitchen. Kennedy changed the filter on the coffee maker then cleaned out the cups. She stood swithering over French or American coffee for some moments. Finally, it was French. She poured out the rich dark granules into the filter with the deliberation of someone who wants to look as though they know what they are doing; then she spoke with authority.

"Professor Peralis, you know a lot about a lot of things. You have your big library," she indicated the back room beyond the kitchen, "you have your certificates and your degrees and such, but..." She fixed me with that challenging stare that young kids like to dish out to older people, "... you know nothing about tramps."

"Isn't he dressed like a tramp?" I replied; I knew a lot more than Kennedy suspected, but street-life was her one qualification. It helped to acknowledge her perceptions on the subject.

"No. Tramps, proper tramps who go from town to town, are dressed for all weathers. Their clothes sort of grow on them, like... like an old house acquiring furniture."

"So, he's not a proper tramp."

"No, and he's not from round here because I'd know him. Most of the men his age are alcoholics and they smell bad; piss themselves and so on."

"So, he doesn't smell."

"No, he doesn't smell, but then neither do the other men who've just lost their jobs through bad luck and the ones that are homeless but looking for a home, if you know what I mean?" Kennedy brought the coffee over and stared through the two-way mirror.

"Could he be a busker?" I ventured. Kennedy laughed, revealing her beautiful white teeth. "Well, does he look like a busker?" I stood up and examined the man again. His large frame was reclining now on my fake plank chest. One foot was thrust forward with its ridiculous shoe perched on the toe and his trilby was still shading most of his face. He looked like a minister who for some ludicrous forfeit had been encouraged to impersonate a cowboy. He was fast asleep.

"I don't really know what a busker looks like," I said.

The phone rang in the back room. I put my coffee down and urged Kennedy to sit.

"No. I'll get it. I'm expecting a call."

Alone in the back room, through the half-open door, I could see Kennedy's small figure sitting cross-legged on the stool. She looked innocent, like a flower fairy caught in a biker's leather jacket, but I still didn't trust her a centimetre. From the various times that money had gone missing from my purse, I knew that she used me as an easy touch. To her I was a lonely woman playing games in the big city; someone to squat in like a comfortable flat. I was never entirely sure that Kennedy wasn't setting me up for a proper crime. She didn't have the guile to do it herself, but could easily have a man in the background with mischief in mind.

I kept one eye on her and another on the mirror between the bookshelves on the near wall.

It's a habit with me, which used to be vanity I suppose, to stare at myself in the mirror when I talk on the phone. When I was a teenager I would note vivacious laughter, inspect like a movie director the line of the lips, the swift brush of black hair over my forehead. As the years dance on and the phone rings less for pleasure and more for business, I still watch the mirror; now, I suppose, more like a Dame indulging an overplayed role, but I find it does help judge my emotional response to callers.

"Hello, Peralis speaking."

"Hello, could I speak to Mr Peralis please? My name is Bower." The voice was cultured, yet slightly embarrassed, as though the speaker was unaccustomed to using the phone. The name rang a bell, but I couldn't quite place it.

"There is no Mr Peralis, I'm afraid. He died many years ago. Can I help?"

"I think not. I need the services of an expert in religious artefacts. Your husband was recommended to me by a personal friend. I'm sorry to have troubled you."

"I think we are talking at cross purposes, Mr Bower. I am Professor Peralis, the expert you seek. What is the nature of your enquiry?" There was a long silence, during which I observed my mirrored smile. It was a familiar charade. I wondered whether Mr Bower would form one of those obstinate male inquirers who never inquired again. Finally, he spoke.

"You wrote the paper on the authenticity of the Seal of Solomon unearthed some ten years ago in Burrow's private collection?"

"I did."

"And the refutation of that recent argument on Nefertiti's mummy?"

"It had to be done"

"Ah. I've made rather a fool of myself. Please forgive me."

"It's a common error. Consider yourself forgiven." I was warming to the melodious tone of his voice.

"How can I help you?"

" I have a piece that I would like you to see, but I'm afraid it is quite impossible for me to visit you for at least two weeks, by which time the purpose of the visit would have also gone."

"What piece is it?"

"I'm afraid I'd rather not discuss it."

"Can you give me an indication? I may have to do preparatory research."

"I understand and appreciate, Professor Peralis, but, over the phone…" My face in the mirror was frowning but behind this mask I could also see intrigue in the pale blue eyes.

"Well, Mr Bower, for you this may be an expensive waste of time…"

"I'll be happy to take the risk." He gave me an address in

Cheshire. I noted it down and arranged a time for the following week. I only had a few other appointments; the karate club wanted me to judge the new belts, the University had called, but it was never good to give the impression that I was available at the drop of a hat. It also gave me time to make my own discreet enquiries.

Kennedy had risen from the stool. She hitched up her baggy jeans; re-tying the rope bound around her waist in lieu of a belt. She took a sip of coffee and placed the cup on my James II Dresser. I winced. Although the panels were all in need of restoration, and the item was in very poor general condition, it always made me smart to see furniture treated with contempt. As she turned to look again at the giant, I discreetly picked up the cup and put it in the small sink.

"Who was it?" said Kennedy; she always assumed that my business was her business.

"A client with an item he wants me to check over."

"Not detective work then?"

"No, and I'm not a detective."

"I suppose not." She indicated the sleeping man. "Otherwise you wouldn't think he was a busker."

"It was just a suggestion. What do you really think?"

She crinkled her nose and screwed up her eyes. "Buskers are sometimes very middle class; college students, even pro musicians. All sorts go busking and of course he lacks the vital thing…"

"Oh yes, an instrument."

Kennedy raised her eyebrows. "He could have a mouthy or a Jews harp or a whistle or anything in his pocket."

"Would you stop being esoteric, and tell me what he lacks."

"Money, of course; If he was a busker his pockets would be full of small change."

I was about to ask Kennedy how she knew, but she pre-empted me. "I haven't been trying the hand on him. It's just that

Buskers jingle like the Tin Man when they walk. He doesn't jingle, and you can see he has nothing in his pockets. They don't bulge. They've never bulged."

"So, he's not a busker, he's not a proper tramp, he's not homeless or jobless. What is he?"

Kennedy bit her lip. "Don't rush me."

And now the time had come to push Kennedy and see where she fell. "Look. You brought him here, and you told me he was special. You're asking me to help him. So, what's it all about?"

"Honestly, it's like what you say about your research. I think things through aloud and then I know." She ticked her fingers. "There are two things we haven't covered. He might be a crook."

"Is he?"

"No. I know all the crooks." I suppressed a smile. Kennedy may have known a few - mostly pushers of crack, ecstasy and the marijuana that I knew she dabbled in; perhaps some junkies who thieved and then, the odd shadowy figure beyond her circle of street friends who she would know as a name or a face or a suit and tie. I let it pass.

"At first I thought..." she flashed me a rare frown of anxiety. "... I thought he was mad."

I looked through the mirror. Asleep I suppose most people look sane. Perhaps rather, they have the potential to be anything. At the least they have serenity. It was no different with the giant. His trilby had slid over the right side of his face, revealing extremely short black hair, shaved at the sides. He had small ears; at least the one I could see was small, and he was so close shaven that the gleam of his strong jaw caught the passing flicker of cars reflected in the Georgian window. Even in sleep he smiled, as though he knew a private joke that he had been nursing all day.

The joke, whatever its subject, was now wearing thin on me. I wanted to hear the punch line.

"Go through it from the start," I said, fixing Kennedy with my professorial stare, the complement to hers. "Tell me all about it."

Kennedy winced. "Could we have something to eat first?" I suppose it cruel. Kennedy never admitted to not eating. I knew that it was quite possible that she had eaten nothing since last night, but I wanted the story.

"Eat after." I said. "If it's a good story I'll take you for a pizza." Kennedy sighed, drew her legs up under her like a yogi, and settled into the stool.

"Two days ago I was in the square," she said. "The Buddhists had been dishing out food since seven o'clock. I'd been up since dawn. It was a cold morning. This autumn's been cold. I'm dreading the winter. Me and a friend..." It was always difficult to find out the names of Kennedy's intimates, "...slept out on Shudehill. There's one of those cellar windows there. You know all the little glass windows and bars that you walk over. Just at that spot the ventilators for the bakery project out. If you can get a place its warm all through the night. Well, we had a place and three dossers stole it from us. My mate could have knocked shit out of the three of them but they were all drunk, and one old bastard, who I know from the hostels, was threatening to piss all over us. They were all so tanked up on milk and meths that we couldn't hack it in the end. We walked the rest of the night. I was shattered, so, after I'd got the free veggie beans, I couldn't be bothered to move somewhere decent. My friend left me sitting on the bench in the square and I sat watching the derelicts mooching all the food." Kennedy shivered, and drew her legs up under her small body.

"It's a horrible sight, watching grown men queue for something free," she continued quietly. "Most people, the commuters, they don't see anything but a row of ghosts. It's like some people believe in ghosts. They give them a quick glance and then shudder and walk on. They don't want to see ghosts, because it frightens them. And other people, they're worse, because they don't believe in ghosts at all. They walk past a long queue. I honestly think they could walk right through it and not know it was there. That's how distanced some people are from ghosts."

The man stirred in his sleep; I saw the tiny heave of his chest and the slight dropping of his lower mouth as he searched for breath. It was easy, with the alienation of the two-way mirror to dehumanise him, to make him a shade. With the camouflage of his grey suit he could walk out of the door, and but for his size, I would never recognise him again; confined to the other dimension, he might easily become one of Kennedy's town ghosts.

"Sometimes," I said, half to myself, "people have problems of their own." I thought of myself fifteen years ago, and my child, who would be precisely Kennedy's age.

Kennedy shrugged, reasserting her usual defiant pose. "That morning *I* had problems. I was tired, I wanted to find a toilet, I needed some money, I was cold." She slumped again. "I looked at the men shuffling up the queue, staring at the ground or worse staring at the food as though it was going to run away. I knew a lot of the men, but none spoke. They were all intent on the next moment, probably feeling the groans in their belly, or, if they were new to it, feeling the presence of the commuters like a judge and jury. There they were, shambling along; dirty grey like a lot of unwashed socks; what they once called the "criminal classes". And then, out of that mess, one caught my eye."

Kennedy let out a sigh. "It was the other way round when I think about it. I'd like to think I noticed something different about him at the time, but it was only afterwards I could see he was different..."

"How was he different?" I found myself becoming involved. Kennedy had that effect on me. Like the excitement an unknown lover generates over a late meal, her words always dragged me in. She rubbed her belly absently, and I laughed.

"You've been talking about food from the beginning of this thing," I said.

"Can't we finish it over cheese and pineapple?" Her eyes lit up.

"What about him." I nodded to the two-way mirror.

"I tell you now. He won't move."

"He looks well gone. I suppose we could risk it. You eat fast enough."

Kennedy's eyes took on the solemn air that I knew always accompanied her great truths. "It's not that," she said. "He has been up for two days but even then it's more than that. He won't move from there. Never."

I was taken aback by Kennedy's certitude. Her whole attitude was tense. Her little body strained towards me, her eyes fixed. I folded my arms, almost threatened by her. "How do you know?" I said.

"Because, quite simply..." she held her hands out, "...I told him to wait."

Out on the bustling street the sun set behind Piccadilly plaza. I looked back down London road. The sun's rays painted gold the curved sweep of the British Telecom office windows. I loved to watch the play of lights. The skyscape reminded me of the dream worlds of H.P. Lovecraft that I endeavoured to walk myself; sometimes, more prosaically, the desert landscapes of Arabian fantasies. I wondered then at the beauty of this, the synthetic and the natural combining to make the world a wonderful place. I tried to interest Kennedy in the golden mirage, but she was distant. She linked her arm in mine and dragged me up towards Piccadilly. As we played dodgems with the approaching commuters she gripped me tighter and clung insularly into herself.

On past excursions together she would shout to the odd tramp as we walked. Sometimes, partly because she knew it irritated me, she would stop and talk to one of the buskers. Usually, I felt forced to throw a pound into their box out of a mixture of embarrassment and pride. Now, she seemed so intent on her current problem that she even walked past the beggar on the corner of Lenas Street without so much as a glance. He saw her and a look of cunning spread across his haggard face. He made as if to speak, saw me stare, and then cast his face down to the chip tray at his feet. I leaned over my shoulder and read his sign; a sign that changed daily in the manner of news-stand billboards. Today it read "homeless, please help." Then suddenly, as we stopped with a crowd at the traffic lights Kennedy said. "He wasn't humble, and he didn't hate."

"Our giant," I replied. "That's how he was different?"

"Yes. The others, myself included, always hate being grateful and having to thank people for things. It's much better to get something yourself, however you manage to get it. But he didn't mind one bit."

The amber light flashed. We risked a run across the street. "He didn't walk with his head down," she continued. "He didn't shuffle like a chain gang prisoner. He stood straight like a prophet. His eyes shone as he took the bowl from the monk. It was like watching a child being fed by his mother; as though the rice was his by right."

"But it is really," I said. "Food, shelter, it's everyone's right."

Kennedy scowled. "Not everyone knows that," she said. "But he knew."

We walked in silence alongside the winking lights of the small fair in the gardens. I'd never seen Kennedy in this kind of mood. It was difficult to equate what she was saying with the fact that she was only fifteen. Sometimes, like now, she seemed to be more than adult; an experienced mind on a child's body.

She always lied about her age of course, insisting she was seventeen, but she made the odd slip about the school she'd left that gave her away. Running away from home had given her a veneer of confidence. It had given her street talk and an understanding of humanity that some people would never acquire. This was the first unexpected sign that it had also given her a philosophy.

We stopped by the market stall at the garden's north gate. I picked up some tee shirts, fingering the material. All the goods were cheap, the shell suits faked, the earrings gilt, but the tee shirts often had original logos or messages in keeping with current events. The trader, a stocky man who wore one of his own shell suits, nodded to Kennedy.

"Three quid to your friend," he said, digging his hands in his pockets. I smiled, and we dashed across the street avoiding the lumbering orange buses. A light wind swept through from Moseley Street carrying with it a handful of rain. We picked a seat next to the wide windows, and as Kennedy ordered, I watched the people rush hither and thither. The market trader drew in his stall, desperately protecting his gear from the gathering rain. The other traders, sellers of flowers, posters, wind up dolls, umbrellas, withdrew to the doorways of shops. The commuters crowded into the bus shelters like blown autumn leaves. Buses strung out in files like glistening slabs of coloured cake. I shivered and pushed my coat over the back of the chair. Manchester could be a cold place.

The pizzas were huge deep pan affairs. Mine, black olives and ham, had too few olives, and the garlic salt and salad dressing were slightly stale. When you've eaten at top restaurants throughout Europe, fast food is simply an insult. Kennedy finished hers before I even had time to look. We sipped what passed for fresh orange juice and I pushed my half-eaten pizza to one side. Kennedy eyed it. "You haven't finished," she said. I nodded. She opened her duffel bag, wrapped up the crust, and placed it carefully inside. For a second I had the impression I sat opposite a squirrel, but I felt the unkindness of this immediately.

Kennedy didn't know where the next meal was coming from. It could be that even what she had now was to be shared among others. I put my drink down and clasped my chin in my hands.

"This giant," I said, "this huge man who we've left locked in my office, fast asleep with his trilby over his face. I know now what's different about him. He's not been humbled by his poverty or bad luck or whatever. He's a free spirit."

"Something like that," replied Kennedy. I could see she thought I was miles off the mark. She was dissolving into one of her abstract states, a mental journey to a place where I didn't belong. She pulled herself back with an effort.

"He's not really a free spirit. he's oblivious of everything... well, not everything."

"Like an alien?"

"Nearly, but not quite. Like I said, he was like a prophet; someone who has been somewhere and seen things that make this world seem trivial. But I think the experience, whatever it was, damaged him beyond repair."

"I thought you said he wasn't mad."

"He's not mad. He's an ordinary sane man. I'm sure of that. It's just that he's been... drained; drained like an empty can of coke." Kennedy crushed her paper napkin and dropped it on the table. "He's an ordinary man, but more than anybody I ever met he needs help."

"My help?"

Kennedy flashed me a hurt glance. "Professor Peralis, you're the only one I know who can help."

"I ask you every week if you need help, and every week you say "no". And yet you ask me to help a complete stranger, a grown man who's fallen on hard times, probably through some situation of his own making..."

"This is different."

"You've used that word already "different". How do I know that I won't walk back to my office and find out the different thing is that I've had my place rifled by a strange man? How do I know he'll even be there at all? What's to stop him calling the police from the reception desk, or even smashing the window to escape? Tell me."

Kennedy jumped to her feet, knocking her chair back. "Trust," she screamed a whisper through her teeth. "Trust. That's what."

A waiter stared across curiously, but doubtless he had seen more interesting things in his time. I ignored him and picked up my bag, feeling like a probation officer whose probationer has failed to turn up on time. I reached for my purse. I knew that I was the guilty party and that the feeling was misplaced snobbery. I had asked Kennedy out. I had pushed her for a story. I stopped, leaving my purse on the table. Kennedy sat down, looking out of the window at the windswept square.

"I apologise," I said. "I do trust you. I don't trust strange men, and when it comes down to it, the story you've given me isn't the normal run of things. You have to trust me as well. I think you owe it to me to say what makes you stand by this man so dearly."

Kennedy smiled. "You're right," she said. "If I'd been in your place I wouldn't have listened this far. It's ridiculous to ask you to help him…"

"But?"

The restaurant had emptied of the teatime *clientèle*. Outside, a few stragglers waited at the deserted bus stance. Kennedy toyed with the salt cellar, spinning it round from hand to hand.

"He reached the end of the queue," she said finally, "and he sat on the bench beside me. I was aware of him eating; slow deliberate movements like a cow. Then he stopped. He finished what was left and wrapped up the paper bowl. He put it in the bin beside the bench, then settled into the bench. I could see him out of the corner of my eye, staring, with that bland irritating smile, on the pigeons strutting through the square. Then, it was one of those moments that feel predetermined, fate or whatever. I turned around and he did. We gazed into each other's eyes, and everything seemed to take a breath and hold it."

"You... you love him." The words came out before I could stop them.

Kennedy laughed. "Christ no, he must be thirty five." She looked away again, tugged at her lip. "He kept staring, staring and staring. I tried to look away but I couldn't. He had seen something in me that I didn't know was there. Who said "the eyes are the window to the soul"? He saw my soul, like God, like God."

A shadow flitted before my eyes and I got that unnerving sensation, when something otherwise harmless appears in the wrong context. I almost jumped back from my seat. My hands went to my face, and Kennedy made a snatch. She held something in her hands, and with a motion produced a glimpse of a winged insect. With a sneer of distaste, she slapped her hands, and the insect was flattened on the table. One wing rose up, flicking briefly like a yellow leaf.

"You shouldn't have killed it," I said.

"I was frightened."

"So was I, but just because I'm frightened doesn't mean something has to die."

"It's just a moth."

I looked a little closer. "No, not a moth. How unusual." I took out my jeweller's eyeglass. The broken wings rose to my face, the crushed thorax and the head smashed to a pulp, one wing still resplendent with colour. "It's a ...butterfly. How did it get here?"

Kennedy shrugged, wiping her hands. "A butterfly isn't a god. It can't look into your soul."

The waiter dropped the bill on the table. I picked it up, and gave Kennedy my purse. She took it, and returned, moments later. We walked to the door. Outside the rain had stopped. I could hear the singing of the starlings in Market Street, the dripping of gutters in the square. The sky was clear, lit with the street lights' ambience, and the air was fresh. Kennedy held my arm lightly.

"Since then," she said, "three days and three nights he hasn't left my side. He does anything I say. And every time he looks at me..." she shivered, "...he knows."

I clasped her hand.

"You'll help me with him?"

"Until I know what it's all about," I said. "I'll help. To be honest, I'm fascinated."

"He sees something, Professor Peralis, something incredible."

"Don't worry. I'll keep him safe."

"Thanks."

She let go my hand, and was off out the door towards Victoria Station without a backward glance. I put my hands in my pockets. The streets were empty. I walked back to the office alone.

Chapter 2
Ka

A SOLITARY CAR shafted London road. It left the growl of its engine to rebound from the bank buildings standing like temples in Piccadilly Square. I followed the path of the vehicle, jaywalking the deserted central lane. Queen Victoria's statue hovered over my shoulder as though she disapproved of a lady walking alone, but only a novice could assume I was a whore; the whores, mostly young things, hung around Canal Street on the south side of the square. For a second I wondered about Kennedy. Had she gone there before, even tonight? But then I remembered she had left in the opposite direction. Kennedy had left me with her problems again. I drew my coat in as the wind caught me from behind like a prowler.

The city centre was dead at this hour; the shops all shut, the *cafés* and takeaways only just stirring for the night hours. I could see all the way down London road. With the death of the sun, the burning shield of the British Telecom building had transformed to a dark gravestone. The road was so quiet I could see only that single car, like a tiny beetle crawling into the distance. As I walked past the Greek Kebab House I heard a muffled clatter of kitchen utensils and high alien laughter. Fragmented by the red neon window sign, two figures busied themselves within. They looked like small beasts in a lit glass case. Further on a bouncer appeared in the Nite Club's doorway, bringing with him the fragrance of expensive aftershave. As quickly as he had appeared he disappeared, like a shot video-game gangster.

My office came into view. I realised that there was no one in the city streets but me.

In this eerie calm, the consequences of trusting Kennedy came sharply to my mind. Somewhere in the darkened office a giant waited. This huge man had never seen me before in his life. He waited there because a girl he met two days before had told him to wait. The man was simple, perhaps mad. I paused at the corner of Lenas Street and London road. Perhaps I was mad as well. Kennedy's urban glamour had seduced me, as it always did. In the restaurant, it had all seemed so clear. Alone, it seemed ridiculous. I could think of none of my friends who would willingly walk into my office now. I stood for a while, the wind whipping my coat. It was a strong wind. It had been stronger on Aonach Eagach many years ago.

An old Marina hurtled around the corner of the square. It sped through the red lights, radio roaring louder than its engine. Two youths glared out of the open nearside windows. They shouted abuse and threw missiles. I jumped back from the kerb as the objects flew at me. The car raced off, dodging traffic islands before it swerved around the corner. The missiles, two empty cans of cheap lager, were grasped by the wind before they reached me, and tossed into a current of air. They clattered down the slope towards Piccadilly station approach like the fleeing trailers of a phantom wedding car.

The silence became a thing. Everything external was lost to the beat of blood through my temples; everything except the clatter of the cans. My mouth tasted dry, and for some unaccountable reason I felt my hand reach into my purse to pull out my make-up bag. I looked in the little compact mirror at my lips, and quickly reddened them with scarlet lipstick. I suppose it was some sort of defensive reaction, but as soon as I'd done it I felt like a whore. My hands shook and I nearly dropped the compact.

The senseless, petty act of violence was enough to change my mind. I would not fail Kennedy's trust, but I was not going to enter my office. It would be enough for me to leave the man there. He could sleep on the plank chest; there was food in the kitchen that he would no doubt find, and coffee to drink. I had locked the back room, so unless he broke in, my precious books and files were protected. Kennedy might be angry and let down, but I would have fulfilled my obligations. She said that he would wait until she returned. If she was so certain then I could hardly be faulted for leaving him. In fact, if he left I could be justified in saying that Kennedy had failed in her judgement.

But doubt nagged me, instigated by the butterfly in the restaurant. The little creature had thrown me out of sorts. With its strangeness, a fear had been born that I had never really experienced. I have been through a lot in my life, and seen some things people never see. But the incongruity triggered something deep in my subconscious. I tried to shake off this new uncertainty. I rummaged in my bag, anxious to find my car keys. I searched my bag, then my pockets, growing steadily more uneasy.

The keys were gone.

I looked towards the square, and then turned to see the street lights flicker down like a dim bronze bracelet towards the station approach. In unison, all the way down London road, the lights changed from green to amber to red. I cursed under my breath. I knew rationally that I was caught in the lull between the end of work and the beginning of night life. No one lived in inner cities; they were a limbo-land at this hour. But even with this logic a premonition of evil seemed to crouch over my shoulder. The streets were too still. I wanted out. I would have to phone a friend or a taxi. Even as I opened my purse I knew what I would find. Empty. Kennedy had cleaned me out. I had nothing.

And then a low growl tore the air like paper. I dropped my bag, nerves shot. As I picked it up I saw, between the billboards fronting a disused shop, the outline of a man - The Lenas street beggar. He was two metres away, standing between Piccadilly Square and me. I could see bloodshot eyes stare from the haggard florid mask of his face. He grinned horribly, blood and foam flecking his lips. Suddenly, he lurched forward; his feet kicked a half bottle of cheap wine over. The bottle rolled, and both of us watched in fascination as it launched over the kerb, and smashed in the gutter.

"Shhymy botll," he hissed. "Bsstard." He flung his arms out and reached for me.

I threw a kick, catching his leg above the knee, but his initial impetus brought him on to me. His open hand caught my face. I smelled his sweated hand as he struck me under the nose. Somehow I freed myself and staggered backwards across the street, breaking into a run as I turned. For some reason I couldn't scream. I had an absurd certainty that there was no one to hear. Searching for something familiar I pushed myself the few metres to my office door. I heard the slap of his shoes on the wet ground, and the rasp of his heaving breath. I reached my door and turned. No keys; keys in my bag. He half fell, raised himself and grinned. I backed against the door, hands scrabbling. The beggar swayed, his mouth dripping, his eyes glazed. He raised his hand.

And I fell through the unlocked door.

I flipped to my stomach, crawled, turned and stumbled to my feet. The beggar stood on the threshold. His silhouette filled the doorway.

"Shymbttle," he hissed.

I slammed the door, flicked the mortise lock, and fell to the floor, laughing.

Lying in the darkness of the waiting room with blood trickling from my nose, I couldn't stop the laughter. I had been so scared and yet it was senseless. The man was drunk, obviously an alcoholic. He lost his temper because his bottle broke, and with the irrationality of drunks, picked on the nearest face: Mine. Was he really the threat I had imagined - an alcoholic beggar? In my time I had floored some of the best.

I stilled my laughter somehow and listened. I heard a low thump and the door jarred. Panting breath and muttered curses were audible outside. I slumped with my back to it, and stared into the dark.

Something had driven me here. That was how it felt. Because now I knew that Kennedy's madman waited somewhere with me.

The darkness lifted slowly as my eyes adjusted. Light filtered in through the blinds on the high windows. I could see before me the reception desk, the counter, the large mirror with the small two-way section at the top. On my right stood the small modern table with rows of magazines on antiques, city and theatre reviews, old academic journals and a scattering of children's short stories. Just behind it, like the bars of an ornate cage, a row of copy Hepplewhite-splat chairs occupied the far wall. I could hardly bear to look to my left because the fake plank chest rested there under the window; the place where I last saw the man.

He was gone and in his place, caught in the street light and reflected large, there was only the small spider I had last seen on his vacant face.

Out of the corner of my eye I could see the black cavern of the doorway that led to the kitchen, the toilet and my private office. My senses were heightened. I could still smell the dirty sweat on my face where the beggar had struck me. My knees and elbows hurt where I had fallen scrambling to the floor. The blood trickling from my nose tasted hot and salty in my mouth. Listening, the footsteps of the beggar, his panting breath and the purr of distant cars, poured under the door behind me. Yet in the waiting room, sounds seemed lost as though I was submerged beneath a vast ocean. I could still hear deep in my head, the intense *shhh, shhh* of my own lungs syncopated with my heart.

The room was utterly still.

My eyes drew themselves once more to the fake plank chest. The worn wooden surface gleamed like the lid of a small coffin. Even the spider had gone. As I stood up, I wished that Kennedy's man still lay there asleep. To have him visible would have felt safer. Knowing that he was here, hidden somewhere in the dark, was a terrible feeling. And yet, the door had been open. I was virtually certain I had locked it when Kennedy and I left for the restaurant. The most obvious conclusion was that the man had woken up in a strange place, and then let himself out. The theory seemed to make sense. I relaxed a little and worked up the courage to switch on the light. Light flooded the room. For a second the objects: chairs, table, chest and counter, seemed to occupy a space larger than their volume. The feeling dissipated. I was left to stare at my reflection in the mirror.

The red slash of my lips, the dark blood trailing from my nostrils, and my pale agitated face made the mirror look like an early surrealist canvas; denigration of the classical style into a flippant graffiti. I smiled. At last I was beginning to think like my normal arrogant self. The last few minutes had seemed like an age. I drew my confidence together like a cloak, briefly checked behind the counter, and marched through the hallway, switching lights on as I went.

"Hello," I shouted. My voice sounded outwardly brave. No one answered. The kitchen was empty. I checked the cups in the sink; two, unwashed. The cupboards were still shut. I opened them one after another. The teas and coffees, sugar and biscuits, remained apparently untouched. My Lancashire ladder-back was safe against the wall, and the James II dresser was unmarked. Nothing had been moved. There on the floor were my keys. I picked them up. It looked more and more likely that the man had gone unless he had used to the keys to enter my private office. I opened the cutlery drawer, and took out the large bread knife with the vivid red handle.

Taking a deep breath I inserted the key in the lock and

pushed open the door. Shadows retreated to the corners and with them the last of my fears. I thrust the door aside so no one could be behind it.

The rows of the books on the walls remained as I had left them. No tell-tale gaps around the places where the rare books were kept, the glass case unmarked.

I have two desks. The Carlton house table under the far window was designed for ladies; the wall was visible beneath its high tapering legs. It was too small for an intruder to hide behind. The other desk on my right, and just obscured by the door, was a mid century library table. My word processor sat astride it, and the old phone. The desk was big enough to conceal one person.

I switched on the light, gripped the bread knife in my hands and strode towards it.

Nothing.

I dropped the knife, shaking with relief, and sat down on the desk. It was over. Calm enveloped me. My rationality flooded back.

I sat for a while, considering whether I should meditate a little as I had been taught. I had been practising the construction of a mental garden; this exercise would focus my mind and relax me, but as with all things that are good for you, I talked myself out of it. I had things to do in the office; little jobs to tidy up, some research to finish, people to phone. I sat down on the balloon-back chair that I had brought in especially for comfort. Its unique design supported my shoulders and the small of my back so that even hours of typing would leave me feeling no strains. Now, after the tension of the last hour, I sent a little message of congratulations to myself for bringing it to the office. Not meditation but a good substitute. It was nice to be surrounded by quality things. It was better to feel the benefit of their quality by daily use. I felt myself melt into the chair.

After a few minutes sifting and sorting I was completely

absorbed. I picked up the phone. The first task was to check on this morning's Mr Bower.

Part of the reason for Kennedy's assumption that I was a detective was the meticulous way I ran my business. As a child I had always been impressed by ancient Japanese mythological heroes. They always won their victories by prior knowledge.

Sometimes it was training, a higher standard of excellence achieved in an aspect of martial art. Or it would be knowledge of the terrain, the past, anything. But knowledge was the key. The more you knew about the person you were about to meet, and the area or speciality that was theirs, the more chance you had to clinch a deal, make a sale or impress them with your ability. All of these ensured that I made a success of my ventures. Kennedy assumed I was some sort of spy, one of the reasons apart from money why she frequented my office.

"Hello," I said. "Jamie?"

"The one and only Professor Peralis," he replied, his broad Edinburgh accent flattened by the phone. "How can I help you?"

"First let me know if you know a Bower at this address." I gave him the Cheshire address, but he had never heard of it.

"Give me a list of dealers under the name of Bower then, back two generations. List any peculiarities or specialities. I specifically want any religious connection."

"I'll have them for you tomorrow afternoon," he replied.

"Morning?" I said.

"I have some serious drinking to do, Professor Peralis. In fact, why don't you come over, to make it less serious?"

"I can't," I said. I usually decline, as Jamie was always making passes at me. Tonight I felt like company, but I heard no other voices in the background, and I knew Jamie was probably drinking alone. He sighed.

"One day you might come and rescue me," he said. "Well, I've started, so I have to finish, but I'll set the tinkler for around five, and see if I can come up with some addresses and such. Is that it? I have a malt anxious to make the long non-returnable journey."

"Yes - oh, no." There was one other thing. "I may need you to make a trace on a man. I'm afraid I don't have much to go on. It's a job for a friend."

"Fire away."

"Well..." I heard a noise in the background; an innocuous noise, meant nothing. "There's not much." I said. "I may have more by the end of the week. Just keep it on file just now: A dosser, about thirty five, white, around six feet eight, quite well built; in fact something of a giant. Short black hair, strong jaw, clean shaven type." The noise was trivial, everyday, but it bothered me. "He may have been a mental patient." I continued, fingering the bread knife on the desk. "Oh, small delicate ears."

"I see what you mean," said Jamie. "Apart from the size of the beast, I suspect you've described half the city - or at the least, most of the polis in this district. Anything else, like a name, maybe?"

"No name. That's what I want to find out. Name, origin. Just who the damn person is." The noise was a toilet flushing in a distant room. A silly sort of noise to bother a person, but then it had been a strange day.

"I have his clothes;" I said. "A grey suit, cheap. One of those sixty pounds jobs from the outsize shop. Black plastic shoes. White nylon shirt. I don't recall a tie. Oh, he has a tweedy trilby."

"A what?" Jamie had obviously been tippling for a while.

"A trilby. You know - soft felt hat with an indented crown. They were named after the heroine of a novel by George du Maurier."

"Hat will do. I think I know the type you mean. Is that it?"

"That's all I've got. Except that he seems neat and tidy, is possibly mentally retarded, and gets regular meals from the

Buddhists in Piccadilly."

Jamie's voice took on a serious note. "This hasn't anything to do with that Kennedy girl has it?"

"That's not your business, Mr MacDonald."

"That means it does. Well you know my feelings about her. I suppose you understand what you're doing."

"Piss off, you patronising sod, and get back to your highland wonderland."

"It's only because I care," he replied half seriously.

"Anyway, you were never good on advice."

I hung up. Jamie's solicitous side always riled me, and yet he had only expressed the doubts about Kennedy that I carried in my own head.

The noise; I knew now why it bothered me. It was the office toilet.

I was not alone.

Footsteps in the hall. The slow measured steps of a heavy man; a man who was unsure of the way. My hands reached out, the fingers clenching and writhing. I stared at the phone and the bread knife as though only one was an escape route, and I didn't know which. The water in the pipes gurgled around the room. It was all I could hear as the door swung inwards. My hand hit the phone, knocked the receiver off.

The operator's voice began to repeat "please replace the handset and dial again".

Kennedy's man stood in the doorway, hat in hand, smile on face. Not a pleasant smile. There was no intelligence behind it. It was the smile of a moron, a hapless idiot. He lumbered into the room, carefully closed the door and turned to me no longer smiling. His face lit up with a small flame of intelligence. He saw me, walked forward. I couldn't take my eyes off him. As I reached out for the bread knife I hit the handle, and the blade dropped to join the receiver on the floor. He reached the desk as I found my feet and backed up against the bookcase.

I could see his face clearly now. He was fairly thick set with an aquiline nose and full lips. His brow was high and intelligent, and in some ways he was a handsome man.

Except that his eyes, a piercing, blue, were those of a damned soul or a yearning beast. His mouth dropped. Saliva trickled down his chin. He picked up the receiver and listened, then dropped it in disgust. He picked up the bread knife and sidled around the desk.

My hands scrabbled, pulling books out of the bookcase, pens off the desk, searching for a weapon. I threw a book at him but his hand went up to his face. Then, like some comical black and white movie star, he placed his trilby on his head. He held out the knife. I began to scream; little high-pitched sounds emerged from my mouth like a hurt animal. I had faced enemies before, faced them down and beat them - but they had all been human. Like the butterfly in the restaurant, it was his misplacement that caused the terrible fear. His blue eyes, insensible, stared into mine like a blind man searching for something he hardly understood. He held out the knife. I saw its vivid red handle and for a second I thought the handle was the blade and that he'd already cut me. His face pushed into mine, centimetres away. His eyes focussed and unfocussed like a new-born baby and his mouth opened wider and wider with his eyes. I felt his coat against my breasts, his legs brush my skirt. I smelled his oddly sweet breath. His hand reached out and touched the blood on my nose. I shivered and shook.

For some reason I found myself focussing on his neck, and like a machine still performing a redundant function I thought. "He doesn't have a tie. He wears a silver chain."

He looked at the blood, and then my eyes, deep in my eyes.

But whatever he wanted, and he wanted it badly, was not there. He held the knife up as though it had been forgotten, smiled, and placed it on the desk. Then he looked up again with his empty face and words came out of his mouth.

"Ka...Ka.... Ka..."

At that point, or perhaps it was slightly later, I flipped back and knocked myself out.

I can't be sure, because I woke up lying on the floor with a pain in the back of my head. Kennedy's man was sitting on my beautiful balloon back chair. I could see the French *cabriole* legs carved from single pieces of mahogany. I kept thinking that I'd sat on the chair for years, and the best part had been hidden from me. He slouched like a dismantled puppet and although his eyes were open it was as though he, personally, had been turned off at the mains. He looked very comfortable. I knew, I suppose with some of the certainty that Kennedy had tried to convey, that he was going nowhere.

I stood up, face red in spite of his mental absence, and brushed myself down. I'd knocked a cup of coffee over myself in the fall. Without a change of clothes in the office, it was going to be an unpleasant journey home.

And the giant? I had a blanket somewhere. If I couldn't persuade him to go back to the plank chest, I would just have to risk leaving him on my favourite chair.

I picked up the phone. The operator still advised me to replace the handset. I dialled and waited. After a few moments, a bleary Scottish voice answered me.

"Who is it," the words were slurred.

"I have more on the man."

"Professor Peralis, eh?"

"He wears a silver bracelet..."

"Got it...where's my pen. You pick your times, woman."

"And he says "Ka"."

""Ka"?"

"Yes, repeats it over and over; "Ka"."

"What the hell does it mean?"

"It could be the ancient Egyptian term for the attendant spirit that dwells in a man or sometimes a statue. Or…"

"Or what…?"

"Who knows? It's your job to find out. Night, Jamie."

I put the phone down, and went in search of a blanket.

Chapter 3
The Bubble Gum Cards

WITH PAINSTAKING CARE, the old man laid the golden cards in order along the reception counter. His withered hands trembled as each card fell into place. Finally, there were four rows. The first three contained six cards. The fourth row contained five.

"That's them all," he said. "My father's set. Beauties, aren't they?"

The sunlight glanced off the surface of each card. It picked out the flat figures of Egyptian pharaohs and Egyptian gods as though they were embossed in gold.

"They are lovely," I said. ""Ancient Egypt", in mint condition."

"I wouldn't have brought them if I didn't need the money," he continued. "They've been in the family, so to speak. But then, hard times... and I heard about you - an antiquarian." He pronounced it awkwardly. "It's said you're very good, know your stuff and don't cheat."

"This one," I said. "Osiris, the many eyed Judge of the dead and potentate of the kingdom of ghosts. It's quite beautifully done. They really don't make things like this any more."

"See, you know your stuff. They said you did."

I was starting to wonder who "they" were, but I held my tongue. The old man was shabbily dressed and obviously genuine.

"You said you had another set?"

"Nothing like these," he said, holding out his hands in apology. "Only a silly thing I bought for a nephew who didn't want them - Bubble-gum cards."

"I'd still like to have a look."

Digging deep in his pockets, he fished out a plastic bag. It contained a small tin. He emptied this tin, full of coloured cards, and dumped them on the counter. "There they are - space ships and monsters."

Monsters, I thought. I have enough monsters of my own at

the moment. From the kitchen came the low snore of Kennedy's giant who I now called "Ka" since that was the only word he ever uttered. I had made a camp bed up beside the cooker. For the last four days he had spent his hours sleeping like an invalid but eating like a man who has been to the North Pole and back on a solitary diet of Kendal mint.

I poured the coloured cards on to the counter.

Immense Martians shaped like cross-bred octopi ravished semi-clad earth women while the combined might of humanity's soldiery struggled in vain resistance. Wonderful cards. I counted them out slowly, checking for soiled cards and missing numbers. It was a complete set, over twenty years old but again in perfect condition.

"I must congratulate you," I said. "You've kept these in remarkable condition. Bubble gum cards are often damaged when boys swap to make their sets."

"Well, these were never swapped. I bought the lot from a little lad, but my nephew..."

"It's the swapping that counts though, isn't it?"

"That's right. That's right. I never thought of it at the time. When you're a lad you always want to get things bit by bit. You open the packet and wonder if it's that last number you need."

"Yes, I think I understand. I know it's on a grander scale, but I sold a car yesterday; a 1955 Citroen 15 CV. I'd worked on it for years, getting bits here and there. All that was needed to make it utterly genuine was the left-hand front lamp. Then a friend came up with an original lamp and suddenly I didn't want the car any more. Years, I had the thing but... it was finished."

*

I was on my way down to see Bower when I decided that the Citroen had to go. I suppose it had been on my mind for some time. It was really my late husband's car. He had bought it for me as a birthday present. We'd spent weekends cleaning it up together and hawking around motor shows for parts, a labour of love; but the love of the car was his. For me it had been the hours together. The more I thought about the car, the more I thought it pretentious and outmoded. Conrad had been dead for years now and it was time for a change; time for something that reflected my own self image, not that of a dead man.

The roads through Cheshire were quiet. Autumn leaves swept across them like golden sequinned scarves. As always, I was avoiding the motorway; the Citroen had a book top speed of 80mph, but it was more comfortable cruising just below 50mph. In any case I had to stop at a small private garage not far from Altrincham.

As I drove I replayed the tape that contained the information that Jamie had gleaned about the mysterious Mr Bower. Jamie's voice was hoarse and faint. "There are two Bowers in Cheshire," he croaked, "but only one at the address you've given me, so I've presumed that's your man. He's a bit like yourself, a dabbler in all sorts, but he earns his bread from a small antique shop in Knutsford. I should watch your fee because I think he's probably short of ready money. The rumour is that the shop is going down the tubes. He hasn't been seen there for months, some kind of car accident that I'm still investigating. As to specialities I have nothing to offer. He's a drop-out from St Andrews University though. He did two years' worth of Ancient History and that could lead to your only clue. His grandfather was an archaeologist, an independent type. Journeyed to Tibet around the time of Alexandra David-Neel. Travelled widely east and wrote a few unpublished journals on occult artefacts and one on occult teachings of an obscure Tibetan sect that was published privately but destroyed by a fire.

"The private manuscripts were known of in the thirties but not much sought after because not only were his theories outlandish nonsense—something about life after death all worked out like a railway timetable—they were also badly written both grammatically and legibility or whatever the word is. Bower senior was probably dyslexic and died mad. So, as well as being unstructured and unfinished, the manuscripts are virtually unreadable.

"Well, I'm afraid that's all I could dig up. I have a shocking hangover, all your fault. If you'd shared the evening with me I would have been a terribly good boy. Oh, one other thing that you'd probably deduce yourself: Bower will probably be broke and he'll try to sell you some artefacts that his grandfather picked up on his travels. All the good stuff was sold a long time ago. Either that or he may offer you the manuscripts. They really are worthless. Don't buy them unless you're out of toilet paper."

I switched the tape off. Before breakfast I'd checked my museum contacts for any gifts that Bower senior may have dished out to the community - nothing. Private collections had unearthed one or two minor items sold by his grandson in the past months. The manuscripts were unknown except to a friend at the Scottish National Museum who had reviewed them four years before and pronounced them "illegible, unreadable and irrational". As I pulled into the garage, I envisaged a sad sort of day.

Bert and his son, a youth of about eighteen, greeted me with stoic calm as I got out of the car.

"Is it the axle?" said Bert, wiping his hands on a cloth.

"No," I said. "It's the whole car. I want to sell it."

"Well, well," he replied.

His son's eyes lit up. "Spiral bevel drive on the front wheels, three forward speeds. The best car the French ever made." He turned to his father. "What do you think?"

Bert paused in his intractable way, then spoke with authority. "They made less than fifty thousand in the ten years after the war. This was one of the last models, so it'll have Deesse's hydro-pneumatic suspension. I believe the car's pristine, except one of the lamps is a copy."

I laughed. "I got another lamp by chance, an original."

"I always had you down for a lucky sod."

"What about rust?" The youth got down on his haunches and examined the chassis.

"I've heard these were a bugger for rust."

Bert laughed. "That's where her luck held. This one seems to be made of gold. It's never shown a sign of rust in all the days I've known it. Two careful owners, one of them an angel."

"So, you think it'll be easy to sell. I need another car, you see?"

"It's definitely going, then." Bert eyed me up and down. "It was never meant for a lady, this one. They was very popular with bank robbers way back, but they used to say a lady couldn't handle the steering; very poor on the lower gears and a turning circle of over forty feet. Still a damn fine car though. I can hardly believe you're selling it."

His son chipped in, "Wasn't it Conrad, your husband - his car?"

"Shush," said Bert.

"No, it's ok, Bert. It was a long time ago. It helps to talk"

"Mountaineering accident if I remember right."

"Yes, it was a funny business. Conrad made off from Glencoe in that bad winter…"

"It was in the papers as I recall."

"Yes, the party split when the weather became doubtful; the main group made for a bothy, but Conrad and another… person, went on."

"Those scotch mountains can be a bugger. Better off down here, Mrs Peralis."

"Too right, Bert. Anyway, it was long ago and frankly, I want to drive something that doesn't get gawked at when you stop at the traffic lights."

"Well, I know what you mean there. Around here though there's always some vintage rally going on, and those who like to drive the old classics can lose themselves in the crowd."

"So, how long do you think before I can get myself a new car?"

Bert laughed. "Oh, you can take mine if you like. You've already sold yours." He pointed at his son who was already under the bonnet. "I'd lose my best worker if I didn't snap up this old Citroen."

I left the Chester road in a 1983 Morris Ital and thousands of pounds in my purse as Bert still didn't trust a bank with his money and always dealt in cash. The only unusual thing about the Ital was that some kid had welded the undercarriage as a racer, but as this couldn't be seen, the car was as anonymous as you could wish.

The small country road curved and twisted before me and even though the estate was a cumbersome car by anyone's standards, it was still a relief to be in something designed for modern life. I had a chance to take in the view.

I always thought Cheshire a beautiful English county. Conrad had loved it. The cool autumn sun topped its trees, spreading a thin luminosity over the underbellies of the low clouds. Oak, beech and sweet chestnuts lined the road and marked the patchwork squares of farmland in all directions. The crowns of these beautiful trees were shedding golden leaves. Zephyrs caught the leaves and, like rushing children or scattered confetti, they swirled and sprayed over my bonnet and windscreen; almost as though the car was being circled by a funeral wreath.

Twice I lost myself, following ambiguous little village signs. The second occasion I pulled on to the verge beside a long fence and sat beside late flowering yellow-gold cinquefoils with a flask of coffee and a cheese and sweet pickle sandwich I had made for the journey. The grass was still slightly damp from the dew, but the whipping wind made the coffee taste hot and bitter the way it should. The sandwiches were awful, as they always are when made by yourself. It was too early for lunch really, but my appointment with Bower was at twelve fifteen and I'd very little idea how much time I would spend with him. I wanted to concentrate on work rather than my stomach when I arrived.

Since Bower's call I'd found myself conjuring up a picture of him in idle moments. His voice on the phone had been sensitive and cultured, perhaps a little restrained. Jamie's rather damning biography made me envisage a small man living in the shadow of his grandfather. He would be mildly snobbish and carry a pained expression of frustration around his eyes. However, I was almost sure he would be handsome in a sort of rakish fashion like the English cad in a fifties film. I was looking forward to being entertained.

The more I considered this the more I felt that a change moved through me. It was a need that had been growing for a number of years. I saw its reflection in all sorts of little things. My intimacy with Kennedy, my successful little business, my flirtation with Jamie. Little things all growing up at once. Even taking on Ka, the giant imbecile, as a guest in my office - although God knows he needed little looking after - he cleaned himself regularly and ate a continuous diet of cheese and pasta that he seemed to have become obsessed with after finding loose jars of pasta shells in the fridge - I think the penultimate touch to this change was the demise of the Citroen 15 CV.

As I looked at the old estate leaning on the verge, I felt the stab of tears in my eye. To me a car was just, and always had been, a thing to get you from one place to another. To Conrad, my Citroen was like a favourite member of the family. Of course, although I had enthused, it had really been a birthday present for him. If he hadn't been dead for years he would certainly have died now, seeing me on the grass verge staring at an ordinary family car.

Through the tears I felt a little anger creep through.

Although I loved Conrad and always would, I realised now with the gift of hindsight that he had been a patronising bastard, a chauvinist obsessed with his work at the university, his cars and his mountains. Of course, he had always looked after me; he was the soul of kindness; generous, courteous. But with all these qualities he had that insecurity many men have. He simply did not want his wife to compete with him. Always I walked in his shadow and my ambitions had to dawdle behind his. Young as I was to make Professor, I would have made it even earlier had I not followed his advice. He had masked his inferiority with a Gentleman Jim attitude that always stunted any of the few attempts I made to assert myself. There had always been that look when I talked about Kirsty, the child that had been taken from me at birth. The look that told me that his family wouldn't have produced a love child, that they were above indiscretion.

I had no idea where she was. I wondered for a second if that was why I allowed Kennedy so much latitude. She would have been the same age. I shook my head. It was a time to forget all pain and grief. To look ahead.

Without any bitterness or rancour, without any guilt or hesitation, I made my second decision of the day. Rising to my feet, I wiped myself down, took off my golden wedding ring and threw it as far as I could into the field behind me. Now it was missing from my life as they would both remain, missing and forgotten

Back on the road I wound the window down and let the wind rip through my hair. At first I drove fast, taking risks on the bends, but then I was forced to slow down as I neared Bower's address. For some reason he had insisted I meet him at the head of a junction. I had my sketch of the area but no map. At the time I remember thinking it unusual, especially his insistence on meeting at exactly twelve fifteen. Personally, I always turned up on time, but found it bad grace to repeat instructions unless someone was habitually late. As I turned a bend shielded by a gaunt hedgerow, I saw why Bower wanted me to be punctual.

On my left, the hedgerow bounded the road for hundreds of metres until it disappeared around another bend. On the right, through a lattice of silver birch gilded by sunlight, the white shapes of touring caravans appeared like tombstones. On this side, at a gravel turn-off, a bearded man sat in a wheel chair facing the road. As I swung over on to the gravel he waved to me, with a hesitant querulous expression on his face.

"Bower?" I said.

"Professor Peralis, I presume." The expression left his face and was replaced by a saturnine gloom. "You can park your car over there." He indicated a site a few lengths away. "I'm up on the right. I have difficulty on this gravel surface. The damned site owner won't put in a path, so I'll struggle up there and you can follow on. I had to be specific about times because I can't hang about. Damned wind"

I thought this was because of his injuries but it was not quite like that.

Bower was a handsome man, but nothing like the slim rakish con man I had invented. He had a heavy beard and thick blonde hair. His blue eyes were full of a hesitant deception. It was apparent that he currently deceived himself. In that brief first impression they had shown hope, self doubt and anger.

I watched his thickset frame wheel up the gravelled side road, his long blonde hair hanging over his broad shoulders. I sensed his frustration as the chair laboured in the gravel. His name was familiar to me. There had been a Bower in the past, but where, I could not trace. I would ask Jamie when I saw him. He was better at names.

Bower parked his wheel chair under a porch alongside a battered forty five foot caravan. Struggling with a tarpaulin, he grunted and swore until he had covered the chair - somehow I sensed it would be wrong to offer him help. Then he dragged himself up the porch steps and through a glass fronted door. I followed him in, and he gestured to a seat on an old divan.

For a while I sat, as he stoked up the boiler in the small hall, just out of sight. While he was occupied, I had a chance to examine the room.

The thin walls had handrails stuck to them at varying heights. The rails had been made from a wooden banister. They had been stapled to the wall in an untidy, haphazard fashion. Curtains made from sacking had been tacked to the walls. In places they hung down to let in light. They shook as the wind beat on the caravan walls.

There was little furniture in the room; a few pieces made of cheap second-hand chipboard, the divan and a set of drawers under the far window. Through a large hole in the far wall I could see the outline of a mattress on the floor in the only other room. The caravan smelt of damp wood and old socks, but underneath this mustiness, the lingering scent of incense tainted the air.

The only remarkable thing about the place, excepting its sparsity, was the number of different religious artefacts around the room. A catholic sacred heart hung on the wall alongside rosary beads and a wooden cross. The Koran, the Bhagavad-Gita and a copy of "The Prophet" by Kahlil Ghibran lay on the floor. There were also some Maasai beads and Egyptian scarabs, but most interesting was a small Buddha, about three feet high and made apparently of pure gold. It stood on the drawers facing east. At its feet a withered flower that may have been a dandelion lay rotting in a votive tray. The Buddha looked down at me. I wondered whether he assessed me as his next owner - if anyone can *own* a Buddha.

Bower pulled himself in from the hall and lurched over to the sink. "Would you like a coffee," he said in his mellow, unplaceable accent. "I'm afraid I've no milk." He cast about in the kitchen area looking for cups.

"No thanks. I had an early lunch. I'd like to get straight down to business."

He found a cup and started to fill up a pan of water. "Well, I'll have one. I'm paying for your time." He lit the gas and placed the pan over the burning flame. "I forgot to apologise for the mess. Actually, I have few... guests and the apologies are getting much simpler as the furniture gets sold. Soon I'll have nothing and then I won't have to apologise at all. Did you park the car where I told you?"

"Yes, some distance up the drive."

"Good, it's just as well. In fact, it's a fairly ordinary car isn't it? I'd advise you to sell it after you leave here. The less people that trace you here the better."

I smiled. "Why the secrecy?"

"That will become apparent."

He poured out his coffee and struggled over to a seat, spilling half a cup over the floor as he missed a handhold. "Damn, it's not the tennis I miss; it's never getting a full cup of coffee."

"Would you like me...?"

"No," he growled. "No sympathy. It makes me sick."

"I wasn't offering sympathy," I replied. "Just practical help. I can make coffee."

He sighed and swept the blonde hair from his face. "Sorry. I've only had this disability six months and I still haven't learned to handle it."

"Would it be impolite to ask how it happened?"

"Not impolite – dangerous perhaps but... I suppose you could find out." He took a sip from the cup and grimaced. "In a sense it's the real reason I asked you here." He held his hand up in a negative gesture as I started to rise. "No, I do want you utilise your skill, in fact I'm desperate for you to do so. It's just that I wished I hadn't asked you seeing you here now." His voice lowered. "It seems rather pathetic but I didn't expect you to be an attractive woman."

"Yes, it does seem rather pathetic," I said. "You think it all right to lead unattractive people into dangerous situations?"

"No, no. On the phone you were just a voice. Someone, who had knowledge that I need, need desperately. At least let me explain…"

I rose from the divan and tugged at the sack curtain. A goldcrest had flitted on to the neighbouring fence gusted by the wind and maintaining its perch with difficulty. Behind it I saw the curtains of the opposing caravan twitch. A face disappeared from view. I would have smiled at the absurdity of the situation but there was something uncanny about it. On the one hand I felt as though I were in some sort of elaborate conspiracy, like a birthday party game, on the other I felt a nagging dread. A little like the feeling that had come over me when I saw the butterfly in the restaurant; a feeling of dislocation. I decided to stay a little longer. As I did I saw a vague blonde-haired girl stare briefly from the opposing window and disappear. Just some curious country girl. I turned from the window to Bower. He looked relieved.

"I lost the use of my legs in a car accident," he continued after a space. "Well, not so much of an accident. The driver of the vehicle hit me as I was walking home from the local pub. I was lying on the ground with my pelvis shattered, half-conscious and screaming. But I still had the awareness to watch as he looked back from his car and then reversed hard straight for me."

"He wanted you dead?"

"If I hadn't crawled across the road like an animal I would be dead. As it was he went over my legs. Only the arrival of another car prevented him finishing me. He took off into the night."

"This is quite awful, but what does it have to do with your wanting me?"

Bower stared at me. "I'm sorry," he said. "I've involved you now whether you like it or not. I shouldn't have done, but I have. Your coming here may have been seen. Possibly not."

"Seen by whom?"

"The people who are trying to kill me."

"Hmm," I said. "I'm seriously considering raising my fee. Who are these people?"

"If I knew, I wouldn't be here now." He gripped the arms of the chair. "It's something to do with my grandfather, his work out East. I've been making some investigations. He was always held to be a crank but…"

I sat down again wondering if this might be the lead up to an elaborate con. "Wait." I said. "Before you go any further let me see this object."

Bower pointed. "It's in the top drawer. I'll let you get it."

As I opened the dank drawer Bower started to speak in a rush. "This man, the driver - he's one of a group, some sort of secret cult. A very ancient cult. I don't even know why they want me dead. I had been making some extensive research into my grandfather's work: Perhaps my investigations were leading me too close to something nasty, but I suspect it has something to do with the artefact. Perhaps it has ritual significance."

For some time I stared into the drawer. Something, some power in me, did not want to lift up the object. It was not a sense of evil. The object had no evil in it, but it had no good either. As Nietzsche said in a different context, it was beyond good and evil. I was looking at something alien to everything I knew. After some time I picked it up.

"I have the chain," said Bower. "For years, since my grandfather's death I have worn the object without knowing its significance. He willed it to me on his death. Now it looks as though it's going to cause mine."

I hardly heard Bower. I found myself talking like a surgeon explaining a simple dissection to eager students. "The object is pure silver: the figure of a man holding in two hands a smaller effigy. The effigy itself is holding a circle of some sorts." I took out my eyeglass and peered at the circle. "A serpent eating its tail. Inside a Tau, the Egyptian symbol of resurrection; a swastika symbolic of the tremendous forces of nature; interlaced triangles, the seal of Solomon, otherwise known as the star of David; Finally, the sign of *Aum*, naked reality. There is writing here around the serpent. Some of it is effaced. It says…"

"…"there is no religion"." Bower broke my speech. "If you look, I think you'll find the writing is not effaced."

My palm was sweating, glowing with the weight of the object.

"How old would you say this is?"

"It was old in my grandfather's time."

"I'll have to date it for verification."

Bower stared. "Anything to add?"

"The writing appears to be incomplete. It should read, "There is no religion higher than truth.""

"Then you think…"

" … A Theosophical talisman of some sort. It contains all their diverse symbolism. But if it's as old as you're suggesting it could be extremely valuable, a prototype for the modern emblem, perhaps one of those made by Blavatsky or an intimate. Or…" I paused, hesitating to suggest it. "… If it is much earlier, pre-dating Blavatsky it could lend substantial weight to her claims that her work was simply the transmission of deeper, ancient thought. It could be proof of immortality, the birth of a new religion."

"Blavatsky, eh? The founder of the Theosophical movement?" Bower grinned. "This is all you can tell me?"

I flushed. "You've only just shown me the object. Given time…"

"Time," Bower's blue eyes stared through me. "I don't have

time, woman."

I put the object back in the drawer. It seemed unnaturally heavy as though it contained a greater mass than its appearance suggested. It was a relief to let it go. "I'll leave," I said. "The fee will be nominal; my expenses and time."

Bower slumped into the chair. "You are the best in the field…"

"That's right." I put the eyeglass back in my purse. "I learned from the best, and they are now dead, so I am the best."

"It wasn't a question, but a statement. I researched you. I won't see you out. You can charge your standard fee, but I have no cash."

"It seems, then, you have wasted my time, as well as me wasting yours."

"No. Let me tell you, Professor Peralis. I am a disappointed man. You, in fact, were my last hope." Bower sighed deeply. "I would like you to take as your fee the Buddha, something my grandfather picked up in his travels. It's quite priceless."

"I cannot accept it."

"But you must. Firstly because it is all I have left and secondly because I shall have no use for it."

"Mr Bower, this is quite unnecessary."

His face grew livid with anger. "Would you rather I sold it down town to some market stall because, believe me, that is what I shall do." He surged across the room, gripping the handrails. He took the Buddha from its shelf and thrust it into my hands. "It's yours, by God. At least you'll appreciate its worth." The votive tray fell, dashing the flower and the rotten water on the floor. A rank smell rose up between us.

"I shall keep it until you change your mind," I said. It was clear I wouldn't be leaving the caravan without it.

Bower pulled the drawer out and took the chain from around his neck. He placed the chain and the strange emblem in a paper bag. "I feel like I'm casting the runes here," he said, pushing the bag towards me. "But I have to go through with it."

"I won't be working for you again, Bower. I regret your condition and the reasons behind it, but I'm not in this business to be insulted."

"You say you're the best, but you are entirely wrong in your assumptions about this device." He held the bag out under my nose. "At the very least, you'll want to find out your mistake."

I hesitated. It was not just my professional pride; there was something quite repellent about the thing. I didn't want it... but Bower knew I would be unable to resist not knowing. For some moments we stood opposed; the crippled second-hand dealer with his world in ruins and the rich antiquarian.

Disgusted with myself and the whole business, I took the bag. Bower fell back on to his chair, almost as though his support had been rocked from under him. "That's it," he muttered. "That's it, then."

I walked out feeling weighted and dirty. When I got to the porch, I shouted to Bower. "I'll let you know what I find."

There was a moment's silence and then he replied, his voice faint and distant.

"Don't bother," he said. "That's it now, finished."

His words had lingered with me all day, and through my dreams at night I had seen the talisman and Bowers embittered face.

I couldn't bear to open the bag when I returned to the office. The next morning I'd been busy seeing clients on various trivial matters, and then this old man, sent no doubt by Kennedy, with his cigarette and bubble gum cards. He stared at me now, with his kind old face and his cap in his hand like the archetypal grandfather.

*

"Well," I held up one of the Egyptian cards and smiled.

"Cavanders is the company that issued these quite beautiful cards. It was in 1928, six years after the discovery of the tomb of Tutankhamen king of the eighteenth dynasty of Egypt. The excavations inspired a great popular revival of Egyptology. These cards were part of that revival. Lovely."

"Marvellous. You wouldn't credit it. Just a set of tobacco cards."

"On the other hand these bubble gum cards are quite, quite special. "Mars Attacks". They were issued by A. and B.C. Gum a subsidiary of Tops but were actually withdrawn from sale because they were considered too horrific. Ghastly, wonderful cards."

"Well, well, withdrawn from sale. Nowadays that would be called censorship. So, they're not much good, then?"

"Don't be too hasty. I do know a man who would be very pleased to see these cards in his collection."

"The Egyptian or the...other?"

"The other. You see, the Egyptian set is incomplete."

"Missing cards?"

"Yes, unless you have any more?" The old man shook his head sadly. "You've shown me twenty three cards and there should be twenty five. Let's see. Number two and number eighteen are missing."

"And my old dad used to bring them out all those times as though it was the full set." He shook his head slowly. "So, they're not worth much after all."

"Not worth you selling them."

His face wilted. He began to pick the cards up in his trembling hands.

"But that's the bad news. The good news is that the bubble gum cards are worth at least five hundred pounds, and I know just the man who wants them."

"Five hundred pounds?" He dropped the cards.

"And, I shall insist that the only way you'll part with the

cards is if he completes your Egyptian set. He has contacts all over, so there should be no difficulty."

"Five hundred. Well, well. They cost me sixpence too."

I gave the old man his money. He stood holding the notes as though they might disappear and then he said in a quiet voice. "I'm glad about my old dad's cards. I didn't really fancy giving them up. I wish you luck lady because you deserve it."

I need it, I thought, after yesterday.

"She was right about you, you know your stuff," he said to himself.

"Kennedy?"

"The young girl I met at the Quaker's hall," he said, half turning. "Too serious for her age."

"Kennedy," I said.

Chapter 4
It Begins

MR JARVIS was a small man with bright, penetrating eyes. When he spoke he did not seem to look at, but through me, as though I was glass. He scratched at the elbow of his shabby tweed suit and offered me a glass of mineral water.

""Kennedy", you say. That's an unusual name for a girl." His voice held a permanent tinge of surprise.

"It's the only name she gave me. It may be a first name or a surname…"

"Or a fictitious name, a pseudonym perhaps. And you say she comes here?"

I described Kennedy - the biker's jacket, the rope around the baggy jeans; clothes that had not changed in the months I had known her.

Jarvis scratched his chin. "There are a few girls who might vaguely fit that description. Why don't you come to the meeting tomorrow and see for yourself." He gave me a thin lipped smile. "It's the music of the Vedas; perhaps you might learn something significant, unexpected."

There was something about Jarvis, despite his apparent friendliness and willingness to help, that repelled me. I felt that any invitation would have some ulterior motive.

"I'm busy tomorrow."

"Pity." He seemed instantly to lose interest.

I walked around the Quaker's hall taking in the atmosphere. There were some huddled groups of grey looking individuals discussing various religious ideas or making general chit-chat in a cold draughty hallway. These people would meet in one of the rooms beyond to listen to some "expert" in the paranormal or some spiritualist with a new theory.

There was a sense that it was all over really. The heyday of spiritualism of this nature had dissipated in the early 1900's but always there were groups of outsiders who persisted in reviving interest. From my experience these groups spent a lot of time bemoaning the current state of the world, seeking new recruits, and discussing deep symbolism, as a replacement for sex. In fact, it was exactly the type of place that Kennedy would find, and its members would delight in finding her, a new naive vessel to fill in a number of ways.

I avoided the huddled groups. I felt the eyes of one or two of the more alert ones cast across and almost will me into their arms, although in the main they seemed preoccupied with each other. I looked at the shabby stalls that contained a few pamphlets. A bookstall was laid out. It displayed various modern religious texts. Posters of starving children and old crippled men glared out at me. I picked up one of the books, and then dropped it as though it were hot.

On the cover was the symbol. I looked behind me as though impelled by some sixth sense. Mr Jarvis stood talking to an old woman. The woman was dressed in a grey raincoat. She had a grey scarf around her neck and her hair was grey. Her eyes were gunmetal grey. They stared from a pale face that had only the hint of red rimming the eyes and flushing the cheeks. She stared at me as I stared at her, and in the moment I felt what it must be like to be a virus on a slide. An old fashioned monocle magnified one of her eyes; it gave her face a peculiar lopsided appearance, as though she permanently stared askance. While she watched me I dropped my glance and stared at the cover of the book. I still felt her eyes in me and I glanced up quickly. She was staring at my neck. Involuntarily my hands crept to my throat and I felt the silver chain that I still wore and for some reason I felt a tingling surge through my loins. It was an unwitting, unwilling feeling. It began deep in the flesh of my groin and extended around my whole loins. It felt as though a hand gripped me between the sacrum and the perineum. I can only describe it as a kind of exploratory handling almost as though someone were laying on hands, but obviously whoever was exerting this psychic force was no priest.

I felt the book tremble in my hand. I tried to concentrate on the cover, read the title, but I could not continue. It was the symbol, and of course at a theosophical meeting it should be visible. But it should not have written beneath it "There is no religion." I knew it just as I knew that I had to get out before the feeling submerged me. It was so intrusive, personal to me, but with a feeling of complete impersonality on the part of the giver. I felt a light sweat break out on my forehead. I willed myself to drop the book. It fell from my hands, and it seemed an eternity before it hit the bookstall. I walked rigidly towards the door. As I did I risked a glance to my left.

The monocled woman now stood next to Jarvis but she beamed across at me with her face fixed in a kind of rictus that another might call a smile. It was as though the face of a corpse had been tampered with. I had never seen anything so obscene.

Mr Jarvis looked on like a rather abstracted referee. He examined his fingernails and whispered something to the woman. Inside me I felt something snap as though a cord had been released and I had been set free. I looked back to the notice board behind the two figures. "The Vedas; a talk by Miss Shadfri on Eastern Angels." The woman with the monocle smiled again. Was she Shadfri? Some occultist with a sadistic bent. I walked outside into the rain.

Manchester was a black and white movie. Like extras in a silent film, late nighters hurried by in the pouring rain. Despite the rain I sat down on a bench in the street. I felt physically drained, as though I had donated soul instead of blood to a supernatural institution. A young man sat down beside me dressed in patched jeans and a big leather coat. "I need money," he said in quite a casual voice.

"Don't we all," I said.

"Yeah, but I need it to eat. You need it to spend on clothes."

In the dripping rain his hair was like grey-green seaweed. His face had been washed away to anonymity. Only his grey eyes stared with a bleak intensity from his thin face.

"Why are you wearing sixty quid trainers if you spend all your money on food?"

"Piss off you old git. Things aren't always as they seem." His face took on a sudden drab life as though a marble statue given up by the sea had suddenly begun to walk up the beach. He gave a scowl. "You might not always be so well off."

He rose to his feet and then with a curse, paced away into the rain. I followed his retreating form and threw him some small change. He turned and scrabbled on the ground and in the gutter looking for the grey discs that lay like spilled pools of light against the dark shining concrete.

Now I felt really stupid and sickened to the guts by the human condition. I walked to the car trying to pull myself together. Why hadn't I bought the book? Even now I could back and get a copy, start discovering things I ought to know.

Still I felt my feet taking me further away from the Quaker's hall.

Was it the monocled woman driving me away, somehow? Had she been the author of that intimate and distasteful attack or had it been my imagination? I was no sceptic. Although I believed in logic, rationality; I had explored through meditation the non-rational symbolic world of dreams and trance. I was conducting my own psychic and spiritual experiments. I knew it "worked". I had also seen enough out east to convince me that there was more to life than would fill the journals of western science. Yet this was really the first time that any thing so clearly external to me had intruded on my own space.

Perhaps it was the events of the last days.

I drove to Jamie's cottage. The lights were on and the old

place, with its stone and its rose bushes and its views of the distant hills, seemed so ordinary that it was comforting. I spent most of my youth and childhood in this village; the hills were like the familiar face of an old friend. Jamie had come later to the village and was doubtless still regarded as a stranger after fifteen years. He was surprised to see me.

"I need help," I said. "I need you?"

He looked me up and down. "Let's go out for a bit," he said. "There's a party at Conal's place. We'll go for an hour. You know everyone there."

"I'm..."

"...going. I know what's good for you."

He was right. Conal lived in the village. There were people I hadn't seen in years. Old family friends. The old priest was on form, gathering a crowd around the fire, sitting at the old bridge table where I had played chess and beaten him to his astonishment when I was thirteen. He greeted me with a smile, but his face looked older, greyer. I had one of those moments best described in Joyce's "The Dead" where you see that others may not see another year. You could read it in his eyes.

"Dr Peralis! No, Professor now - or should I call you Annie?" he said reaching for a glass.

"Annie will do, Father."

"She beat me at chess, you know," he turned to the crowd. "You were only ten."

"Thirteen, Father. Age makes you exaggerate"

"An old man in a draughty house under a windy knob..."

"...Eliot," I said before he could finish.

"Good Heavens, beating me at quotations now. I just don't stand a chance."

Everyone was there. Making the usual jokes and telling the old stories. It was as though my youth and childhood were being replayed again by friends and distant relatives. I think that for the first time I felt saddened by the spectacle. Once I had revelled in my brilliant career and the implicit compliments that only people who have known you for years can give by not mentioning any of it. Now it all seemed a little tired, as though some of the runners were dropping out of the race.

"Are you staying?" continued Conal, hardly listening to my replies. "I convinced Andy to bring his fiddle," he continued, "and one of his friends plays something. What was it...?" Conal shouted across the room. "he's in the kitchen. Jamie, get yourself a whiskey, only a small one, mind. I know what you Scots are like. Charades later, as always."

"I can't stay, Father."

"On a case, Annie, eh? You can't put it past me. Here, come over by the fire and let's talk. It's been too long."

Jamie jigged off to the kitchen, taking the daughter of one of my cousins off with a whoop.

We sat by the fire and Conal gripped my hand as he always did. "Now don't spoil your beauty with those frowns and tell me what's up."

"There's too much to tell, really."

"Never."

I thought I might show Conal the amulet, but I knew that he would strongly disapprove of anything remotely connected with the occult. All I would get were his warnings, and I didn't want to upset him. Suddenly I blurted out. "Do you believe in hell?"

He looked at me in surprise. "Gosh, that's a bit heavy. Is it a confession you're after?"

"No, No. Just what you think. Academically if you like."

"There's no such thing as a purely academic question when it comes to your soul, Annie."

"Just tell me."

"Yes, there is a hell, Annie, just as there is a heaven and a purgatory. If I'm lucky I'll settle for the last." He grinned.

"So you die and then there's the afterlife?"

"Well, that's about it?"

"Does evil exist?"

"Oh yes, Annie, and you don't want any of it."

"Can it exist in an object?"

"Now, that's open to debate. I mean what is an object? We could go all scholastic here."

"You know what I mean. You hear about these weapons of power, and then there's the crucifix and all sorts."

"Well, all I'll say is that in the transubstantiation Christ's body enters a wafer, and that's the power of good. Now Satan, he's a nasty dog and maybe he can get in an object as well, but I wouldn't want to know about it. Now, Annie, are you going to tell me what you've found? Is it something awful?"

"I don't know Father. It worries me but it was the way I found it. I got it from a man very fearful for his life." I showed him my neck, and in that second I was aware that he was looking at the valley of my breasts. It was only an instant, but I felt the power of it and a fraction of disgust. The look passed and the feeling too. Conal looked at the amulet. He shook his head. "It means nothing to me, Annie. All I can say is that you should wear a decent Christian cross."

Jamie looked over my shoulder with a glass of wine and a whiskey. "Let's not get too good, Father, we can't all be good."

Conal laughed. "Music," he shouted. "Give us a good reel, the Mason's Apron, Andy! Where's that lad with the Bodrhan."

The dancing helped me forget, but at some point I had to get away. My last vision of the party was Conal up looking old and brave, playing charades.

When we got outside the wind was gusting about with intent. I was glad to get back to the warmth and stillness of Jamie's cottage.

Jamie poured me a large whiskey; poured himself a larger one. He sat down beside the open fire, toyed with the poker, his handsome face perturbed and looking slightly satanic in the light of the flames. "This is serious," he said eventually. "I heard some of what you were saying to old Conal. I can't seem to find any suitable jokes."

"Good. I'm not looking for jokes. Have you read anything on witchcraft?"

"Now I can think of some jokes, although none are particularly good." Jamie saw my face and changed tack. "A little. Mostly Hammer Horror stuff."

"I'm not talking about upturned crucifixes or exorcisms or indeed new ageism."

"Then what are you talking about."

"I'm talking about the power to influence someone from a distance."

"Some psychic phenomenon?"

"Sort of." I explained a little about the monocled woman; told him about what I had seen with Conal, the ugliness of it.

"Interesting." said Jamie. "But then is it not true that you have been stressed out lately?"

"My job is fairly stressful and now is a stressful time, but I do know my own mind, Jamie."

He smiled. "I'll grant you that."

"Bower himself told me about this symbol and the evil influence it was effecting on him."

"The object on the silver chain? Do you have it still?"

"I took the chain from around my neck. Jamie examined the object. Under the light from the fire it took on an unnatural glow, as though it were about into flare into light. Slowly, he handed it back.

"And this is the same object that your madman, Ka, has around his neck."

I nodded.

Jamie took a large gulp of whiskey. "It seems too pat to be a coincidence. Now don't shout me down. Kennedy could have set you up for this."

I bit my lip. But the thought had been sneaking around the back of my mind. I was unwilling to concede anything to Jamie on this, though. "Have you found anything on Ka?"

Jamie smiled. "Something. I've traced his description to an extent. You didn't give me a lot to go on but I've narrowed him down to three possible institutions in the Northwest. The photograph helped. I expect I'll have some sort of residence mapped out shortly. My friend at the station is looking up mug shots and the finger prints, and so on."

"Ka is the solution to this. I know it. There is something about him, a marred innocence."

"Perhaps," said Jamie. He swirled his whiskey around in the glass. "You see Bower as a sidelined figure, then."

"Bower is terribly afraid, and perhaps a little mad."

"Not a good combination. If you do go to see him again, take me with you."

I smiled at Jamie. Under the Edinburgh gentility he was a hard man. He had earned a black belt in karate in his teens. In some ways he was like a brother to me. He looked out for me, tolerated my moods; he understood me as Conrad never had. On some of those trips up north before we were married I remembered him walking alongside Conrad. Jamie was the bigger man and I wondered now when his drinking had started.

"Do you remember our winter traverse on Aonach Eagach?"

"I'll never forget it. Conrad in the lead. You almost slipped on that harmless Glacis."

"He held me."

"Yes," said Jamie. "He did." He swirled his glass. "You married him the following year."

There was a long silence. "He loved the mountains but they took him in the end."

The irony did not escape me. "Yes he loved the mountains. Why do you think he split from the party in the Inchnadamph?"

Jamie frowned. "I don't remember much about it." I could tell he was lying. "We wanted to try the Suilven. He…"

"…and the girl - what was her name?"

"Sarah, attractive girl."

"But they…"

"They were lovers. I knew anyway."

"He never betrayed you. But I know that the reason he parted with us was the girl. He had…taken a shine to her. Wanted to impress her I suppose."

"Like me."

"Nobody is like you but …they wanted to go off on their own. Who am I to say? We warned him"

"Long ago."

"And they are both dead now."

"Missing somewhere in the northern highlands."

"It's a bleak place. They never found the bodies; highly unusual. He wouldn't say where they were going, totally against the code - but they should have found them. The girl, Sarah; It's coming back to me" He jumped to his feet. "She was a Bower. Sarah Bower. I'm sure of it."

"A coincidence?"

"Some coincidence. I'd like to see this Bower. I remember the girl's face. He couldn't bear some grudge, could he?"

I walked to the window and opened the curtains. The night was dark. Was there something moving in the garden? I shuddered "I don't think so. Why should he bear a grudge against me?"

I felt my head spin. I remembered Bower's agitated face. I felt a tingling in my thighs, unexpected in its intensity.

"Perhaps it was his cousin or sister. How do we know? It'll have to be looked at."

"It's a common enough name."

The night sky was charcoal grey on the window, like a tapestry. *I could seduce Jamie now.* Where had that thought come from? *I could open my legs for him.* The whiskey seemed to burn like a fire tightrope between my sacrum and my perineum. Outside I saw a cat on the far wall. I wouldn't have noticed it except for its bright green eyes staring intently like twin stars.

"Jamie," I said. "Please shut the curtains." It was my voice speaking. Not the inner voice that seemed to speak from my sensations ; not my soul.

I heard Jamie rise from his chair, and sensed his presence next to mine. His hand brushed against my bare shoulder as he drew the curtains.

"Fuck me." I said.

"What!"

The feelings melted through my body. I felt the trembling all along my frame and I moved quickly away from Jamie, and sat on the edge of the sofa.

"It was the cat." I said.

"It was you saying..."fuck me"." said Jamie, bewildered. "I don't quite know how to take that."

"No it was the cat outside. It manifested some sort of power latent in me. It drew me down to bodily sensations. Of course I'm physically attracted to you, that's what it worked on."

"You're still upset. I'll get rid of the cat if it bothers you." He made to open the curtains again but I stopped him.

"Don't. This is witching. That cat is a transmitter of someone else's energy force."

Jamie sat down heavily. "I think you'd better explain things."

"There isn't much to explain. Bower says some group is hunting him down. I believe him. He gave me a talisman that the group wants. Now that group is hunting me."

"Wait a minute. You've only had this thing a matter of moments. How are they hunting you?"

"Not me then, the talisman. It attracts them." I could see it all.

Jamie looked at me as though he was going to laugh, and then he changed his mind. "If you really believe that, throw it away."

I clutched the silver talisman in my hand. It glowed with its sickly Inner Light, felt heavy in my palm: It was not something that one idly cast aside.

Jamie could see that I wasn't going to part with it. "Stay the night here," he said. "And before you say it, I'm locking my door in case you come after me this time." I laughed, despite the growing chill that seemed to enervate my insides; "Don't they have witches in Edinburgh, then?"

Jamie nodded. Flicked the black curls from his forehead, poured himself another scotch. "We have witches." He rose from the chair and brought the bottle over to me. Poured a large glass, and stood by the window. "They burned the last witch in the borders in the seventeenth century. Some old women, no doubt falsely accused, probably a herb gatherer, one of the old school of medicine."

"Ireland killed their last witch much later."

"The Celtic race still carries trace elements of its ancient barbarism, or so they say. I know myself some of the old customs still carry on. Up on the Pentlands for example, and Arthur's Seat in Edinburgh, there are still people who will climb the hill on All Hallows eve to light a fire. They burn stones in the fire. Each stone is marked with an initial. If any stones are thrown from the fire, cracked or broken, the initialled person will die within the year."

"Ever tried it?"

"No. Unlike you, I don't believe in witches."

"But you Celts have always had a thing about seers, people who could see into the future. The second sight."

"Yes. They say that the left-hand side of our brain is utilised more than you Angles. I believe it's one of Wilson's pet theories: The left-hand side controls the symbols and imagery, the right hand side controls the rationalisation. The Celts are supposed to be more intuitive, less rational than their neighbours. Personally, I think it's a lot of hogwash. Some Celts are intuitive types, some are rational, and some like me after a few drinks are utterly irrational, and unintuitive, if that's a word." Jamie gulped down his glassful. He was starting to slur his words slightly. In a few minutes I knew he would probably forget his good intentions and start thinking about how to get my knickers off. These thoughts would no doubt be assisted by my recent announcements.

The room began to swim slightly before my eyes. The heavily brocaded curtain was blocking out any air from outside, the fire was consuming air from inside and the whiskey was robbing me of oxygen. I felt the fatigue and the stress of the day draw me into the welcoming arms of the sofa.

I woke up with a blanket over my knees and the sun streaming like the shaft of a spear from the seam of the curtain. I smiled to myself, thinking of Jamie staggering about tending to me like a befuddled old nun. I got up, found the bathroom empty and the shower waiting. The water was hot. Steam rose around me like clouds of mist, the shower pelting me with pearls.

I turned, and towelled myself down in front of the mirror, examining what time had done with my body. My breasts were small, which was fortunate; the nipples were dark, the result of bearing Kirsty some fifteen years before. My waist was trim and my hips seemed to swell out more than I remembered. My legs were thin, as were my arms yet they had the strength imbued of karate, yoga and swimming. In all I looked pretty well for my age. Clearly, I was still attractive enough to lure Jamie.

God, when I thought of the things I'd said to him the night before. Was it the whiskey, the stress? No. I knew for certain that it was some psychic power. Witchcraft had the power to enwrap you in the night and then persuade you in the morning that it had all been an illusion or some private introspection. It was not an illusion; I never offered my body to friends after a few whiskies. I had been persuaded by some external force to do so.

I had a good idea where that external force emanated from: The monocled woman, or maybe Jarvis. Either one looked like they might have the power to do something nasty. Evil often hid itself in something insignificant. As nothing had ever attacked me before the passing of the talisman, I could only assume that this object was the cause of their interest in me.

I had left the talisman around my neck. I held the chain up and curved the hot silver in my palm, staring at the swastika symbol in the centre. I felt for a second that the wheel was spinning. I found my eyes drawn to the mirror. I watched my breasts rise and fall with my breathing. I looked quickly to my eyes. I looked like a stranger, some erotic, Sapphic woman. My breasts shone white like silver, the red nipples leering like two twin roses. I watched as my left hand curved the swell of my belly. My fingers found the handles of my pelvis. There I rested them before sinking to the floor and opening my legs in front of the mirror.

Slowly, with great deliberation and unwilling, willing intent I began to urinate; the yellow stream of piss bleeding on to the carpeted floor. Unable to find an object with my scrabbling hands I watched the mirror woman using her fingers. Sudden flashes of what she was about to do rocketed through the shocked stratosphere of my brain. I saw myself searching for my private places, ramming my fingers inside myself like a boy chopping holes with the edges of his hands in wet thin card. I saw all this and with a tremendous effort of will prevented it. Shutting my eyes, clinging to a little decent bit of myself.

And then like a woman who had narrowly avoided rape I lay back on the floor wondering what had happened. How I had been chosen out of nameless millions to have this horrible attempt on my self-respect. I sat up, staring in disbelief at the urine in between my legs. Then I looked at my own face in the mirror. I was smiling, although inside I felt disgust. My mirror eyes were smiling, the eyes still of stranger. A dissatisfied predator lurking outside the windows of my soul.

I turned away from the mirror. Here was a challenge for the

moment beyond me.

I searched for a cloth.

When I got downstairs Jamie was struggling with the coffee. His face had all the hallmarks of a disgraceful hangover. I took over, sorting out cups and saucers. He sat down after washing his face in the cold water at the sink. "You made me drink more whiskey," he said when I handed him the coffee.

"I hardly threw it down your throat."

"It was the changed character," he replied taking a slug of coffee and wincing.

"That wasn't me, Jamie."

"I'm glad," he replied. He smiled through the sweating mask of his face. "I like a little romantic prelude."

"In fact, I want to get down to the reason for the whole thing. Can I use your phone?"

We walked through to the lounge. "Listen in please, Jamie, I want you to assess the character of the man".

I phoned Bower; there was a pause then the hollow atmosphere of an answering machine. Bower's modulated tones sounded. I left my message.

When I'd finished, Jamie said "He sounded just as you would imagine him; a bit of a loser, a little bitter, a bit of a put-on accent."

"Does he sound honest?"

"No. And can I say something else. Is it wise to ask a man you hardly know whether a talisman he recently passed to you could result in attacks of erotic behaviour?"

"That is not quite what I asked."

Jamie opened the curtains and groaned as the bright lights of the greying dawn sky hit his eyes.

"Christ. I'm glad I'm not working today.

"That's where you're wrong," I said. "I need you to interview Ka at the office."

"Favours for friends," groaned Jamie...

Jamie closed the door on the cottage. He didn't bother to lock it, which always made me feel good, and we both turned, looking out over the hills and sucked in a little fresh air. As we walked up the path Jamie paused and clutched my sleeve.

"My word," he said.

Under the bush, in a hopelessly contorted position, lay a cat. Its body was stiff and grey; where its eyes had been were burnt charcoal holes.

"It looks as though it has been short circuited," said Jamie. "Like an electric machine".

"Like a body that has contained too much or too different an energy source," I replied.

"I'm beginning to believe all this stuff wholesale," said Jamie. "That cat isn't the only thing you know. The bathroom floor has an immense patch of water all across it. I wonder if it's associated with the cat"

I smiled. "Perhaps it is in a sense, but I don't think you'd believe me if I told you about it."

Jamie followed me in the car until Manchester central; there he side-stepped, and we agreed to meet at the office in an hour.

*

As I crawled through the city centre the drab grey punters crawled through the grey streets. I felt drained, seeing in them only a reflection of my inner self. I knew that I was being influenced, and I had to do something about it. Jamie would provide the answers I needed about Ka, but Bower knew about the talisman. I resolved to hunt out the truth behind it. Clearly it was not a Theosophical cross. It had to be some kind of sect who had robbed the Theosophical images. I could guess who was involved. Jarvis and the monocled woman could easily be members. It seemed impossible that it was all a coincidence.

When I entered the office, Ka stood like a statue in the

doorway. He was exactly where I had left him, as though by some uncanny intuition he knew precisely when I was coming back and had adopted the pose; it was either that or he had stood for hours in the same position. He smiled at me, and I led him through the back room. "Ka" he said as I sat down. He had given me the usual thorough examination to determine whether or not I was Kennedy. When he found out I was not, he sat down in repose as though the world was waiting for him.

I shuffled through the papers on the desk, searching for the answer to the talisman. Each symbol was in the place one would expect from a Theosophical talisman, yet there was an uncanny difference. The single changed phrase "There is no religion", which seemed to turn all the meanings on their head. It could only be a refutation of the Theosophical Society. But what were the motivations behind the opposing society or individual? I had numerous contacts in what could loosely be called the New Age circuit but none of them had the depth of experience I required. There was a woman, though, whom I knew of through one of the contacts. I had never met her, but her reputation resounded through the esoteric circles. I reached for the phone. After a few moments I was speaking to Ms Pontefract.

When she divined the urgency of my need she offered to come and see me in the afternoon. I put the phone down as Jamie walked through the door. He placed a book of mug shots before me. "Mustn't breathe a word of this," he said.

"I got this specially."

He looked across at Ka, said "Hello." Ka got out of his seat and walked up to Jamie. He paused towering over the Scotsman, breathing in his face. Jamie stared at him for a few seconds.

"Ka," said Ka. He sat down.

"What was that about?" said Jamie.

"He was just establishing that you are not Kennedy".

"Ah," said Jamie. "That explains it."

We looked through the books, each taking one half of the page. Eventually, after an hour, we had our man. He was registered in a Manchester home, under 'care assistants'. Prior to this, he had been comatose in a small south England coastal hospital and after this in a mental institution for three years. Incredibly his name was registered as Banberry in the mental institution and Cross in the hospital. Someone with a poor sense of humour was playing an elaborate game with his identity.

"Then who is he?" said Jamie in frustration. "He can't be both Banberry and Cross, and it's incredible that the modern welfare state should get his name wrong and not notice."

"I suppose it's possible. But I wonder if he is either of these names."

Jamie went to the office phone with the hospital number. I went through to the office and turned on the computer. It was possible my private records might throw something up. I stuck his height in. It was unusual enough for something to come up somewhere.

Jamie came through a little later. "The nurse who registered him in hospital is dead. She died in a car crash shortly afterwards." Jamie looked a little pale. "It's like that book on witchcraft in the Bocage. Once you open the box, every incident seems pregnant with adverse possibilities, and they're all directed at you."

I nodded abstractly and tried "missing persons".

"The care assistants have all left. It's a transient job really. The head of their section knew nothing. He looked up the register and found his name and a note that he was officially registered under "Cross" but he seems to think that was just a convenience as he was an unknown.

"Try newspapers," I said. "The date when he went in a coma might show something. An accident or whatever that led to him being comatose."

"I'll go to the central library. See you in about an hour or so."

I sat down for lunch, all the time watching Ka in the office kitchen munching on Pasta he had made himself. It was an incredible sight - like a Goliath wearing an apron or ironing underwear. His motions were like simple motor functions but there seemed to be echoes of something else, some form of defensive psychic behaviour. I left him eating and went back to the computer.

Two hours later Jamie entered. "I got something," he said. "Not much but a small article from the date." He held up a piece of paper. "Man found in street. A brief description. It is him, I'm sure, but they know less than we do. There was no follow up."

I tried in academic records. A few clicks and I had him.

Jamie leaned over my shoulder at the picture. "It's him, but he's not Banbury or Cross."

"Keran Westwood. Born, Edinburgh. Thirty-five years old. Height, six foot eight."

"God!" exclaimed Jamie, "Look at his former occupation".

I looked down at the displayed files of the yearbook. Keran Westwood had been head of philosophy at a major university.

We both stared at the big man sitting on the chair. The witless unintelligent eyes were fixed with hopeless lassitude on the back of his hand. An idle smile played on his handsome lips. Even as we watched a trickle of spittle ran down the side of his mouth.

"What did David Hume say? "Too much philosophy depresses you.""

"Something like that."

"I think we should trace relatives next," said Jamie after a pause.

"What about Kennedy?"

"What about Kennedy? She's dumped him on you. And anyway his folks should know. God knows how he got out of the institution."

I nodded. Jamie was right. We owed it to his people to take him home.

Then the phone rang. I picked it up. It was Bower. He sounded distant.

"You're feeling under threat," he said in a matter of fact voice.

"Yes."

"Is it taking on an unexpectedly personal and intimate character?"

I thought of the various recent events. "I would say it is," I replied.

"It gets worse, really. It's something to do with the root of your being. It operates at various levels. The psychic effects are deep and subtle. There all sorts of manifestations - depression, anger, revelations - all false, of course - and on the physical plane, you get these ridiculous, what could you call them, erotic assaults. They would be comic if they did not imply great danger. Initially, they are the more disturbing because they are so personal, but they're the least of your worries"

"Enough to worry you?"

"You'll be able to control it up to a point when you're among friends."

"I've already made propositions to friends."

Jamie grinned in the background.

"Yes, initially you might. I did, but then there comes a point where you can control that. Afterwards," he hesitated. "You wish to be much more private, auto-eroticism, and then casual liaisons will appeal to you. It's an attempt to disable your concentration. I'm not saying you will succumb to them, but you may well think about it."

I thought of the Lenas street beggar and I felt a tingle in my thighs.

"Yes, I can imagine that," I said.

"You can resist it all if you're a person of fairly moral character, but the real question comes when a stranger approaches you."

"What do you mean?"

"Well people you know are hedged with social ties, they chain you in past relationships, expectations of how to behave, rules and regulations. You can fit in with their pattern. When you meet a stranger, it's different. If that stranger is trying to bend your will, you'll find it much more difficult to resist. It could be you'll do anything for them. That's part of the effect. It's a lowering of your spirit so you become enslaved to their purpose. Remember, quite simply they want that talisman. The auto-eroticism crap is a by-product of the deeper manifestations; an absurd and pathetic debilitation. All they want is that talisman."

"Bower, how do you know this?"

"Isn't it obvious?"

"So you met these people?"

There was a silence.

"If you met them, how did you not manage to ascertain the meanings behind the symbol?"

"I resisted the temptations. That's when they got angry. I investigated on my own, and that's where a blank was drawn. I found out certain things but not enough - that's why they're going to kill me."

"Do you have any advice?"

"Give them back the talisman at the first opportunity."

"I can't do that."

There was a pause; the space in between the telephone wires seemed to echo emptiness. "Then, like me, you're lost," said Bower. He rang off.

Jamie poured out a whiskey. He poured another, but I shook my head. He sat down at the desk. "Listen," he said. "You know I've always been concerned about this Kennedy girl, warned you off and so on. Well, she is nothing compared to Bower. He has got to go, and his talisman has also got to go - back to him if possible, or in the Mersey. Either would be suitable."

"It's not as simple as that, Jamie. Look at Ka...Keran, look around his neck."

The silver talisman shone, half-hidden by his shirt and the black hairs on his chest.

Jamie shrugged. "I suppose you're right. It's the sort of thing you have to investigate even if it kills you, and it probably will."

"Inchnadamph didn't kill me, nor K2."

"Nor that debacle with the Russians, I suppose," said Jamie, sighing.

"Nor those diamond "collectors" from the Netherlands, and they were nasty."

"Jamie emptied his glass, shuffled the papers on the desk. "I'll inform Professor Westwood's folks if we can trace them. In the meantime let's see that silver talisman again. You ought to compare it to Westwood's and see if there is any anomaly."

I took the talisman out of my pocket as Jamie picked up the phone. Switching on the desk lamp, I placed it on the table. Ka looked at it with a baffled and unexpected anxiety. Jamie stopped dialling as Ka leaned forward, his nostrils sniffing, his eyes wide. He took the chain from around his own neck and placed it alongside the other. Superficially, the two were exactly alike. Ka seemed pleased with this. Then on a sudden he retracted his own Talisman and pointed at Bower's. He laughed.

A horrible empty sound.

"Kennedy" he said, and then again "Kennedy." He shook his head, dropped his face in his hands and began to slowly sob.

Jamie sighed, put the phone down. "Did you see the difference?" he said.

"Yes," I replied. "His is the Theosophical symbol with the words unchanged. Mine…"

Jamie nodded. "I can hardly wait for this afternoon. I need some theosophical knowledge almost as much as I need a double malt."

Chapter 5
The Theosophist

WE HUSTLED Keran to the kitchen when the buzzer rang. In the two-way mirror, I saw the woman I assumed to be Ms Pontefract. She was young, blonde, beautiful; dressed in a white two piece suit that looked hopelessly impractical for the city. An air of impossibility hung around her, as though she had blazoned into our dimension and was somewhat surprised to find it so dingy. She sat on the Hepplewhite splat chair, her gaze resting languidly on the books and magazines.

"Stay here," I whispered to Jamie. "See what you think of her."

I walked out into the waiting room. She rose with dignity. I saw then that she was older than I had first supposed, but her make-up was subtle, her skin soft, and her pale blue eyes had a degree of attraction that led one away from any possible imperfections in her face. In the first seconds of our introduction, two amazing things happened. Firstly, I felt a rush of sexual pleasure suffusing my body - the first time I had ever been attracted to a woman. It made me blush like a girl. I could only attribute the feeling to the hex on me. The second thing was more remarkable. As we spoke, her eyes never left my face. We were talking normally and then, as though time had gone out for lunch, her left eye slowly winked, a movement that seemed impossible. All the while she talked in a level tone, in total contrast to the movement of her eyes. The feeling gave me a sense of nausea, as though I was being turned inside out. Then, as though I had failed a test, her eye slowly opened. I became aware that she was saying something about the chair.

"I don't much like copies, but I suppose they are functional in an office waiting room. Do you think it's wise to have a first edition of Tolkien's "The Hobbit" left out with the magazines on the table?"

"Ah," I said. "I'm pleased you noticed that. It's a test. Silly sort of idea, really." She kept looking at me as I talked and I felt that within that gaze I was utterly silly.

"The second edition is more valuable. The first wasn't illustrated. Does that pass your... test?"

"It gets a distinction," I said, trying to recover from the girlish feeling.

"I don't mind tests," she continued. "They can sometimes be fun, but I thoroughly dislike being spied on." She nodded to the mirror. "Do you really need to have that thing there?"

I coloured. Ms Pontefract was humbling me without even trying. "I find it useful," I said "to assess the character of customers. Also, a woman alone in the big city needs to be forewarned of any trouble."

She did not reply.

"Jamie," I said. "You can come out." I invited her through to the office. Jamie followed, with his eyes fixed to Ms Pontefract's swaying hips. He glanced at me with eyebrows raised and a wicked smile on his face.

"I came because you said it was a very serious matter," said Ms Pontefract. She had ensconced herself immediately in my favourite balloon back chair. I glanced at the French *cabriole* legs, and comparing their elegance to hers. "I wouldn't have come otherwise as I'm very busy," she continued, sipping the coffee that Jamie had made. "The Society is my life work. It takes up most of my time."

"Before I come to the point," I said. "I'd be very grateful if you could tell me about the aims and purposes of the Theosophical Society. I ask this only because it may have a bearing on the matter I wish to discuss with you."

Ms Pontefract ranged her elegant fingers through her blonde hair. I could smell the natural fragrance of her body as she spoke. "Theosophy is a spiritual science open to anyone from any religion, or indeed to any atheist or agnostic who wishes to join, provided they have two referees." She gazed at me intently, as if I would struggle to find two referees in a stadium full of Theosophists.

"That's just that Ron Hubbard thing. Diatribes…" said Jamie, crumbling as Ms Pontefract directed her Athenian eyes towards him

"Dianetics," she said. "No it has nothing to do with that, although anyone who followed that creed could apply for membership. There is no exclusion."

"Even for someone who was a practising witch."

She nodded.

"What about a black witch?" I said.

"We would not welcome anyone who wished to practice evil of any description. One of the purposes of the Society is to seek and share knowledge. Let me make it clearer: Most members believe in three simple truths. Firstly, that the spirit of man is immortal. It is a continual process of growth. Secondly, this spirit can be observed by the perceptive. Thirdly, each person is the author of their own universe. He or she," she looked at me again, "is the author of their own punishment or reward, their own heaven or hell."

"Forgive me," said Jamie. "I'm a practical type. That all sounds very laudable to me, but a little abstract, like "love your neighbour". Nice and simple, but means very little. What marks out the difference between you and someone who just wants to be nice?"

"We pursue truth," said Ms Pontefract.

"Doesn't everyone?" said Jamie. He was beginning to feel more comfortable now, and if I knew him would attempt, somehow, to wheedle an evening out with Ms Pontefract. I butted in.

"What would motivate someone to join your organisation?" I said.

"There are a number of reasons why a person would be

attracted to it. Good reasons are that it explains how life is a unity, it shows how our nature has seven parts, renders life intelligible, removes fear of death. I could go on and on."

"What are its views on spirit?" I said.

"Theosophists often hold differing viewpoints, but most would accept that we are all divine in our essential nature. Our bodies are mortal, but contain spirit."

"Are you connected with the Spiritualists?" Jamie asked the question innocently enough, but it seemed to go down like a lead balloon with Ms Pontefract.

"No. Spiritualists in my view are misguided, having failed to see that the spirit they try to recall is simply ego."

"Could you explain that more fully?"

She sighed, looked at her watch. "A spiritualist tries to recall a spirit back to this plane. In a sense that is like asking a dummy to pose as a human. Once spirit has left this plane there is no purpose in returning. A medium, in my view, either talks to herself or to an ego, not to a spirit."

Jamie sat down at the desk. His hands searched for a whiskey that was not there.

"Theosophists regard the spirit as immortal. It exists after death, its object is to realise itself, to become aware of its divinity, not to return as a side-show for lonely people."

"So, you believe in reincarnation?"

"I know that reincarnation is the near inevitable result of living in this corporeal form."

"How can you know?" said Jamie.

"I know because I have been reincarnated several times."

"You remember your previous incarnations?" I said.

"Yes, back to Babylon."

"I'll get some whiskey," said Jamie. He left.

Silence descended on us. Little things seemed enlarged in the claustrophobia of the room and the silence. I was strongly conscious of the unperfumed yet sweet fragrance of her body. I raised my eyes from on her legs; felt embarrassment colour my cheeks. She stared back at me, holding the white saucer in one elegant hand. Her nails were unpainted, and I could make out the tiny half moon cuticles of her fingernails. Her white dress glowed like a bright snowy morning; her intense eyes, like pale moons, held to my chair;

Whether it was the glow of the desk lamp or my bad eyesight, or perhaps something half understood, I became aware of an aura surrounding her body. It seemed to emerge from behind her like an angelic suffusion. For the first time, she smiled.

Jamie came in with a decanter full of whiskey. The bright lights seemed to whirl in and on the decanter as he poured a glass out. He offered one to Ms Pontefract, but she declined. I took a glass and swirled it around in my hand. "Would I be right, then, in thinking that you see the soul as an evolving entity, that this body is just an envelope?"

"Yes, we reincarnate. The root of this belief is Buddhism."

"You are a Buddhist?"

"I favour much of what is said in Buddhism, but as a Theosophist I don't take it all on board without thought. I am always searching for enlightenment - through science, through religion, through self-perception, poetry. There is more truth in few lines of Kahlil Ghibran or Omar Khayyam than bundles of textbooks."

"So, you believe that I've been dead and come back again?" said Jamie, downing his whiskey.

"Yes. I believe that."

"Was it me though," he continued. "Would I recognise myself as a medieval knight or a pirate or something?"

"No. You wouldn't recognise yourself unless you were aware of your astral shape. Your physical body would not be the same. Only the soul is eternal. The shape it inhabits is different."

"So, Jamie could have been anything before," I said.

"Yes, he might have been a pig for all I know," said Ms Pontefract.

"Steady on," said Jamie.

"Pigs are very intelligent," she continued. "If you lead a fairly reprehensible life on this plane," she nodded at the empty glass of whiskey, "You might find yourself a pig on the next plane." I laughed. The sound fell on a silent room. Ms Pontefract clearly thought there was nothing funny in what she had said. Jamie was also less than amused.

"We all choose our direction. Each action obeys the cosmic law of Karma, and rebounds throughout the universe. The consequence of all our actions comes back on us in equal measure. Therefore every choice that we make determines our future. You," she indicated Jamie, "choose to expend yourself on whiskey, where another person chooses to develop their consciousness through yoga and meditation. You make the choice, no-one else."

"What about background, doesn't that make a difference?" I knew that Jamie was thinking about his alcoholic mother, and for the first time I realised that he drank so much to prove that he was not like her. It was a strange paradox; and within half an hour Ms Pontefract's presence had brought to light something unknown about a friend whom I had known for years.

"Yes," I said in defence of Jamie, who seemed to be getting steadily more melancholic.

"It seems rather élitist. Many people are victims of their social background. What chance to develop along the path of evolution would a baby have who lived only a few minutes?"

"Who knows?" said Ms Pontefract, "And I feel that I've answered many of your questions already. One way to answer more would be for you to come to our regular meetings on Wednesday night at the Quakers' Hall." She put her coffee down on the Carlton house table. "Nice table," she said patting the surface. "This at least is original. I dislike copies. Now, you have some questions of a more serious nature, some help I can give, but before we get down to that - I sense that there is someone else in this place."

I nodded.

"I really wasn't sure," she said. She closed her eyes, and suddenly a look of pain stretched across her brows, she winced, her hand stretched out clasped, and then she controlled it.

"Empty," she gasped. She stared around the room as though the shadows contained more than darkness

"Please, could I have a glass of water?"

Jamie went off for a glass.

"At first I thought it was a child," she continued when she had taken a few sips of water. "There was emptiness, but it wasn't a child."

"We have a man here;" I said "he's mentally defective."

"That might account for you thinking it was a child," said Jamie, guessing.

"Empty, quite empty. Not a child, not mentally defective, just nothing there, a curtain drawn."

For the first time Ms Pontefract seemed utterly thrown. She kept shaking her head. And, as though a defensive wall had been breached, this gave me a chance to examine her more fully. It was as though I had been restrained by her talk, by her masterful appearance. My eyes travelled up and down the contours of her body, quickly, surreptitiously imagining how she might be naked, how it might feel to invade her limbs, touch her belly. My mouth grew dry with contemplation. I had to look away or it would become obvious. As I did I saw Jamie glance at me with a jealous, strange look. Ms Pontefract recovered herself. "I'm sorry. What did you want to know?"

"Well," I said, "it's bound up with the man who you sensed was here."

Ms Pontefract held up her hand, palm forward. I could see the white lines on her palm like an immeasurable map. "Believe me, there is no man in this place except him." She pointed at Jamie. "At least..." she hesitated. It seemed like a crime in someone so confident and assured. "...at least there are only the vestiges of someone who was once a man - shadows, emptiness, evil even, but of such a negative nature."

"At least you don't think I'm a pig." Jamie's flippancy seemed entirely out of place.

"If all you say is true, then we really need your help," I said quickly.

She swallowed, nodded, and dropped her hands to her lap.

"I was given this." I drew out the talisman. For some reason I did not want to pass it to Ms Pontefract. Instead, I held it up by its chain where it shone argent in the light of the desk lamp.

Ms Pontefract leaned forward, pale eyes absorbed with interest. "It is the Theosophical emblem; an amalgamation of symbols. The Crux Ansata for resurrection, the interlaced triangles that suggest the unending conflict between light and dark, the serpent associated with wisdom, the swastika..." She leaned closer," ...but the words." She drew back, eyes flicking to left and to right as though expecting some sort of attack. For seconds we seemed to operate on a different time scale. I was intensely aware of her body smell; the sweet perfume livened with sweat, her skin colour blushing away from paleness, the sound of her deep breathing merging and susurrating like a distant ocean. I wanted to move forward and touch her, caress her, but it was as though she was somehow cut off, encircled by some kind of power.

The moment passed. I quickly looked to Jamie. He was staring at his whiskey, unconcerned. Ms Pontefract rose to her feet.

She stood tall in the centre of my office, as though she owned it. "I want to leave," she said quietly.

"Can't you help us?"

"You must help yourself."

"Can't you tell us anything about this thing?" I held the talisman out to her, then retracted it, and put it in my pocket.

"It is not a Theosophical talisman. What you have done to me is difficult to describe." She began striding to the door.

"Well, at least try to describe it," shouted Jamie suddenly. Ms Pontefract stood at the threshold of the door.

"Imagine a Christian," she said. "Imagine being a Christian in a church. Then imagine a man came towards you holding a cross. You smile because this is appropriate behaviour. Then you look again. The man is holding the cross upside down."

She walked out of the office. I rushed to the mirror followed by Jamie. She strode out of the door. As she walked out of the door she looked to left and right, her eyes taking in the whole street. Then she was gone, and Jamie, Keran and I were left to consider events.

Jamie breathed annoyance. "Why did she walk out?" he said through his teeth. "How rude can you get?"

"It was the talisman." I said.

"What was all that stuff about Christians and crosses?"

"Oh don't be thick, Jamie. She was saying that this thing is the dark side - the black, the devil, as compared to her side - the white, goodness."

"Oh," said Jamie he was calming down. "God what a desirable woman," he said, plumping down on the ladder-back. "That's why she left. She thought we were in league with the enemy."

"You know, I think she was really scared."

"What? She frightened the life out of me. She was so formidable. Nothing could scare a woman like that."

"I'm not so sure. I think she wanted out of here so that she could get back to her own patch, to safety; like a white spider in a silver-stranded web."

Jamie had carried the whiskey decanter into the kitchen. He took a slug straight from the decanter. "You're drinking too much." I said

"Sorry. Do you think I'm turning into a pig?" He tweaked my breast.

"Don't, Jamie," I said. "I'm vulnerable at the moment, and that kind of behaviour is always offensive anyway."

"I don't think you would have found *her* offensive. I'm sorry," he said. "It's this damn drink." He put the decanter down on the table. "I think I'd better go."

"Yes. I think you'd better."

He rose; shoulders slumped, looking older, smaller. "You know," he said, "She didn't answer any of the questions we wanted her to, yet she made me understand something about you I'd never have guessed." Jamie obviously thought I was gay. Maybe I was. And yet it was true. She had made me see Jamie for what he was. A broken disillusioned man, trying to prove that he was not a drunk by drinking himself to death.

I stopped Jamie at the door. "Look, I'm sorry about all this. Our nerves have been strained by events, we've been working too hard," I laughed. "And what for, Keran?" I pointed to the witless professor who sat immobile in the corner of the kitchen. "Kennedy had left us with a man who can't think. The Theosophists think he isn't even here at all, and all I've got for my trouble is a gold Buddha that I don't want and this crazy talisman that is inhabited by evil spirits. I think it's time we saw the funny side of things. Let's have another whiskey."

"No," said Jamie. His eyes fell. "I better go. You think you're vulnerable? Well, I'm struggling, woman." He made for the door. "One thing. Promise me you'll get rid of that talisman. If a woman like Pontefract is scared of it, I'm inclined to be terrified."

"I promise." I said, "In the morning, I'll drive down to Bowers and I'll throw it at him if he won't take it. Will you come?"

"Maybe," said Jamie. He smiled and was gone.

In the quiet, I sat and played over events in my mind. Every time my thoughts strayed to Ms Pontefract, I saw her long legs her slim body, her golden hair. It was like a reeling fantasy enervating my own body. I fought to control it. This was Bower's attack of erotics. I thought they might name it, like "priapism", after him: "Bowerism". I laughed out loud, but the laughter triggered a wave of passion. I visualised Ms Pontefract naked, but between her legs I saw an erect penis, throbbing with life and blood. I imagined it entering me brutally. I began to search for my private parts. I quickly looked at Keran who sat on the kitchen floor. I had become accustomed to him there was nothing inside his head or indeed, if Pontefract was right, inside his soul. I tugged at my panties, uncaring. Keran stared at me with his blank visage.

"Kennedy," he said, in a faintly superior tone. "Where is she?"

Chapter 6
North

"I DON'T KNOW," I replied. "Kennedy has been gone for days now."

Slowly, I removed my hands from my knickers. Keran lapsed into silence again. All the doubts came rushing in. Was Keran who he seemed to be? Was he witless? Was he a spy, a criminal set up by Kennedy to rob me? The list was endless. I examined his face. It may have been my imagination, but his eyes seemed to betray some intelligence; an intelligence that had been previously lacking. Could a man have kept up such a profound deception for days? I doubted it.

"Do you understand me?" I said.

He looked up, did not answer.

"Why Kennedy?" I tried. It seemed to be his hobby.

"Kennedy," he said. "I... I want Kennedy."

The magic word. "I know you want Kennedy. Why do you want Kennedy?"

It was too much for him. His hands fell to his lap, his eyes slid around the room, in search of Kennedy, no doubt.

"I've had enough, Keran." I said. "I'm sick of being worried, sick of responsibility and sick of enforced eroticism. I'm taking you back up to Aberdeen to your people or your damned institution, I don't care which."

"Want Kennedy," he said.

"Kennedy later," I replied. "Home now."

I threw two sleeping bags and my three-man tent into the back of the Ital. I packed a few bits and pieces, some peanuts and some fruit. Then like the owner of a petulant poodle, I led Keran Westwood, Professor in Philosophy, out of the office. I looked up and down the street. Piccadilly square was thronged with people. Too many to weigh up if any were watching me. I saw the Lenas street beggar some metres up the way, his polystyrene tray with some message unreadable from this distance. He did not even look at me, immersed no doubt in alcohol, or perhaps fears of getting no alcohol. Then I stuck Keran in the front seat beside me where he sat like an inflatable dummy. A traffic warden rushed to book me for sitting on double yellow lines, but I was smart enough to rush off without noticing.

In half an hour I was on the M6 heading for the roads north. I phoned Jamie from the service station at Preston and cancelled the morning appointment with Bower.

His answering machine played some obscure highland melody. It amused me because of my appropriate destination. The smile was wiped off my face as I got back in the car.

Parked a few metres from me in a Range Rover, a young man stared at me and grinned. It was an unpleasant smile. His companion, a dark haired girl dressed in a denim jacket lifted up a rag doll to the windscreen. She deliberately showed it me.

Then, with a quick imperious gesture, she held it out of the open window and tossed it out in front of the Range Rover. I started the engine of the Ital and coasted out of the parking area. Behind me in the mirror I could see the two young people, their fixed unnatural smiles like little white nail clippings. The doll staring with a tiny face; a face crushed a moment later as the large wheels of the Range Rover rolled over it, and then began to run a course contingent with my own. I pushed out on to the slip road. The morning traffic had died down. In the encompassing space of the free way I felt the liberty of escape tinged only by the threat behind me. Because it *was* a threat. There was no mistaking the look in those almost inhuman eyes.

The Range Rover stayed some fifty metres behind, hugging the path of my car. As I pulled to overtake a van it aped the movement of the car almost as though an invisible tow rope bridged the gap between us. Hours later, as we by-passed Carlisle and took the smaller winding roads, the Range Rover was there, its occupants still grinning as though they knew no other facial expression.

I have a car phone that I never use. Conrad bought it for himself a long time ago. If he had taken it with him on the mountains so long ago he might have survived, but then he was always impulsive. I had transferred the phone from the Citroen to the Ital out of habit. It began to ring. The first time I had heard it ring for a number of months, as I refuse to give out the number. The more I thought about it, the more I realised the impossibility of its ringing. No one had the number. I didn't even know the number myself. I let it ring.

The Scottish border country sped past me, rolling low hills only tinged by purple heather and yellow speckled gorse and broom. I looked at the speedometer. I was travelling too fast. The remorseless pace of the Range Rover, the continual ringing; my nerves were fraying again. I slowed down deliberately. The Range Rover slowed down. I crawled to around twenty miles an hour; the Range Rover crawled, its occupants staring at me with their empty grins. Finally I took the road as fast as I could, throwing the car into lower gears as we hit corners. The phone rang like a mechanical chant, out of step with the erratic movements of the Ital.

I can drive fast, I know various things about cars learned from Bert and other friends in the trade; how to swerve out of a skid, sensing when the back end glides, pushing the hand brake on, dropping the gears and turning into the skid to pull out; welding the chassis lower and reinforcing it with steel girders; little things you learn over the years. But it's one thing to know these things, and another thing to drive an old banger. Each corner I turned, my mirror revealed the Range Rover, the occupants grinning their smug grins. It was apparent that I couldn't escape them on the road. I slowed down. They tagged my movements like adept mimics.

In my mirror I could see the amorphous girl holding her phone, willing me to pick mine up. In the end I had to.

"Hello," I said.

"I heard the sound of breathing, not a woman's breath but a man's. Then a voice spoke like shells breaking against rocks. "You have something I want," it said. In the rear view mirror I watched as the girl's mouth opened wide. Suddenly, as though it was the most natural thing in the world her head separated from her body and disappeared.

It appeared through the receiver of my phone, beginning to emerge like the word-bubble in a cartoon. I poked it with my finger and like a balloon it burst. A faint smell of gasoline permeated the air. I glanced again in my rear view mirror. The Range Rover had dropped back a few metres; the women's pale head had reappeared, its inane grin still fixed.

My heart beat fast and my neck seemed constricted as though a snake had curled around it. In contrast, my lower body was infused with tingling as though some lewd stranger groped me. Ahead the road veered around bends. The border hills rose up around me like statements of grim intent. I had a desperate feeling of failure, despair. Suddenly, Keran croaked out in an unnatural voice, "Stop. There!" His large hand pointed forward.

On the road standing as nonchalantly as anyone could, a scruffy hitch-hiker held out his thumb. I was in no mood for questioning judgements; even those of an idiot who had never spoken sense before. I braked hard, sending the Ital into an ungainly skid. Pushing the door open, I shouted. "Get in the back for Christ's sake, get in. Quick." The hitch-hiker got in nervelessly. The Range Rover had pulled up bumper to bumper behind the Ital.

The Hiker bundled his small bag in the back, bring in with him the musty smell of days on the road and no baths.

"Where are you going?" he said.

"Does it matter?" I replied

"No." he said. In the mirror I saw his deep, dark hair, weather beaten face. A man of around thirty-five, assured, relaxed. "He craned his head around. "You got some trouble?"

"It's a long story." I replied.

"Well," he slouched back in his chair, "if it doesn't matter where we're going, we might have time for the story."

I sucked in my breath, felt the tingling again in my crotch, watched the image of the hiker in my mirror easing in and out of male and female aspects. But the effects of the spells were weaker, as though the presence of another person had dissipated the strength. His face resolved itself into that of a man, thin lipped but handsome.

"The man in the back is a professor of philosophy," I said. "he's been turned into a mental cripple by someone. The people in the car behind have got something to do with it."

"They the police?"

"No, I think they belong to a coven of witches."

"Ah," he said "The Golden Dawn or someone's being dropping LSD in your drinks."

"Whatever way you look at it, the perception of events is what counts. I think they're trying to kill me, or perhaps something worse, so they're a threat."

"True enough." he said. "Is it going to help running away from this?"

"What do you mean?"

"Well, if the threat is real, why not face it? If it's only a perceived threat, why not face it down too?"

"How?"

"Can you fight?"

"Black belt, six Dan. But lately I've lost a little confidence."

"I know a few tricks. Stop the car. We'll get out see what happens." I slowed down, stared at him for seconds, his dark hair, dark eyes. He looked old inside. His eyes wise depths.

"Who are you?" I said, fearing the answer.

"The hero," he replied grinning.

Ahead, glinting in the afternoon sun, a blue parking sign appeared. Four hundred metres to a lay by, the tingling in my loins had become more intense. The association of lay-by with illicit sex began to send waves of anticipation through my body. I fought the irrepressible feeling, damping it down.

We came to a series of bends. Hills rose on either side, wooded land rising upwards so the sun caught the declivity and made the world hot. I wound down the window, heard the air rush by outside.

"Keran," I whispered. "Can you fight?"

There was no reply. I felt an overwhelming sense of loss, like bereavement. The thought swirled around in my head that this new man could be the anti-hero, another actor in the conspiracy that seemed to be building around me. If I stopped the car in this deserted spot, what was I going to receive?

The white and blue parking sign appeared. I looked in my mirror. The enemy car had dropped back, as though it was waiting for events.

I had to take the chance. The Ital crunched into third gear, and then down to second. I pulled up in the lay by half way down to where a bin had been spilled open, its entrails shining cups and magazines. The hiker got out of the car immediately and stood by the bin. Pulling out a pack of cigarettes, he threw the pack down among the rubbish and lit one with a small plastic lighter. I waited and then, drawing in my breath, opened the door. "Stay in the car, Keran," I said. The instruction was unnecessary. Keran remained immobile, entranced by the backs of his hands.

As I stepped out of the car and turned, I heard a light bump. The bumper of the Range Rover was scraping the rear of the Ital. The two faces remained in the Range Rover, still grinning. I had seen the grin before, perhaps in the death's heads at a

Mexican festival many years before, perhaps in dreams where I imagined the face of my dead husband frozen in snow. The fear ate my insides.

The hiker looked across the bonnet of the car at me. He took a draw on his cigarette. "Do you smoke?" he said.

I shook my head.

We waited. The sun disappeared behind some clouds. The wind caught up. I was cold, shivering. The hiker glanced at the car, as papers began to blow over the road.

We waited a long time.

"Something is badly wrong," the hiker said. His dark eyes penetrated me. "These are very bleak times." He examined his cigarette and then threw it to the ground.

"Don't touch the Range Rover," he said. "don't leave any prints on the door and whatever you do, don't open the door. But, if you feel up to it, I think you should have a closer look."

Together, with the breadth of the Ital separating us we walked over to the car. He on the passenger side, me on that of the driver.

The grins were fearful things, bared teeth on waxen dummies. The eyes - I have no idea how they were preserved but they were, glistening artificially.

"Dead." spat the hitch-hiker." Both of them, a long time dead, but kept alive like someone might keep fruit artificially, superficially wholesome, by waxing it outside. Inside, about to burst with rot. "He looked at me solicitously, "Better to see it," he said. "To know…"

I reeled back from the image of the two young people. Felt my stomach going over. Suddenly the hiker leapt the bonnet, sliding towards me. I tried to react, making a pass with my hands, the way I had been taught. But he had been taught too. He twisted the arm, pressed me towards the open door of the car. The tingling erotic sensations had gone. I felt only the desperate horror of what he was about to do. He forced me downwards over the seat, head hitting the raised steering wheel. I threw up, struggling against the inevitable.

He held me close.

"Finished?" he said. "If you'd thrown up over the ground, we might have found ourselves having to answer a lot of awkward questions. He sat me down. "Drive. You'll feel better with something to do."

As he walked around the front of the car I felt the urge to run him down. The engine ticked over, embalming the silence with its resonance. It seemed to be growling at me, persuading my drowning inclinations. The moment passed and became something infinitely worse. Papers thrashed up in the wind, hitting the windscreen.

As he sat beside me in the passenger seat, I pointed, voiceless, to the window.

"I know," he said. "I saw it earlier in the spewed contents of the bin."

Some women's magazine. The faces normally, anonymous, forgettable, two happy socialites. The two rotted things in the car behind, staring at us from the pages flattened on the windscreen.

"No use keeping it," he said. "If we tried to take the page it would be probably be caught in the wind. If we did get it somehow, by tomorrow the faces would have reverted, changed into something we couldn't remember."

I put the car into first gear and began to drive. The page of the magazine was caught and tossed into the slipstream. I observed it in the mirror, rolling down the incline of the road.

For an hour I drove into a gathering gloom. The rain began to spatter the windscreen. To me this seemed like an attempt to cleanse the windscreen, an attempt that would fail. The car smelled of acrid sick, the seat uncleaned. Beside me, the hiker was apparently asleep. I felt tired, drained, but at least the feeling in my loins had gone. I felt almost human. Perhaps the presence of the hiker was a reassurance. He had a presence, a natural safety net around him like a halo of security. It made feel better. We stopped in a small village. I gave the hiker some money and he returned with some milk and biscuits. He had procured a pail of water and he swilled out the car. I put some expensive perfume down on the seat but it only masked the bad smell. We ate some biscuits in the car, and he drank all the milk. I could barely touch it.

Only when we were some ten miles from Glencoe on the west of Scotland and the rain was thundering down, did I bring myself to raise the subject.

"What do you know?" I said.

He smiled. "I could be covert and say I know nothing, but I'm not Socrates. I know some things, many things in fact. What do you want to know?"

"Was it a coincidence - me picking you up, you being there when I needed you?"

"Nothing is a coincidence."

I looked to see if he was joking, but his face retained an enigmatic calm.

"Bullshit." I said.

He shrugged. "I know it," he replied. He was assured, certain.

"Did you wait for me?"

"You picked me up, didn't you? Other cars passed by."

"Where were you going?"

"Here," he replied.

"That's a stupid answer."

He shrugged again.

"I'm sorry," I said. "They're stupid questions."

He lit a cigarette. "As long as you're asking questions, you're still alive," he said. "This is a complex game you've entered, lady. There is a lot of things it's better not to know, but I think you might benefit from knowledge of a few things." He drew on his cigarette and blew the smoke out slowly. "Nobody knows everything. Don't assume that there is a single path. We all take routes towards what we want, and some are misguided."

"Which path are you on?" I said tentatively.

He smiled laconically.

"Left or right?"

"Neither," he replied eventually. "The ones we left back on the road, the two corpses - once they had a life, desire, energy, thoughts. Someone took that from them, killed their physical body..."

"Who took it?" I slipped my fingers into my dress, pulled out the silver chain. "Was it the people who made this?" I slowed the car down, put the hazard lights on and pulled into the side.

For a long time he looked at the talisman, not touching, looking. "That's a thing of chaos," he said. "I could be simplistic and say those on the left hand path..."

"Brothers of the shadow?"

"Evil," He laughed. "Misguided, whatever. But..." He paused, took another drag. "It could be something altogether different. A Theosophical symbol twisted like that. It's not the standard conception of evil."

"You don't know, then, who it is, where they are?"

"I can tell you one thing, lady. I don't know who they are that I'd be willing to find out. Where they are - the only reason I'd want to know that would be to run from the road that leads there." His blue eyes stared at me with genuine compassion.

I put the talisman back in my dress; felt the disappointment, the fear. "Would you help me?" I said, knowing the answer.

"The only help I would give is advice," he said. "It's there if you want it."

"What is it?" I said.

"Most times, life is apparently a series of choices. Each choice leads you down a certain path. You choose the path and hopefully you choose one that leads you to a spiritual evolution.

However, there are times when any choice you make is bad. This is one of them. You could change your name; run, hide and maybe you would be physically safe; I question whether your spirit would evolve in such a claustrophobic existence. Normally, I would say face whatever you have to face, but now, here, this thing you have - it gives me a very bad feeling... a feeling that you should get out, fast."

He lapsed into silence. The rain beat down on the windscreen "What about my friend in the back - can you give him advice?"

"He worries me. Doesn't say much, does he?"

"He says "Ka"".

"Egyptian?"

"Short for something else, maybe, "Kennedy", a girl he likes."

The hitch-hiker looked in the mirror at the giant, who stared straight ahead with a faint smile.

"You all right, my friend?" said the hitch-hiker.

There was no reply.

The silence extended. There was no let up in the rain. The hitch-hiker seemed to consider something for a while, and then he said, "Let me have a look at your man."

I stopped the car. Like parents with a large child, we persuaded Keran out into the rain. The three of us stood in a parking place beside a large black loch. The hill over the road was steep and impassable; the dark loch spilled out like an inkblot, and the vague mountains could be seen through the drizzle, overhung with black edged clouds. Keran, amidst the ragged splendour of the landscape, looked like one of its features. The hitch-hiker took him over to the small stone wall overlooking the loch. Below us, the tops of pine trees like a diorama, spread out towards a tiny shelf of stony beach. Ka seemed to be in charge of the world as he stared out over it all.

The hitch-hiker slowly took off the giant's jacket. Standing in his nylon shirt, Keran's musculature seemed to be bursting through the material. The rain began to show the shape of his huge powerful body. Then the hitch-hiker took his shoulders, staring upwards at his face. For fully an hour, the two locked eyes. The hitch-hiker seemed to be meditating, but there was a feeling, an aura around him. The air between the two seemed charged with something else. The rain began to drive, and there was a sudden crack of electrical energy from the mountains over the east side of the loch. This was followed by the low rumble of thunder. As the lightening forked over the hills, the hitch-hiker dropped on to his back like a felled ox. He lay there staring up at the sky with pained eyes. I rushed to his side and slowly pulled him up. He was visibly shaken. Keran, on the other hand, remained motionless and apparently unchanged. The rain ran in rivulets over his immense body, in the same way that it might follow the course of the mountains.

Slowly, the hitch-hiker pulled himself together. He seemed visibly upset, shaking with cold and pain. I helped him to the car, and Keran followed without hesitation.

I started up the engine and allowed the warmth of the fan to pile in. We set off in silence.

For a long while the silence remained between us.

Suddenly, the hitch-hiker made a low cry. I watched his face contort. His hand reached out for the dashboard, clutching.

"God. I feel bad, something bad in me."

"What?"

He felt his stomach, stared at the driving rain. "It's passed," he said. "I think I'm okay but I don't want to talk about the big guy, about what just happened. Talk to me about something else."

"What would you advise about the talisman?"

"You call it a 'talisman'," he said quietly.

"An object, in this case metal, inscribed with magical drawings, sigils, specially prepared."

"I'd call it an amulet."

"But an amulet was originally based on an image, and normally used as a protective device against the evil eye. I could understand if the imagery was grotesque. This thing; it's hardly a prophylactic."

"Amulets were not simply designed for protection. Some, they say, were designed by diabolic means…"

"The Malleus Maleficarum of 1486, of course, I should have guessed. Seven rules - seven rules for detecting the evil. "There is no religion" - surely a sign that the amulet is designed for evil…"

"I'm not so sure…" said the hiker. His face twisted with pain. "The Malleus Maleficarum was a bogus, ill informed work utilised by witch hunters to justify their actions, not…" He groaned. I clutched his arm. "Not… divinely inspired. The amulet," he said finally. "I think it's beyond evil. There is something else. God." His face turned white, his eyes bulged. Suddenly he doubled over his voice an urgent whisper "Let me out, now. I need to get out." His hand clawed at his throat. He lurched sideways, opened the door with difficulty. And then, without speaking, the door swinging outwards, I watched him disappear into the driving rain.

Thirty minutes later, he had not returned. It was ten miles to Glencoe, and I felt lonely and afraid. Darkness was falling fast around me. I heard Keran breathing deep, asleep in the back seat, the rain beating on the roof of the car. I got out the car and walked around. The hills rose above me. It was impossible to see more than a few hundred metres. He was gone. I walked over the road in the direction he had taken but it seemed impassable. Further up the road the same and back down the same. For all I knew he could be dead. Twice I waited, and twice I walked out into the increasing rain.

Then I began to hear the voices.

In the car I drove for a few miles before switching the radio on. For a few minutes the music played, drowning the rain.

But then the voices started whispering between the music and I had to switch the radio off and pray that the fearful things they said didn't infect the elements around me.

*

In Glencoe there is a place beneath the visitors' centre where tents are often pitched. The hill walkers' pub is some metres to the north, and the river is far enough to the west and down the slope to prevent it taking your tent away. Some foolish people pitch theirs near the river, and in bad weather the river can rise three metres. I knew the area reasonably well, but I had always approached in daylight. The beam of the headlights picked out the scattering of tents through the driving rain. The wheels of the Ital crunched on the loose stone road. I could see, like spotlight actors or a shadow play, the campers bedding down for the night.

I could go to the hotel, of course. Even if full, they would find a spot in the pub, on the seats or in a corner, but I was now abjectly terrified. Any contact with people of any form posed a potential threat. With that in my mind, I took my car through the sheltering camp and beyond, some three miles down the river where it was forbidden to camp. In a lull in the rain, I ran out. Only my previous training and experience with this tent enabled me to erect it in the night. I felt like an SAS sergeant as I ushered Keran into the awnings of the erected tent, and he showed as much appreciation as a squaddie as he lay down under some blankets on top of his sleeping bag. I huddled in close to him, still too scared to undress. For a long time I lay in the darkness, trying not to listen to the wind.

In the night, the gale reached force ten. I heard the voices screech down the glen like the misted cries of the dead clanswomen. But at least I was safe. Around my neck I clutched the amulet. Perhaps it was a kind of spiritual 'magnet', neither good nor evil. Only people are good or evil. The dead voices were just that - dead - and the dead cannot harm the living. I kept telling myself that, but it didn't help me to sleep.

Chapter 7
Book Dealing

WHEN I AWOKE, it was seven a.m. The tent had collapsed in on us. Keran lay on his side, facing away from me, the vague bulk of his body mostly covered by the awnings of the tent. I was wet, cold and hungry.

Outside, the rain was unrelenting. I roused Keran and walked out into it. Ours was the only tent visible in any direction. The cold hills rose above me, obscured by the rain and low clouds. The car parked on the rough track glittered in the rain like a bejewelled and writhing lizard. I made towards it, only vaguely aware of Keran, behind me somewhere.

When I reached the car, I turned to see the shambling giant crouched over the collapsed tent. At first, I thought he was being sick, defecating - some infantile response to his environment, but then it dawned on me - he was recovering the tent. For a few moments I watched him crouched like a sedate gorilla in his shabby clothes, his big hands methodically pulling the aluminium tent pegs and placing them in the nylon bag. His movements were systematic. In a few minutes he had the entire tent packed, the sleeping bags rolled and the few personal possessions that had scattered where they had fallen the night before, secreted in his pockets. He advanced with the gear and placed it carefully in the back of the Ital. I sat in the driver's seat and waited for him to enter. His enormous bulk engulfed the seat beside me. He gazed thoughtfully over the vista before us, the forbidding hills, the driving rain, the flood-gutted river. "Bad day," he said.

"Keran," I said, "Switch the heater on."

For a moment, he looked around aimlessly at the dashboard, and then he found the switch and flipped it. He sat back in the chair, easing his enormous body into a more comfortable position.

"Keran, how do you feel?"

"How?" he said.

It was the last word he spoke until we reached Aberdeen in the afternoon.

I parked the car near a small fish market, not far from Albert Basin. The rain had stopped, but the sky echoed the granite features of the bleak Aberdonian architecture. My clothes were dried, but I felt sick and hungry. For a few minutes I tried unsuccessfully to call Jamie MacDonald, but the car phone was dead. I threw it away, and, leaving Keran in the car, made my way to the Mechanics Institute Library. There I found a phone. I phoned my mother. The phone rang for a long time, and no one answered it. I tried Jamie, and within seconds I was speaking with him. His voice sounded faint, lost in a buzz of static, but he managed to give me some addresses on the North side of Aberdeen. Apparently, he had made extensive enquiries and had traced a police officer who had been involved with the professor, and also what might have been a relative, based in a house in a council estate. He gave me the address and then he kept asking me if I was all right.

"I've been worried," he said.

"I'm okay. How are you?" I said, not really interested.

"Well," there was a pause and I recognised in his breathing that he was drunk again.

"The reason I've been worried about you is because I'm now worried about me."

"What do you mean?"

"Let's put it this way. Remember I had doubts about this Satanist, Dennis Wheatley thing you've got involved in?"

"Yes."

"Well, now I have none at all. None whatsoever. I'm shit scared; things…things have been happening down at the house."

His voice became fuzzy, static building on the line. "Nothing I can… but…"

"I can't hear you," I said. And then, horribly a voice came through that was not Jamie.

"Hello." It said.

I did not reply.

"Hello… again."

I put the phone down quickly as though I had picked up a slug in the garden by mistake.

I walked out of the Mechanics Institute Library and back to the car. The door hung open: Keran was gone.

I felt a lurch in my stomach. Quietly, I closed the door. I looked up at the street around me. It was fairly quiet, a few shoppers browsing through the tatty junk shops and takeaways, small newsagents. No giant figure; no tramp with a trilby and plastic shoes. I don't know if it was the blow that Jamie had dealt me - The feeling that one of my closest friends was being driven over the edge by the same fearful, horrible thing that gunned after me. Whatever it was, the sense of loss was huge. And it was not simply the mystery surrounding Keran that could maybe be solved with or without him. I had realised that throughout the last hours the one thing I had liked on the landscape was the big, rambling figure of the giant. I really liked the man and for some stupid reason, felt safer when he was around than when he was not.

I walked up the street until I found a café. I ordered an omelette and some coffee for a late breakfast. Although I didn't feel like eating, I had to get strength from something. When the omelette came, I wished I hadn't bothered. It was greasy, steeped in animal fat. The coffee, however, was drinkable. I savoured the bitter taste, surveying the street outside.

It seemed incredible that ordinary people walked there, unaware of the impossibilities that I had faced. I felt my breath getting out of control, panic, reaction. I meditated for a moment, drawing into myself, recovering strength. I needed to think things out. I counted the numbers in my head, one, two, three four; dropping into a trance, walking down the steps in my mind to an inner garden that I had created over the years. It always calmed me.

Mentally I surveyed the familiar lawn, the high hedge, the fuchsia bush, and heard the murmur of the hidden fountain and the small wrought iron bench. Mentally, I sat down, creating my own tranquillity at peace. There, ensconced in my head, away from the real world, I breathed deep fresh air and tried to work through the problems that confronted me.

At last I was beginning to appreciate what Bower might have meant, stuck as he was in a rotting caravan, surrounded by dwindling objects and twin auras of conspiracy and fear. Like him, I could not deny that something was after me. It would be easy to say it was all subjective: most of my experiences could be taken a number of ways, but they all predominantly crept with a sense of dread that was more than ordinary anxiety. I suppose I could look to my own derangement for the answers: the loss of my child so long ago, depression of some sort creeping up on me. I fingered the amulet around my neck. No, it was more than that. My life had been briefly and terribly changed. I was as certain about the reality of my feelings as I was about my dislike of the café's omelette. Something stank, something was rancid, and whatever it was did not like me. I believed it to be real. It was real.

And now Keran was gone, taking with him part of the jigsaw that made up the gruesome picture

Just maybe I would be left alone if they had Keran. It was a possibility, but I somehow doubted it. In any case, I had no wish to stop. I wanted to get to the bottom of the thing; I needed to know the answers. After all, I wasn't simply hunting out the price of an antique, checking on playing cards or the weight of a gold coin. This was concerned with the ultimate: life and death, and the displacement of everything I had previously accepted as real. I had watched a face come out of a telephone. If it was a trick, it was one hell of a fancy trick. Whoever played tricks like that had powers that I wanted for myself - if only because, without them, I was liable to meet a very early, very unwelcome grave.

I pulled out of the garden in my mind, left the wrought iron bench, the murmur of the hidden fountain and ascended the short steps back to reality. I faced my cup of coffee and the omelette sitting in its cold grease. I felt a flicker of nausea in my stomach, so I got to my feet and left some money on the table. Outside the rain was subsiding. Raindrops spat from the sky, but with gradually decreasing force. I pushed my hands in my pocket and began to walk back to the car.

But I didn't walk for long. I felt it sharply in the back of my neck and in between my legs; the vague tickle of dread, of being watched, of being turned inside out. The calm I had created in the restaurant was a cheat; a lie reserved for islands of ordinary reality, for places that knew nothing of terror.

I don't know how it happened, but I began to run. I ran, blindly, pushing people aside, vaguely aware of the flash of colour as I passed shop windows. Then, incredibly, I saw him - Keran. He was standing across the street, hunched over some books laid out on a stall outside a junk shop. I nearly rushed to grab him in relief, but some curiosity prompted me to hold back.

He had picked up a book. Briefly, he examined it and then, like an expert thief, he tore something from it and secreted it in his pocket. The movement was so quick, fox like, that I hardly noticed its disappearance. He looked straight ahead, through the open door of the junk shop to the eaves, where a tall, swarthy man stared with an equal intensity.

Through the gloom, which hung like a halo in the shop, and the ancient furniture that arched like a forest, I could vaguely discern the piercing eyes of the shopkeeper. I was about to walk forward when suddenly the shopkeeper advanced, his eyes fixing on Keran. Keran walked backwards, as though some external force was pushing him. On either side, the few pedestrians seemed to be disappearing like extras in a western. It was as though they sensed something. I felt it, even across the street. Evil, darkness; dead things in a dead room. Keran kept backing away; I kept looking. And then there was a flash of light, a chance reflection from a passing vehicle that struck the window of the opposing shop like a brief beam of light from a lighthouse. I saw in a moment of terror that Keran was about to walk backwards into the road, that he was about to die under the wheels of a car. In that moment I shouted.

The shout was not loud. In fact, it was more of a whimper, yet despite the distance, Keran must have heard it. His body hesitated, tottered on the brink of the kerb. He began to fall backwards. The car, a jaguar, swerved slightly with a screech of brakes and Keran, like an acrobatic diver, sailed backwards. His great body suddenly struck the wing of the jaguar, and in a single rushed moment hurtled backwards, sideways towards the shop window.

In that second I saw a look of pure hatred from the wide eyes of the shopkeeper. I rushed forward, nearly being hit myself. I was the first to reach Keran. The shopkeeper and another man crowded in behind me. Keran looked up. The driver of the jaguar slammed his door and I could hear him shouting that it was not his fault. Keran winced. He tried to get up. The shopkeeper began to speak in a calm, heavy voice. "Lie down," he said. "Lie down." The voice was deep and somehow insistent. "Stay calm, lie down…" And then I heard it. Under the words, from the mind, or some black soul beneath words and beneath mind, the voice was saying over and over gain. "DIE, DIE, DIE."

I found myself shouting at Keran, "Get up, get up. You are

going to be all right." A struggle evinced itself across his features and as we two shouted like two punters at a racehorse he began to struggle to his feet. The shopkeeper put out his arms. I saw a heavy palm with black hairs and long fingers, each with a silver ring. The hand rested on his chest. I don't know how I knew, but I did know that this hand was trying to pull out his heart, to pull it out and squeeze it like a mouse. Keran visibly jerked, and then his eyes opened wide, his nostrils flared and his own huge hand grasped outwards, clutching at the throat of the shopkeeper. There was a brief intense struggle, and Keran's free hand snacked out into the face of the other man. As the shopkeeper toppled, his mass pulled Keran up.

The astonished crowd began to shout, remonstrating, assuming I suppose that this was shock or terror or drunkenness: anything but what it was.

Keran let the man drop, and then he stared at me. "Now!" he said. "Run. Run while we still have a chance."

Incredibly, we began to run.

We ran to the car, Keran's breath labouring; myself, whimpering and feeling cold and small. Footsteps resounded behind us, but I didn't look. The car door was still open, and for a second I thought I saw a shadow in there, but it was a briefcase or some such object. I jumped in the driver's seat and Keran managed to thrust his bulk into the passenger seat. In a second, we were off, and I saw a few dwindling figures run, stop and then stare as we turned a corner out of sight.

"Get rid of the car," said Keran. We had driven into a side street about two miles from the shop. "Get rid of the car."

I stopped and we both got out. I looked at Keran.

"Why?" I said, and I waited for that brief light in his eyes to die. But the star in his retina remained in view, the flickering of humanity. "Dangerous..." He held his head as though it contained too many things. "It's...dangerous, I don't know why."

He might know very little, but he knew something, and he could talk and listen. For the moment, at least, he was no longer Ka, the witless giant.

The street was empty, a back yard full of huge waste bins, with cobbled stones and scattered cardboard boxes; a place of big rats and smells of stale kitchen vegetables.

"My name is... Keran," he said suddenly. "I... I remember." He gripped me by the shoulders. The movement was sudden, full of raw energy, and I felt his great hands crush my bones in a vice of flesh. "Oh God." His eyes stared beyond and through me, to something so ghastly that it blinded his senses. He retreated backwards, hands grasping at the air. His large body knocked against a standing bin. He seemed not to notice its weight against his back. For a moment it appeared that he might weep. This in itself seemed a horrible thing. I watched his face move from utter impassivity to such a well of deep emotion it was as though I was seeing the gamut of possible human communication encapsulated in a single person. If Keran broke down and wept, he would carry my sanity with him.

And then, he managed to hold himself, recover. His hands clutched at his pockets, feeling for something he had lost, long ago. Incredibly, his hands left his pockets and, as though each had a working brain, moved like snakes towards his throat. For a brief second I thought he was about to strangle himself; his hands inched toward his neck, towards the amulet. Footsteps arrested his movement. My own heart leapt to my mouth.

"Come on, Keran, let's get out of here."

"But where?" he said.

"To your recent history" I replied.

At that moment, Keran turned me round slowly. I looked at the Ital. Slowly, inexorably, from the brief case that had undoubtedly been planted on the back seat; the car was filling with inky black smoke.

I found a children's park. There was a seat, decorated with

obscene graffiti, away from the colourful rides, and hidden by some bushes. A small river, filled with plastic cups and bin bags, ran beside it. The seat was wet, but the rain had stopped and the sky was clearing. We sat there, huddled together for warmth. Keran was staring ahead, but I could see that he was no longer completely vacant. His eyes were staring at the past, struggling to remember.

"I can tell you what I know." I said.

He nodded.

I told him everything that I had found out - his name, his occupation, how long he had been out. Then slowly, with care, and checking his face for looks of disbelief, I began to outline the experiences of the past few days: Bower, Pontefract, the amulet, the two occultists, Jarvis, and the monocled woman. At each point, when I looked at his face expecting to see disbelief, he simply nodded slowly. When I reached the point over the loch where the hitch-hiker had attempted to contact him, a pained look came over his eyes. "Occult training," he said. "An adept. He tried to find me and he did, but I think he would never have tried if he had really known…"

Keran explained that he had "come round" shortly after, although he was clearly not fully alive. He had left, looking for me, because he had become aware that I was a friend. When I mentioned the junk shop dealer, he simply nodded. "Yes he was trying to kill me. I think there was a reason, but…there are too many gaps."

Then he said something in response to my explanation of the attack.

"No, that wasn't hatred in his eyes, merely indifference." These words were said with such certitude they made me ponder. But how could he know?

We decided to seek out some ordinary places, try to get a change of clothes somewhere and rest up. Then we would find his relatives. When I mentioned the police officer, Keran shook his head. "One of them, I think. He betrayed me at some point," he said, "but the other, my uncle…" here his eyes narrowed "… might be able to help. In the meantime we should try to do something entirely ordinary; it's the most effective weapon against the forces of the occult. It helps to root you."

So we found a bookshop in a side street and killed several hours staring through the shelves. First editions, local history, philosophy. I picked up a few books on the Cabbala, on astral projection. Keran frowned, sitting on a chair provided by the book dealer. I bought the books, and Keran took them off me in the shop. He sat down again, and began to read. The shopkeeper brought a coffee. He had noted my interest in the occult, and began to speak, while Keran read on.

His interest was purely academic. He had a private collection with some stunning works of necromancy, but none were for sale. As he eyed me with his toad eyes, I felt a creeping sensation run through my body. It was not the sinister abandon that afflicted me like a force. This was simply the natural reaction to a man who was obviously perverse.

As the conversation wore on, I began to think of seeking out a new haven, perhaps a quiet restaurant, while Keran and I gathered strength to visit Keran's uncle in the dark of the evening. And then the opportunity invited itself. The bookseller offered to let me view his collection. It was somewhat distressing to realise that his toad eyes had found a kindred reflection in mine. But it was a place to go and be unobserved. I stressed the need for secrecy, giving hints that I might belong to some deviant Masonic lodge with women members, and an even darker hint of my involvement in a Manchester Coven. It was enough. The book dealer's trembling fingers had his antique keys out of the drawer, and we headed swiftly behind him towards some back streets.

The book dealer's house was small; a modern flat inside, but with one private room that he said he would reserve for a little later. Dubious surreal art decorated the walls. Certain ugly themes repeated themselves, mitigated by some good Ming vases that appeared original. It was a place I understood, taste I could identify with, if not share. The juxtaposition of objects was intended to shock. After what I'd been through, it hardly caused a ripple.

The little man, in his incongruous tweed plus fours, began preparing some green tea. Keran and I sat facing each other on a couch. Outside it began to rain again, a light drizzle that brushed the window and obscured the view to the flat across the narrow street. On a silver tray, the small cups of green tea were set. With an elaborate and womanish gesture, the book dealer began to pour the tea. I watched his trembling fingers. The veins stood out on his hands. He had a surprise for me. Something to do with Yeats. I had expressed an interest in Yeats' symbolic work, then, shown my knowledge of his involvement with the Golden Dawn, the eighteenth century sect who counted Crowley as one of their more memorable members. His claims to be the Beast were implicitly echoed by the dealer. He was a smaller beast, easier to manage, I presumed.

The book dealer nodded above me, and said he would show me his works as soon as I had finished my tea. I looked at Keran. It was difficult to say whether he was lost in thought, tired or as blank as a sheet of paper again. I sat sipping the tea. It tasted good, if a little bitter. I made some small chat about a certain *grimoire* that had been lost in the eighteenth century, and which was little known. It was a test that the book dealer passed.

"You're referring to the Mammeron of Nice," he said relaxing. He eased his thin frame on to a small rocking chair. Ugly carved gargoyles projected from its arms. "I saw a copy once at a private fair."

I glanced quickly at him.

"Oh, yes. It was everything they said. Someone has it, not a friend, someone who can't be named. They have allowed some copies out. Would you care to...?" He gestured vaguely to the recesses of the flat. I got up. Keran seemed preoccupied with his introspections, or nothingness. I stretched, and followed the book dealer's gesture. A small hallway led to a low door, behind which a desk with a philosopher's skull lay for decoration. The room, although small, resembled an antiquated library. Leather-bound volumes soared to the ceiling like sepulchral catacombs. I stared with the joy of a collector, at things that I felt it unlikely I would see again. For a moment, I felt myself forgetting the disasters of the past few days. A distant tingling was beginning over my body, but I put it down to the effects of my enemies, and I managed to suppress it. I pointed at one of the prominent books:

"This is "Martyrology" by Samuel Clark. Circa 1660."

"1651," the dealer said. "I purchased it privately."

There were copies of original mystic poems by Yeats. I could swear some had never been seen before. They were authentic. Of that I was certain. But there was so much to see. I looked at a scattering of ancient manuscripts on the desk. "These Italian writings. They are they are original inquisitors' confessions circa 1680 and this," I could not touch it. "It's an original drawing from Mandeville's Travels. How..?" Suddenly, the room began to feel small. I felt like Alice on the entrance to Wonderland, unable to get in to the garden beyond the door. "My head?" I clutched the chair before me. Felt my head strike the desk. I heard a voice behind me, breathing through a deep cavern. The voice was telling me to relax. In a small corner of my mind, I began to panic. I felt trembling hands scrabbling at my skirt, my knickers being pulled down. Fingers forcing my buttocks apart.

Even in the moment of waiting, I was conscious of the illustration by Mandeville, a devil's face gradually swimming into obscurity, changing in and out of reality. At times it seemed like a sketch of the devil, the original drawing, at times it appeared like simple pornographic scrawl. I waited like a cadaver about to by sliced open.

I heard a voice.

"You are not very strong, Professor Peralis. This is only the beginning of the humiliation."

Hands pulled my head to the side. My vision was cloudy, as though looking through an opaque glass. Horribly I felt my body make an involuntary response that my mind rejected with pure loathing. The book dealer adjusted my head on the table so that he could see my face.

I could see his. Leering down at me with glistering toad like eyes. He let go of my buttocks, stroked my breasts, relishing the moment, staring at me in triumph. Behind him I could see the door half ajar. And then, slowly, imperceptibly it opened further. A swaying shadow blocked the room beyond. I felt the book dealer's hand reaching down between my buttocks, heard his trousers drop to the floor.

Then I watched as a silk scarf wound around his neck and his face, purpling like a kipper, was withdrawn from my sight. I could hear the sounds of a struggle. I saw kicking legs hit books. There was a silence. I waited, trying to find my limbs, trying to work my mouth. The silence continued. I could not speak. All that was left was my distorting vision, my touch and my hearing. I could hear something externally, like the sound of bellows distantly breathing, but that was all. Internally, I felt my heart palpitating wickedly. My mouth was drying out, and my exposed buttocks and legs were chilling like a fish.

Beyond the fear, my heart raced. The total paralysis was due to some drug. I tried to think of the drug that would produce this effect, but my mind was playing more tricks than a troupe of tumblers. Was it a fatal dose? I couldn't hold the concentration necessary to rationalise. And then, as the row of books took on the properties of a series of ancient, opening doors, I knew that there was an extra variable I had not anticipated. Whatever the drug, it was not simply physically debilitating. It was beginning to produce what I knew were a series of mind destroying hallucinations. The hallucinations were too severe for any known LSD. I could only conclude, assuming this was not part of the paranoia induced by the substance, that I was about to be taken on a mental trip to hell. The drug was a form of raw peyote, or worse, devil's root.

If the book dealer had not intended me to die from the physically debilitating drug, he knew there was a chance that I would die of the devil's root.

And if he knew I might die, he had clearly known that Keran would be unable to help me. Which meant that Keran might be dead behind me, or…? The books exploded into a tapestry of colours as the doors became living mouths, entrances to a thousand private mansions of hell. The drug had me held in its sinuous grip, my mind became plastic, my sense of self lost in a hurtling chain of auto-suggestion, hidden nightmares and subconscious terrors. I joined the lonely thoughts that inhabit the fringes of lunacy.

They began to dance.

Chapter 8
Words

I AWOKE on the floor. Someone was dripping water on to my lips and face. I saw a vague, shadowy bulk above my head. I felt a moment of pure terror, as though a lift floor had opened suddenly beneath my feet. My face must have convulsed in fear because a voice responded instantly,

"Quiet, quiet, everything is fine, easy."

The voice was Keran's. I began to weep quietly, Keran all the while stroking my hair and face. I clung to him, and then slowly sat up, staring at the brightness of the day. "Where?"

"He's in the library."

"Is he..?"

"He's very dead."

I held my face in my hands, looking out of the shutters of my fingers. "Tell me about it."

"First drink this."

I took the coffee, staring at it warily. Keran smiled, his eyes bright and compassionate. I took a sip. The bitter taste fought with the bad tastes in my mouth; the toxins in my head responded by advertising the headache of headaches. "Poison?"

Keran nodded. "Some devil's root. I don't know exactly what. I'd guess there were around six tabs of acid in the cup as a mixer. It's only a guess. My head is hurting as much as yours, if it's any consolation."

I nodded. "How could I have been so stupid?"

"Not just you." Keran grimaced, picked up his coffee. "We were both tired. The events of the day…the last few years." he smiled wanly.

"Speaking of day, how long have I been out?"

"Three days."

I spat out some coffee. "Three days. No wonder I don't feel

too great."

"You nearly died." Keran gulped back his coffee. "In fact, we both nearly died." He nodded behind me. "He did."

I looked across the room, turning my head in slow agony. Beyond the half-shut door of the library room, I could see the booted feet of the book dealer sticking out like those of a Guy Fawkes doll. I heard Keran's voice beside me, low and tense. "He must have misjudged the dose for me. I suppose he had to be really careful. I'm certain he didn't intend either of us to die. It would have been difficult getting our bodies out of the flat."

"Would that have mattered to him? If he's one of these ... people; they don't seem too interested in that kind of detail."

"I don't think he is one of them. His motive as far as I can tell was purely sexual. I made a thorough search of his apartment. I've found details of some of the members of his coven. Most are ordinary occultists, but there are a few useful addresses of paedophiles and rapists. Two murderers among them."

"Useful?" I said.

"Oh, yes. When you are hiding there is no better place to hide than among those sorts of people. They won't be too quick to reveal us when their own backgrounds are so dubious." I shuddered. Keran seemed unmoved. "If you question the morals of it, look at these." He pushed an envelope towards me.

The photographic evidence was sickeningly graphic, hypnotic in its horror. The book dealer had been a meticulous man. I lingered over the photos of the abused children, noting the names of the abusers and the other detailed records. One lawyer from Manchester held my attention. I knew him professionally. His victim was a girl of around thirteen. He had raped her before killing her. He seemed to enjoy being photographed. I could hardly tear myself from her ordeal.

Keran nodded sympathetically. He took the papers from me.

"I think he intended to drug us both," he continued. "The man thought me a moron. From what you said in the library you led him to believe you were in some sort of sick satanic sect; possibly one involving tantric magic - a stupid ploy if I may say, and I would guess your judgement has been affected by the sect. He no doubt thought he had bluffed you with superior witchcraft. He was going to have you and then probably have us bundled into a car, say we were drunk, probably stick us out in street somewhere. Perhaps invite a few friends around for some sick fun. I don't know, I'm not a pervert."

"Why did you kill him?" the words came out unforced.

"I was reeling from the drug. I thought that at any minute I might collapse. I was too clouded to guess his motives. I saw you…well," Keran grimaced "I think you can guess. The only way to stop him was to get him then and there. Even as I got that scarf around his throat I was collapsing to the floor. Fortunately my bulk took him down. I kept squeezing until I fell unconscious. The fact that the man's dead is just one of those things."

"It's going to be difficult to explain to the police."

Keran smiled. "Police?" He took a last sip of coffee. "Our chances of talking our way out of the crime would be next to nothing. We have no motive for being here, and the people we are up against would find the police a trivial barrier to their purposes. An accident could easily be arranged; both of us hung up like lumps of meat, or maybe they would arrange for a sentence of thirty years. Once inside, they could simply let us rot, or worse…"

"What should we do?"

"I don't know. I've been awake for two days now thinking about just that. He pulled a black book from his pocket and tossed it over to me. There was an envelope tucked in the book.

"Take that, for a start."

I picked it up. There were about thirty names and addresses, with some coded writing next to them.

"I found the original in our man's safe, along with a few other trinkets that I've appropriated. They are all members of his coven."

"The coded letters?"

"Somewhat characteristic of the membership of a satanic coven is a lack of basic trust. Our man compiled a dossier, and the coded letters represent what he had on them. The envelope expands the code. With the murderers, I've given the names and in some cases the location of the body. The rest are paedophiles. He managed to contrive incriminating photos in each case."

"How will these be of use?"

"We may need safe addresses. We need only convince the home owner that we have tucked away the proof with lawyers or such, and we have a resting place for the night."

"I hope it doesn't come to that."

"It probably will,"

"And now?"

"I've been thinking about that… and thinking about a lot of other things."

I smiled. "You've recovered your memory?"

"Not all of it." His face took on that look I had seen before, the haunted pallor of a man with no past. "I remember parts, a lot, in fact largely too much." He frowned. "As soon as we are out of this immediate mess, I'll tell you all I know." He pulled a fragmented leaf of manuscript paper from his pocket. "For the moment, this is significant in some way. I found it in the book shop - if "found" is the right word."

I looked it over. It was old, the language Tibetan. On first glance, it appeared to be some fragment of the Book of the Dead.

"You read Tibetan," said Keran.

"I read twenty six languages fluently and about fourteen dialects. Tibetan is easy enough, but this manuscript is fragmentary, and the script..."

"...Not easy, I agree. The Book of the Dead would give us the perils of the afterlife, the burning holes to avoid, copulating couples, the savagery of the early interpretations. This has similar themes, if I'm not mistaken..."

"...but it's not the Book of the Dead. It's some non buddhisitic sect, ritualistic, esoteric." For some reason I thought of Bower's grandfather, but surely that was too fantastic? I handed the sheet back. Keran looked at it for a few moments longer. "It would be a mistake to keep this," he said finally. "Whatever our inclinations..."

I couldn't help but agree. There were too many coincidences. It produced the uncomfortable feeling that it might simply be another magnet to our whereabouts. There were more pressing issues. I looked at Keran's face. He frowned.

"It's coming back to me," he said, returning the glance. "Slowly, in awful detail." For a second, he looked as a child might look to a mother, and then his face changed. He put his arms around me and kissed me on the cheek, in a brotherly fashion. "Let's get something to eat."

Keran prepared a breakfast of oats and soya milk. As he took the milk from the fridge, he wiped over all the surfaces, and then the milk carton. "We'll have to wash up, and replace the bowls exactly where they were found."

I stared for a long while at the cereal. The floating patterns of the oats began to swirl in sludge before me. I stared upwards like a frightened deer.

"The acid," said Keran; "the flashbacks will be with you for a few days, you may get some peripheral memories..."

"The psychics say six months even a year. Acid is a moral adventure. Most of us are not up to it."

Keran smiled. "I'm sorry, I'm making assumptions. You'll have to forgive me."

I laughed. "I've just realised how funny all of this is. We've both been together almost without a break for over a week. I've spent the whole of that time simply trying to find out who you are; you've spent the whole time observing me, and yet neither of us knows the slightest thing about the other."

Keran laughed. "It's like some sort of surreal, romantic novel."

"Gothic." I replied.

"I hope not in the Shelley sense. "

He paused, put his spoon down, and looked at me very intently, and with a sudden hint of suspicion. "Tell me about yourself."

I paused, surveying his face. A face made handsome by the light in his eyes. The light had not been there before. I realised in that moment that man is a soul, not a mind in a machine. Everything was in that light that exists in the eyes of a living being. The body is nothing but an envelope, an animal without a dream, without a purpose. I could tell Keran anything. I found the words coming out naturally, easily, as though I were speaking to an old friend; perhaps more than that.

"My name is Professor Peralis. I'm an antiquarian. I deal in fine objects. I'm well-off, some might say rich. As a hobby I transliterate Egyptian hieroglyphics. I used to collect antique cars…"

"You're the amateur female detective," he said suddenly. "The one they compared to Holmes." He laughed.

I laughed. "That awful article. It's adequately summarised by the complete balls-up I've made of this."

"I've read your papers, though. They're very good. All except…"

I nodded.

"The occult," he said. "In that respect, you are limited."

"I know a lot…"

"You know it intellectually," Keran said. "But you don't emote it. You're articles are dry, unreal. I…I can add a lot to that tale."

I waited, but Keran was not offering. He took a spoonful of oats in his mouth. For a second, I thought I had lost him again, as his eyes stared unresponsively to the table. I felt a yawning abyss where my stomach should be. I didn't want to lose him. And then he looked up; gave a quick smile. I thought then how each moment must be like that. How many times do we stare into space? In that second of loss, where we are no longer social beings, do we genuinely exist as people? Or are we nothing, non-existent? I closed the thought path down. The acid would probably bring back these melancholic reveries at intervals. I would have to face that. Keran looked at me anxiously, and then his face relaxed. He began to speak.

"I'm starting to remember a lot. I have stories of university, family, childhood; I'm getting some of it back. It's very comforting in one sense. Like finding old friends at parties, but then...there is another side to it. The nightmare that exists on the other side of the room, the darkness where the light of the party doesn't fall. That's there."

"It's probably a product of the acid, it's getting you down. I felt it moments before; drawing me down to intense visions. They're like pale shadows of reality but ...intensely believable."

"It's not just the acid," he said. "I know about the acid. I tried it at university when I was eighteen. I've used it on other occasions by way of...experiment. I've used devil's root. I'm not frightened of the effects. It's..."

I waited, watching the nervous play of the muscles on his jaw.

"It's the..." He seemed to be losing it. Then he got up quickly, paced around the kitchen. For a second he stared at me and then at the table. Slowly, deeply affected, he picked up a pen. "You know about words of power. Well this is one. You don't say these things lightly. I'll write it down and then destroy it." He began writing on the paper, a short two-syllable word. He showed it to me. "Remember this, "he said. "I will never show you it again but there will come a time; I see it clearly, a room empty of furniture, a spell of some sort, words, an Indian death spell." He stared into my eyes. "Remember it, because at the moment of extremity you will need it." He picked up the paper and ate it.

As far as I know, the act was one of re-assimilation with the god - A rite of possession. Keran seemed to know what he was doing. I didn't doubt for a second that he acted in a rational way. He knew that word was bad and I could tell with deep intuition that he had somehow been looking into the future. From the point of view of the western mind, the eating of the word would have ritual significance - psychological, if you like - to him. He needed to contain it within his person.

"I feel better having passed this on to you." He laughed. "It's a bit like the casting of the runes. You know the story. The powerful spell is written on a card. You pass the card to someone else, and the devil gets them."

"You've got to get rid of the card to someone else, or the devil gets you."

"A great story," he said.

"But it's not a story really, is it?"

"In this case, no. You're involved now. You were involved before, to the point where your life was at risk."

"What can be worse than that?" I said. I wish I hadn't. Keran gave me look of bewildering horror.

"Believe me;" he said "I gave you this word because I have seen a point where without it you would... How can I put it? The very act of telling it to you would make a superior magician dread the consequences. These consequential events are so great that you would probably commit suicide now if I told you the truth." He looked to the floor. "But only if you believed me."

"What do you mean, 'Believed you'?"

"I could tell you and you simply would choose to accept whatever I said at your spiritual level. I probably sound like I'm talking nonsense. Anyway, I wouldn't involve you in this unless I though that you were in so deep they would have you anyway." His face darkened. "Believe me; these people would have all of you. In a way, that's why I wasn't remotely shocked when I saw what that pervert was about to do. The body, it's nothing, just an envelope. If it gets hurt you can get back up. Even the mental damage, it's nothing. What these people can do is so bad ...it's...it's..."

I held his hand. He stared vacantly at the floor, shook his head. After a while he breathed out deeply. "I sometimes think it's fortunate that I forget bits."

"I can help," I said, squeezing his hand in an inadequately pathetic gesture. "After all, I took you on as a case even before I knew that... that you had a mind. A mind that I..."

He looked up with a dog-like gratitude, a complete contrast to the arrogance of the moment before.

Over an hour later, we had brushed down the flat, trying hard to remove our every trace. A forensic expert would, of course, find something, but we had made it difficult. No one had seen us coming in. At night, we would leave, and no one would see us go. The bookshop would be the give-away. A week, maybe two, and they would investigate. There was nothing to link us with the man, and, judging by his collection of books, a sinister motive for his death could be assumed without the need for additional suspects. With this in mind, Keran pulled up a chair from under the desk in the spare room. He took the scarf from around the neck of the dead man, and stood on the chair.

I watched as he tugged the scarf around the light switch, and hung with all his weight. The plaster cracked, but the roof did not cave in. He walked through to the kitchen.

While he was gone, I found myself staring at the desk, anything, in fact, to avoid looking at the purpled, decomposing face of the book dealer, and the grotesque mockery of his naked thighs, trousers rumpled above his boots. The contents of the desk were not as I remembered them. For example, what I'd taken to be an original of Mandeville was no such thing. It was simply a facsimile, that under normal circumstances I would have spotted quickly. I scoured the shelves looking for the first editions, the rare volumes I had imagined. However, most of the books were not rare. Some were first editions, but of late works on witchcraft, others were simple copies that could have been purchased for ten or twenty pounds at any New Age store. The man had been a sham. I risked a glance at his corpse. His boots sticking outwith his crumpled trousers, his scrawny thighs, his deflated penis. Worst, his purple face, and a tongue that seemed to have burst from his body. I sensed Keran behind me. He was silent for a moment and then he said, "Just an envelope."

We crossed town on a bus, Keran going separately to a prearranged stop. He had picked up a long black coat in a charity shop that almost fitted. I had also changed into jeans and a sweatshirt that made me look scruffy and dissolute. We had boarded the bus separately, Keran walking to the next stop. All the time, I watched and listened and waited for some grasping horror to emblazon itself on the scene. The one thing that had become an advantage to me was this spell that had been thrust on me. I sensed that if that unnatural bodily reaction affected me they would be close.

The bus took a long route around an estate. Finally, by late afternoon, we reached the street. We both got off, waited for the bus to go, and then walked up the street. There were a few children playing on bikes, some three or four year old cars on immaculate drives. The houses were well kept. It was a typical suburban area with nothing to either recommend or condemn it. The number of the house was thirteen. By this stage, I was beginning to take a cabalist's view that the number was inauspicious.

He opened the door, a man of about sixty but tall and athletic for his years. For a second, he seemed taken aback, and then he recovered himself. "Keran," he said, "I can scarcely believe it's you."

Keran stared hard at him. "Rodin, you need to help me." For a second I saw the older man wince, hesitate, and then he opened the door.

Inside, the front room was conventionally furnished. There was no television. A series of abstract paintings lining the walls. A violin was laid in an open case on a simple couch. There was a bookcase with a few paperback novels on the far wall. Rodin stood uncomfortably in the centre of the uncarpeted floor.

"You can't stay long, Keran." He said.

"I don't want to."

"Who is this?" He pointed to me.

"A friend."

"That's not enough."

"She's an antiquarian, not one of yours."

"You're a mason." I said flatly. I had seen something.

"For one of the profane you read well. Are you sympathetic to the brotherhood?"

"I treat people as they come."

"Again that's not enough."

"Look," said Keran. "We need help. It's simple enough; there's blood between us."

He paused, thrashed the air with his hand. "What do you want?"

Keran looked at me. "There are gaps in my memory. I need to fill them."

Rodin looked briefly relieved. A glint that I did not like appeared for a second in his eye.

"Come through to the back room, "he said.

The contrast was incredible. From a conventional house we entered a temple. The room was bare, the floor black, obsidian, the walls dark as night. On the far side of the room was an altar, on the polished floor a huge circle was laid in mosaic. The smell of incense clung to the air. On the altar was placed a pantacle, sword, a bell and some holy oil. Rodin made a signal that I missed, took up a robe, and indicated for us to do the same. He drew a wand from somewhere, and disappeared. I felt a lurch in my stomach. Rodin reappeared by the altar and motioned us into the circle. My mind kept saying it was an elaborate trick, done with mirrors, anything but what it might have been: a human disappeared into thin air. Rodin spoke and his words echoed softly through the dark room.

"We are going to have to be quick, Keran but meticulous. If we miss anything the consequences will be dire."

"What are you going to do?" I said.

"There's little time for explanation."

"No," I said. "Before this goes further, I need to know what we're getting into."

Rodin frowned, looked to Keran.

Keran shrugged. "She deserves an explanation."

"It's one thing to deserve an explanation, another to get it."

Keran looked at me. "We go back a long way. Rodin is my uncle, but he was also for a long time my master."

I felt a shaking fear begin to crawl up my spine. "Which path?"

Rodin looked at me and smiled. "My magic is unselfish, for others."

Keran broke in. "We made several successful invocations. We were following a path of knowledge, always risky, but our intention was to utilise anything we managed to learn for the benefit of others."

"Keran was young, only seventeen when he took the oath. It was not something I pressed on him. He sought me, wanted to learn. I resisted his pleas, but when he threatened to go to the left-hand path I decided I would have to do something. For over twenty years we worked together on the mysteries."

"But you stopped?"

Rodin's face darkened. Keran frowned.

There was a pause as Keran rubbed his forehead. "We didn't stop...."

Rodin nodded. "You remember?"

Keran dropped to his haunches, stared at the black polished surface of the floor, traced his fingers idly over the embossed runes. "We didn't stop," he said. "We were *stopped*."

Rodin nodded. "Do you still want to carry on?"

Keran looked at me, his eyes welling with a fierce terror. It was a quick glance, only an instant of terrifying pain and then his eyes hardened, steeled. "I'm not sure. It's not all there. I think maybe I'm not capable of taking it at the moment."

Rodin said, "I know you're not."

"But I don't remember. I need to remember."

"The great work is beyond you," said Rodin. He dropped to Keran's side. "Believe me, it's simply a fight for survival now. The forces of darkness are all around us. I've had to live with it for the last few years, the appalling attacks. Frankly, I don't know how I've borne up. I don't know why they've let me carry on, unless they regard me as too insignificant."

"And what about me?"

"Clearly, you've taken the full force of their power. You don't remember because you can't bear to remember."

Keran gripped Rodin's hand. I watched as their eyes met. "I need to take the steps towards knowing it all." said Keran finally. "Don't you see? I've got these vague memories of the last years, a drifting shambolic hulk, wandering from place to place, from walls to walls. I get images all the time: places - institutions I think. I've memories of being abused, of being laughed at, of being comforted. It goes back and back and then there's nothing - don't you understand, *nothing*. I can't have just 'nothing'. Even if it's bad, I've got to go beyond and see that there was something there, anything. Anything at all."

Rodin got to his feet. He paced around, looking, for the first time, nervous, agitated. Then he controlled himself. "Don't you realise how much I'd give to have you back, all of you? You talk about your existence. At least you didn't know I existed. I had to think of you as dead. I didn't know what had happened to you, only that you had disappeared. I tried to trace you through the university, but I had to watch my step. They are everywhere, and they watch and they wait like spiders. I carried on trying to go further, trying to see beyond, and all the time the mocking, beyond the abyss."

I felt I had listened enough. "Look, what are you saying, it seems confused to me. Couldn't you have easily traced Keran? You're his uncle, for God's sake."

Rodin sighed, looked at the black floor.

"There were two distinct problems," he said finally. "on the one hand, Keran was physically removed from me. He went somewhere and never came back."

"Where?" I said.

"I don't know. I tried to find him. I was still looking when he walked in the door."

I nodded. "And the other problem."

His face took on an ashen hue. He half turned, as if to walk to the altar.

Keran took his arm. "She knows the word."

Rodin started, visibly shocked.

"She's in it up to her neck," continued Keran. "And I let her know the word because she will need it."

"For your own reasons or someone else's," said Rodin. There was no sympathy in him. His body emoted coldness.

"I had to do it," replied Keran flatly. "Because I saw ahead. I saw something where the word was necessary." He stared at Rodin. "And it's possible I did it to force you to go further."

Rodin faced me, his eyes piercing me through, and then he

relaxed, giving up. He began to speak, indicating objects as he went.

"This is the path of the magician," he said. "Your high altar should always face east: On each side, an obelisk with counter charges in black and white; a dais of three steps, similarly black and white; above, a super altar, with the holy book enfronted by four candles and ensided by six candles; below this, the graal. The candles should ideally be made of human grease. Each sacred object - pantacle, graal, sword, holy bell - all of these must be made by hand, from materials found for yourself. No other must touch these materials: years of craft industry, failures small successes. Always secret, always under cover, for reason both of persecution by the profane and of investing total spirituality in the object of veneration."

"I know," I said. "I know all of this, and I know that he's diminished this word by sharing it-"

"You don't know enough, Professor, or you wouldn't be quite so cheerful about the significance of Keran's actions." At this Rodin gave a silent chuckle, and then he began to laugh, quite horribly. "The other problem," he said, "has nothing to do with physical removal." He drew his cloak around him. "Have you ever stepped beyond the boundaries of the physical, Professor?"

"Until my recent experiences, I would have been quite happy to accept most magic as the play of unconscious forces. I have walked dream landscapes in what you might call the etheric or astral body. I'm not sure how I would define these experiences. Sometimes I lean to Castaneda's description of the magician's way; at other times I am happy to accept the views of the Jungian psychiatric tradition."

"Basically, you are a curious amateur, Professor. Don't be offended. I'm not denying your intellect, which is fine; I simply deny your experience and understanding, both of which are constrained by your intellect. Neither you nor Keran, I'm afraid, are in any shape ready to enter into the conflict. Keran is lost forever. He would crumble like dust in any attempt to cross the abyss that divides reality and the world of moral etheric experience. You might have the fortitude, but you will have to face that alone, in your own time, and in a place, however, not of your own choosing."

"Gloomy words, Rodin."

He shrugged. "You'll remember them some time."

Keran broke in. "Rodin, I accept what you say. To go back to some kind of spiritual quest is an impossibility for me. I wouldn't know where to start. It is possible, though, that I can face this thing on the physical plane. To some extent I may be able to gradually build some defence."

"Ignorance was your defence."

"I'm no longer ignorant."

"No, that's true. You can trace your physical past back to your initial institutionalisation. Prior to that I would guess that you wandered witless over the earth. They did something to you before this, something at which even I am only grasping."

"It may be enough for me to go back to that time and place, to confront the group who did this thing to me"

"I doubt it," said Rodin. "But anything is worth a try."

"How can you help?" I said.

Rodin shrugged. "I could tease the memory back easily enough. That would be a simple hypnotist's trick, but I need to stand in between Keran and the direct experience that did this to his mind and his soul. That is the way of the magician; fraught with dangers, involving a sharing of psychic experience and risk to both of us. I am very reluctant to do it"

Rodin looked at me. "You see, you didn't know Keran when he was a whole man. If you did, you might have some comprehension of the force of the…evil that has done this."

Rodin took Keran by the shoulders and looked him directly in the eyes. Keran stared back impassively, questions crouching behind his mental shield. For a second my memory led me back to my office, the two way mirror revealing the witless giant in his cheap grey suit, his plastic shoes and grubby nylon shirt; the battered trilby perched like a small uncomfortable animal on his large head. Then I looked closer drawn to his eyes. I was brought back forcibly to the here and now.

"I can do it if you want, Keran," said Rodin. "It's up to you."

Keran paused, reflecting only for a moment. "I need to know," he said.

"I assert only one condition," said Rodin.

"Say it."

"Neither you nor this woman make any attempt in the future, spiritually, physically or otherwise, to contact me in any way whatever. From the moment after this act we are finished. We are parted for ever."

A bitter spasm crossed Keran's face. Then he looked to me. I nodded, and finally he nodded too.

"Swear it on the altar."

We both crossed over the star of Solomon and faced the altar. Rodin made some gestures, mumbled some rite of cleansing. We both swore to his oath. He asked me to leave, and wait in the front room. As I closed the door behind me, I saw him covering Keran with a black shawl.

The front room seemed preternaturally light. The late afternoon glow sliced through the shutters, making prison bars for the abstract figures in the paintings. The work was depressing. It seemed to be cast by the same melancholy hand, lacking inspiration as though deliberately offered to dull the senses.

I glanced at the bookcase, the shiny paperbacks. It seemed incongruous that a magician should keep cheap best sellers and crime fiction on his bookshelves, that he should have an ordinary television in his front room, with popular videos. But was it a sham? Did he sit back and relax after calling up the devas of the dark spaces, reading cheap novels and watching soaps on Telly? Of course it was quite possible. Magicians are varied in temperament and inclination. A magical escapade could last for a month, or a year, but is followed by a period of "rest" in the secular world. On the other hand, it could simply be what it appeared to me - a conventional front, to delude the profane, the uninitiated.

The minutes clicked past on the garish digital clock. My mind seemed to still; possibly an osmotic effect from the effects of the magic in the next room. An unnatural calm swept over me, and I began to dwell in the past. Recalling first my encounter with Keran, and then a series of faces. Kennedy, the flower fairy in her biker's jacket, her jeans tied with a rope. What had happened to her? Where had she gone? Was she with the enemy, drained in spirit like Keran, or even dead in some back alley? Bower, the poor bitter antique dealer caught up in a web of his own making, making deals with people who were far too big for him. Then there was Pontefract. I felt a chill creep over me, perhaps an LSD flashback, but the image of her body, the shape, the contours rustling under her white dress, followed by the stroke of Fear's fingers, her terror and alarm at the amulet. Poor Jamie caught up in his alcohol, drooling after Pontefract like a drunken terrier. He had no chance. No chance whatsoever. Like the hitch-hiker. What little chance he had and yet what help he had been. I thought then of Jarvis. His face I had forgotten entirely. I could only see a kind of aura like the web of a spider and the monocled woman; she too, beyond the monocle, seemed as empty as the dead faces of the socialites in their Range Rover.

I looked again at the room; its very ordinariness seemed awful. The bookshelves, the clock, the objects seemed to be occupying more space than their volume, extending outwards - they breathed. I shuddered, pulled my body closer to me. Tried to avoid the abstract painting. It was apparent that the painting was not all it seemed. What I had taken to be random markings were something else altogether.

Shapes were beginning to form

With the shapes came the sound of quiet music. I looked for the source, tearing my eyes from the painting.

Perhaps disturbed by some wind shift in the room, the violin in the open case was whispering its harmonics. I could only assume that vibrations of some sort affected it. Perhaps it was the cold. The room had become very cold. I huddled into myself, staring at the books in the bookcase, looking at the carpet, avoiding the painting, trying not to listen to the violin singing its aimless tune. Like a stick falling from a tree, the bow fell from the violin case. It hit the strings with a jarring discordance and then hung for a second, scratching out the low G and D before toppling to the floor. The harsh chord made a hollow space in the room, as though a door had opened in the air, an invisible door into a dark cool realm. I tore myself away from this thought, feeling the tone of the note stretch out before me. Then I caught the abstract painting on the edge of my vision. From this point, not staring directly at the picture, I could sense the flickering of tiny forms like chill fish in a pond, or eels on the bed of a dank river, wriggling. It was more disturbing to keep this picture on the edge of my vision. I stared back again at the painting, licked my drying lips.

I felt that it would be difficult to move; that to move would be a mistake. My body felt naked and isolated, exposed and vulnerable. There was no sense of the body responding sexually. I was sure of that, only a cold and pitiful loneliness.

The painting began to flicker as I stared at it. I became aware that it was composed, not of abstract shapes, but of things very much like individual beings. Although the figures were inhuman, there was a sense that they were some kind of sentient form. They shifted and changed as I watched. Then, like a kaleidoscope scramble that has been suddenly lit by bright sunshine, the picture seemed to explode, and the diverse shapes scattered outwards. I felt the sensation of being at once tiny and large, of being a microcosm and a macrocosm. The cold dropped like a cloak, and my body suffused with a warm heat. I was losing myself in a colourful world. The light became dazzling, the elements of the abstract painting, the wriggling sentient forms gone, and in their place only a backdrop of light, a foreground of still colours. The colours came to take on a form. One by one they disappeared, until all that was left in the all embracing light was a single square of colour. In this brief second, I sensed a tiny voice in my head. It was calling from very far away, but at the same moment seemed to suggest a nearness. I tried to listen to what the voice was saying, but the words were indistinct. My concentration flicked again to the blank colourful square. I saw that the square had a handle. What little that was left of my reasoning mind suggested that I should turn the handle. I willed myself to go the door, but instead of going forward I realised that the door, like a hungry mouth, was coming to me. I felt a moment's hesitation, and then the warmth, the light, reassured me. Everything I had ever read about light and heat told me that this was the right hand path. If this was a magical experience, or simply an acid flashback, it was a moral question of the same worth, and I sensed a deep contentment. I tried to open the door. The door handle would not turn. I knew now that the door concealed something, something good. I saw a keyhole. I willed myself, and the keyhole came up to my eyes. Through the keyhole I could see my garden. The garden I had last created in my mind in an Aberdeen restaurant, and had built upon through many years of occult training. It looked beautiful and still.

I tried to think to reason in what had become the most vivid dreamscape I had ever entered.

Somehow I had come through, or to, my own mental construct; the place where I felt safe. I was outside or beyond.

Outside the door.

Then there must be something behind me. There was light; there was warmth; a sense of glory. I turned slowly around. All before me was the sense of light and eternal space. It was a wonderful feeling. I felt a joy surge through my soul.

And then there came a knocking on the door.

I did not want to turn around. But I did, forcing myself from the eternal landscape that had enervated my whole form. The door was still there, unchanged. Its handle, its keyhole. The knocking became louder. I heard muffled whispers, sort of grunts, shuffling. I felt a sense of great unease. I bent towards the keyhole.

And looked.

Chapter 9
The Garden

ONLY THE GARDEN.

The grunting noise had disappeared. The garden was still and quiet. I smelt the fragrance of the fuchsia bush just out of sight. In the distance I saw the white cupola of a flowerpot beside the small wrought iron bench where I usually ended my mental sojourn.

I turned the handle of the door, and the door gave in slowly, without any noise. Tentatively, I walked into the space. I was met by a cool breeze and the distant sound of water trickling down the fountain somewhere out of sight. I turned to my left. The fuchsia bush was there, with its complex of red ballet-dancing flowers. Behind it, the tall hedge ran a circuit out into the distance, shielding the view beyond.

Slowly, with growing confidence, I entered the garden proper, and wandered up the small stone flagged path.

I breathed in deep.

This was one of the truly great mystical experiences. Something that might come to a practitioner once or twice in a lifetime. The sense of reality was overwhelming. I knew at the back of my conscious intellectual brain that this place was a mental construct - that, in effect, it did not exist, but to deny the experience would have been foolish. I felt it. I saw it; to all intents and purposes, it was real: each footfall that landed softly on the flagged steps gave forth a corresponding sensation in my foot. Each movement rustled at the edge of my hair. And the wind, if not objectively real, moved, apparently out of my control. After years of patient effort in meditational trance, without real hope of this kind of success, the garden had become an entity unto itself.

I had read of this, of course, in both scientific and occult journals. Anthropologists would probably suggest that I had invested so much of my time and energy into the creation of this mental place, that it had become at least subjectively real. Occultists would say that it *was* real, and that in it I must take on the great moral quest; the meeting of the guardian angel, the subconscious knight, who would test my worth and strength. Psychologists would point to the mental aberrations, the after effects of the LSD. This could be a violent flashback produced from the intense stress of the moment.

None of this, for the moment, mattered. I had found a haven, however momentarily, from the external horror that I had been through.

I walked a little further into the centre of the lawn, examined the single rose bush with its red rose. Looked at the earth, deep ochre and sepia. All around me, the stillness breathed gently. I sat down on the wrought iron bench. I looked at my hands.

Carlos Castaneda had been told by Don Juan, his Mexican master, that the first thing to learn in dreaming is how to get there. His suggestion was that you should try and look at your hands in dream. It was the first thing you should do. Get a good look at the palm of your hands. Most times when you did this you would find that you woke up, or that your hand melted away and you lost control. Finally, however, you would be able to stare at you hands. At that point you would begin to control your dreams. I had reached this stage several years ago. I was able to make limited movements in my dreams. Later, when I became more adept, I was able to travel some distance. However, there were dangers in dream walking. It was possible to meet entities - Jung might have called them evil. There were things that seemed to come unwelcome into dreams, and sometimes it was difficult to wake up.

But this was not a dream. It was my garden, the garden that I had deliberately constructed through long hours of meditation. It was a peaceful place, a retreat from danger, from stress. I assumed now that I must have been induced by the stress of recent events to retreat to this world. If so, I was glad.

I got up slowly, so that the illusion did not pass. This was a fey realm, that might melt away at the sight of an unwelcome guest. I walked slowly, believing in myself and the thing that I had created. The hedges towered above me; magnificent hedges. Before and beyond, the path opened beneath my feet, spreading upwards towards the fountain.

I had only ever heard the fountain. I had never been able to clearly visualise it. I paced forward, feeling my heart beat soft against my neck, my breathing light. I turned the corner, and there it was. Silver spray humming in the air, a coronet with a halo of water droplets steaming out beyond the central core. On top of the fountain, a small statue of a tall slim girl, like an ancient Greek Kore. I walked closer, pausing at the penumbra of the water vapour. The air was cooler here. I sensed the sun going down beyond the towering edges. I looked up. Through the mist of the fountains, I became aware that the sky was reddening. Dark grey clouds clutched out like hands between the drops of scarlet blood that decorated them. The air was chill, but not unpleasant. I walked into the mist of the fountain. The water made a film of dank mist on my face. I sat on the edge of the fountain enveloped in the mist. From the outside, I would appear like a shimmering ghost, blurred colours, an impressionist painting. Inside, it grew cold and damp. Yet this arena was safe, enclosed, and I knew that the external terrors of the world had been left behind. For moments, at least, I could rest. I dipped my hand in the water.

The circular pool of the fountain basin was a deep green, edged with a yellow blue scum at the outer rim. Silt had built up on the bottom of the fountain, and it was not clear how deep the water went. I noticed with an almost idle curiosity that my hand had literally disappeared on touching the water. All I could see was the surface of the water, my arm up to the wrist and then nothing, no hand, only the water, and the silt some indefinite distance below. I pulled my hand out. It was still intact. Clear water dripped from it. I tried the experiment again. Slowly, I dipped my right hand in to the water and watched as it disappeared. I paused for thought, hand deep in the water. My hand felt something shift in the nothingness under the surface of the water.

Suddenly, with inextricable force my hand was gripped as though a steel inquisitor's glove had been wrapped around my living flesh. The pain was intense; fierce pulling tipped my body off balance. I gripped the rim of the fountain, felt my buttocks slid into the water, then my left side; the other arm clinging on desperately as the force kept pulling.

I fell head first, legs kicking. For a second my hand was released. My head turned. I could see one leg kick above the water line, the blood red sky, the sheen of water wrapped around my face and then I fell.

To land on a hard surface.

The room was entirely black, a circular room of some thirty foot radius with no discernible door. Only curtains, draperies all black. I had fallen on to a circular stone table in the centre of the room. There was no other furniture and the only occupant of the room was a thin boy creature or a young girl with its skeletal back to me bowed over something. The room was dank and wet. The table was cold and my clothes clung to it, water dripping down to the black floor.

I felt an ugly sense of fear grip me inside. This was not part of my carefully constructed garden. I had been led out of it, into something awful. I raised myself up slowly. It was as if the creature had not noticed my arrival. I let my gaze slip to the rear. There was nothing behind me - only black, and more drapery. Only a hard black polished floor, dripping wet with ooze. I examined the back of the creature. It was thin, pitiful; almost on the verge of emaciation. The ribs stuck out like those of a Christian sculpture. I edged off the stone table on the farther side from the creature and then slowly reached my hand upward towards the ceiling. As I did, there was the sound of something falling with a wet thud. It came from just beyond the creature.

I hesitated. Let my hand drop. Slowly, I walked around the table, calculating distances as I went. The other sounds alerted me. From behind the draperies, some things were moving. The movement was subtle, insidious, but it was there. My hesitation had drawn my attention slightly from the creature. One of the hands had moved. It was lying slightly to one side. It was an ordinary hand, but pale like the underbelly of a trout.

I walked a little closer, only some five feet from the bowed, emaciated back. On the ground I saw what had fallen. It was a book. Where had I seen it before? My mind raced. It was drawn back to the Aberdeen bookseller. The desk, the *grimoires*, the original prints. I felt my resolve weaken. The sounds behind the curtain came close, creaking dry sounds incongruous in the dank wet room. What was it? I sent my brain scrabbling for a reply. I had not seen it on the desk.

Slowly, as though worked by unseen strings, the head of the creature turned.

The face was dead, but it was, or had been, a beautiful face. At once it reminded me of a Kore by Phaidamos, with that questioning half smile, but the eyes were closed. There was no breath, no movement. The hair was curly, matted, almost bronze in appearance, but bronze that had rusted and become encrusted with a green sulphurous growth. The head remained bowed, and then the eyes opened, and I realised that the thing was not dead.

Sadly, for my peace of mind it was also not alive. It was something in between, beyond, underneath, or anywhere but life and death. The lips parted in a meaningless smile or sneer. Like a puppet, it rose to its feet until it was standing erect, with the half smile fixed on its face. I was frankly scared; dream creature or not. I had read enough of the occult to know that this experience might not be fatal but could easily be such to derange me. I willed myself into action.

"What is your name?" I said. The creaking noise round me paused and then began more frenetically.

"What is your name?" The creature stopped its external movements. Stared with eyes without a soul. A dawning recognition crept on me. I knew where I had seen these eyes before.

"What is your name?"

"Kaaaa…" The creature opened its mouth, to a spilling of dark water. The book too; I recognised the book now. It was the one that Keran had found in the first junk shop. As though impelled by this thought, the drapery began to murmur. I held myself together with a growing desperation

"What is the title of the book?"

There was a sensation of time being turned inside out, of myself being the turning. In what was only a few moments, if it could be measured as such, the creature seemed to say the awful word, the word I had been told never to repeat. As he said it, the draperies began to come down, revealing an audience who desired to participate in the life of the room. As they did, the creature released one limpid hand and casually turned the opened book and shut it. The cover revealed a symbol that I had seen before. It had hung around my neck for a long time, the symbol of the abysmal cult that was trying to destroy me. Somehow, in this inner world, the symbol seemed more alive. It outshone the entire creative world that wefted insubstantially around it. It breathed life and vibrancy. My eyes were fixed to it as the strange occupants of internal space swayed towards me with their hands outstretched. I was in the realm of the worm Ourobouros, the eternal spiral of eating and being eaten, the sigil of the watchers

Something in my mind snapped. My gaze left the book, and in that moment I took my chance, jumped to the stone table, and leapt, as hands leapt towards me, through the roof, and out of the waters of the fountain. My upper body caught the rim of the fountain basin. I felt my legs clutched by innumerable hands, but the momentum took me over. Without looking back, I began to run. Then I checked myself, halted, forced myself to turn. The waters of the fountain bubbled, as though an internal torment was raging. But the surface was unbroken. I saw then that the scene had changed only fractionally. The statue that had adorned the top of the fountain was gone. Apparently it had fallen into the waters below. I had no desire to try to raise it out. Not yet. I looked to the rippling water. For a long time I observed the gradually diminishing play on its surface. Were the things going to reach out? It was apparent to me that my dream landscape was under threat, that beings could penetrate some of the aspects of it, that I must protect it from the outside, and that the only way to do this was through psychic effort.

Gradually, the surface of the water settled to a blankness suitable to my need for security. I waited a little longer, and felt my breathing return to normal. The creature was some kind of symbolic archetype in my mind, some abstraction from the darkness able to unsettle my viewpoint. It had been used as a device to snare me. The other things outside the room, these figures who had encroached on me as I leapt to safety, they had seemed somehow more vibrant, more alive.

It was as though certain aspects of the garden were truly me; the garden itself, the fountain, these were me. But below the surface surely this was simply aspects of my unconscious as yet unbreached; worries, fears, Electra complexes, the baggage and the guilt that we all carry beneath our civilised veneer. I could explain this. But there had been something unnatural, discrete and separate about the other things; the other things that existed in the areas beyond the black room. Somehow it seemed as if they were not part of me, but something alive and unique in themselves.

I pulled myself away from the fountain, walking slowly, wary of surprises. I was aware that the garden was my own construction. As such, I had to have confidence in its inviolability. If I were for one moment to feel that it could be breached by dreadful apparitions, my mind would not be safe. I felt in myself that I had the spiritual or mental ability to resist invasion. I tested the premise, strolling briskly through the shaded avenues, watching with intense interest the clouds form into dark threatening buttresses in the sky. Suddenly, with all the qualities of a genuine dream, I was plunged into shade, and caught in the maze of towering hedges. I had come to a narrow sidewind, a place of disorientation.

I was in a maze. The worry of this was that it was not part of my original psychic intention. Basically, the maze was something I had allowed myself to visualise only as a distant object, a kind of Fun Park that I never really intended to enter.

Instead of entering it, it had entered me.

I now walked slowly, unable to stand still for simple fear. The hedges towered around me. They were not threatening in themselves, but there was a tinge of doubt in my mind that they could conceal things. I walked slowly forward, each footfall a faint dull noise. The path before me was unadorned, a hard grey clay. The hedge was low; its twisting undergrowth only a foot above ground level. The rest of the intertwined leaves rose like a cliff face, green and impenetrable. I seemed to walk in a dual time structure, with minutes passing like hours, hours like minutes. My emotions seemed tagged to the hours, my rational mind the quicker time.

Footsteps, distant, muted, began to trace my own. At first, I thought they were simply echoes, but then there are no echoes in damp hedgerows. The footsteps seemed at some stages to be walking parallel with me; at others they were behind.

Sometimes, more disconcertingly, they were in front of me, but not approaching, going more distant. After a while, my nerves began to frazzle, and then worse followed. The footsteps that had so disturbed me disappeared. I was entirely alone in the maze. An absolute silence emerged around me, like a palpable thing. I sank to the floor amongst the damp shavings of bark, dark mud and grass. I felt the beat of my heart on my chest. The metaphor "trapped bird" seemed appropriate; I heard the shallow breathing of my lungs, tasted the metallic taste of fear, mingled with the scent of resinous trees and undergrowth.

And then the footsteps began again. I could hear them, ever so far away, almost like a ghost sound, so quiet in my ear. I realised they were literally in my ear. The footsteps walked through the archways of my brain as though the whorls in its organic structure were an internal representation of the maze itself. I was becoming very confused; I felt it slip away from me. The towering hedges began to dance in a melting cascade. I pulled myself to my feet, tottering like the deconstructing world around me. I felt my head swim, the footsteps growing louder. And then, as suddenly as they had begun, they ceased.

This was worse. The all-pervasive silence. I struggled to retain reference points. I had none. I was experiencing a form of nirvana without any ecstasy, a limbo where I was literally nothing. This was perhaps what Crowley referred to as the great abyss across which the spirit must leap to bliss or be damned in lunacy. I felt myself slipping…and then a voice far away carried me back.

It was the hiker. I saw his face in the contortions of pain, I saw his back walking away in the nothingness, heard his pleading voice shouting, "Let me out, let me out."

It was something to cling to. Like Descartes mediations. Cogito Ergo Sum; I think therefore I am, and, in thinking, I exist. I knew it was a retreat. That the object of meditation was to suspend thought. Yet I knew I was not ready for nirvana. It was the same mistake that Crowley had hinted at when you washed your soul in the blinding light of the guardian angel. I could not tear the mask from the figure on the chariot because the very sight of naked eternity would burn me into an oblivion from which there was no return. So I retreated, and, in retreating, let those alien presences come rushing in. Footsteps from all sides tearing along corridors, hands ripping through the untrammelled hedgerow of my mind. The authors of evil trying with vehemence to tear down the walls of my being. They were winning. I had to eject them from my mind. I began to run. Blindly, dashing through the maze.

Again I heard a voice call in the distance, an indistinct murmur, seething around me.

And then I saw the door. I rushed to it, beating at first and then calming, turning around away from it. Through the eaves and shadows, for the towering groves of the hedgerows, the shadow creatures came.

They were not black. Neither were they clothed. They were wriggling indistinct unrealities like souls in goldfish bowls, indescribable yet emanating an alien strangeness that was objectively inhuman and hence, to my human perception, evil. I felt my throat constrict, my lips dry. I itched all over, and my eyes and head were sore with pain, muted and dark. I began to shiver with uncontrollable fear, and the parody of an erotic tingling enervated my body.

A voice called from beyond the door behind me. I could not respond. The figures slunk from the hedgerows across the open space of the gloaming garden. They had come for me and they were going to have me. The voice called again. I searched, through a brain that was frozen, for some magical alternative, some hope of rescue. I felt an inner voice as well as the outer call. I forced myself to unbend from the images before me, to turn to stare into the keyhole. The moment in which I turned my back on the most fearful thing in existence was one for a masochist to savour. In the brief seconds before utter destruction, I saw through the keyhole.

Inside, the room was a familiar place - a television, a couch, a small bookcase, a violin lying in an opened case. And a figure on couch, the figure of a woman. A woman with black hair and red lips, good looking. She was in an obvious catatonic state. The man bending over her, in a waxen tableau, was Keran Westwood. He was working some motion with his hand, but the room clearly occupied a frame of reference with a different time signature from the world that paralleled it. It was like a musical score where one piece plays in a discordant syncopation - one world out of time with another, but coexisting on the same piece of notepaper.

Of course I was the woman, and I was in trouble. Keran was trying to snap me out of it. He was saying something. I tried to hear, but it is difficult when you can feel the breath of unnatural evil on your back, and you can hear sounds that should not exist, in a land of shadows whose only purpose is the extinction of your sense of self. And then I heard. I knew what I had to do.

Slowly, with care, I began to knock on the door. Keran turned. Looked around the room, eyes searching walls, ceilings. Then he frowned, and looked towards the picture. I knocked again. Felt hands slip into my own and fingers caress my hair. Keran ran forward, and with a shout pushed open the door.

Suddenly, unbelievably I was free. Keran shouted at me, shouting loud and hard, pulling me, willing me forward. I was aware for a strange second of being in two places at once. Keran's face pressed into my own. I saw my own face blank, staring expressionlessly ahead. Then Keran shouted again. There was a crack - an unbelievable noise, and I suddenly awoke, spluttering, coughing; there was no time for ceremony. The only thing I heard for comfort after the worst of a series of ordeals was Keran shouting, "Run for God's sake run."

Chapter 10
The Body

THE WAVES rolled over the sand on the short beach at Portobello. The white sand reflected the light of a pale, chill sun. The power stations rose against the skyline over at Cockenzie and I could see the gulls like tiny white kites heeling above the flats near Aberlady. The sun occasionally caught one of the great birds in a spear of light, and for a brief moment the eye would feel punished.

In a while, the sun would go down. The flat seas would redden; the waders would cross the beach, searching for exposed lugworms and crabs. Until then, Keran and I would sit in a long silence, staring outwards to the ocean as though it represented some form of escape from the closing horrors around us.

We had said very little since the cataclysm of Rodin's house. It had been a long, long journey; bus, train and at one point, a stolen car. Fear hedged us in on all sides. I felt particularly blasted. Occasionally, my mind drifted back to the cosy years with Conrad but he seemed like a hollow man next to Keran. His stark betrayal in the northern hills seemed glaringly obvious, and his death, an act of stupidity; at other times, I found myself thinking about Jamie MacDonald and the academics at the university. All the happy carefree parties we had attended when I was something in the city. I recognised myself now as only an idle poseur. Sometimes I thought about Kennedy, left behind in Manchester. My daughter Kirsty, lost to adoption, I had never tried to trace her. I thought then of how she would be the same age as Kennedy. I thought of coincidence, synchronicity.

But thoughts like this tended to lead to the unreality of the occult. That grey area of nonsense where common ordinary things became obscene and different. The ocean at these moments seemed to take on a living vital force, the chaos of primeval energy sometimes equated with the devil. I would have to look at the sand. Then this would become a seething fragmentation and I would retreat to the stone slabs beneath the bench where we sat. When I felt particularly brave, I would glance across at Keran.

He seemed less intimidated than I did. He was still crumpled, worn out, but there was a glint to his eye that I knew I did not possess. He had said nothing of any consequence since we had run headlong into the street. He had taken no backward glances; he had simply run. I, on the other hand, had been foolish enough to look back.

I shivered, drew the old coat around my dwindling frame. A few small children ran up the promenade carrying chips, walking a small dog. Their figures seemed to be etched out of the blue sea and the blue sky. A small blonde girl, a small black haired boy. Keran stirred. I felt the nervous reaction kick in. The shuddering pain in the gut, the nausea.

"It's okay," said Keran. His words sounded flat, vaguely empty, as though he had no spare emotional content to dish out. "The kids are just what they seem: kids."

He stood up. Walked out a little way towards the rail that stood before the short drop to the small beach. The adults followed the path of the promenade, a stern couple walking purposefully and silently in the tow of their children. A dog ran along the distant strand, its owner whistling mournfully. For a time, Keran stood with his back to me, a large, hunched figure like a black crow staring at the beach, the flat expanse of water and the solitary distant figure of the dog owner.

Rising from the bench I joined him at the rail. Looking down at the sand, I saw the paper cups and the condoms and the cans and the plastic lollipop sticks that littered the ebb tide mark. The sombre depths of a few dark pools reflected back the light of the sun around the leeward side of the breakwater. Its stanchions rose up in dwindling perspective towards the sea that was now reddening as the sun died.

"I need to talk about it," I said.

Keran did not reply.

"When I looked back -"

"No," said Keran. "Not now."

I bit my lip in frustration.

"Come with me."

He lifted himself with surprising agility over the rail. I slipped in between it and followed him down on to the sand.

He walked out towards the ebbing tide. The wind whisked across the beach, sending the sand flurrying for a brief moment, and then it died as we reached the wet hard sand. The waves pitched on to the shore in a wide sweeping arc. Low waves feeling their way across the sepia sands. As we stood on the shoreline the sun dipped and the sky was dimmed. Grey clouds blossomed in the air fringed with dark red penumbra.

The beach was deserted.

Slowly with appalling grace Keran began to take off his clothes. His coat fell to the sand. He unbuttoned his shirt and peeled it back revealing a tight muscular frame, long arms matted with black hair. Then he bent over like an athlete stripping before a race and removed shoes and trousers. Without looking at me he said, "Take off your clothes."

I undressed.

I made a neat pile of my clothes beside those strewn by Keran. He glanced at me, looked me in the eyes; not once staring at my naked body, and then he took my hand and began to walk out into the sea.

The water was cold on my feet, splashing like ice on my shins and finally my thighs. My stomach gnawed with the cold and my breasts and groin pulled tight as though my skin had shrunk like an envelope around my bones. When we reached hip level, Keran let go off my hand and made a determined dive into the water. I watched him for a few seconds thrusting outwards with measured strokes, and then I dived after him.

The water was freezing but I followed him through the darkness, increasing the pace until we were some three hundred metres from the shore. At this point, Keran stopped, and turned on his back floating like a starfish beneath the darkening sky. For a second I trod water, sweeping my arms in a wide circle, watching his eyes glint almost corpse-like in the half light. He made a few tiny movements with his arms, but when it became clear he was going to simply lie there, I flipped over with less grace and kept afloat. The moon was rising like a nail clipping, somewhere above the now invisible Cockenzie power station. The stars were coming out like tiny raindrops on an erratic mosaic of dark tiles.

I felt like a corpse on the biggest mortuary slab in the world.

Keran murmured something. When it became clear that I had not heard him, he repeated himself

"Starless..."

I felt the chill rising through me from underneath like a sleeping draught

"...Bible black."

The chill became something beyond the physical; a vast absence surrounding and enervating my entire frame. I felt the expanse of ocean, the expanse of sky, the entire macrocosm and me, microscopic beneath it above it, and yet neither. I began to sink. And then Keran was beside me, pulling me under the water into the black. Deep into nothingness. His hands were round me, at once gentle and demanding. He seemed to be manipulating me like a child, and then he was pulling me upwards until we exploded into the cold air. I gasped, teeth chattering.

"Back." he said.

Limbs freezing, body weakening until I felt nothing in my

arms or legs, my whole system shutting down, I was pulled back towards the shore by Keran's sheer physicality. He carried me, like some B-movie monster tottering from a swamp, and then he pitched me on to the wet sand. Kneeling over my face, he pushed his erect penis into my face. I opened my mouth and began like a child to suck. Then the smell of rank seaweed and the taste of bitter salt merged and then there was the grating of sand on my tingling body; all sidelines in a show supervised by his stern, forbidding, shadowed face. Like a bronze of Neptune, he dominated the sky above me, and then with a grunt he shot his sperm into my gagging mouth. I tried to draw back but he would not allow it. After a few seconds he stood up and deliberately urinated over my breasts and belly. And then he turned around began searching the sand for his clothes.

Weakly, I got to my feet and tottered to the beach. Quickly, with violently shaking hands, I splashed water on my face and body. When I got back to the beach, Keran was already half dressed. He stared at me, taciturn, unmoved, his face half in shadow.

I began to put my clothes on but I had only pulled my knickers up when he forced me to the sand on my knees and brutally penetrated my vagina. Then, in a frenzy of thrusting and grunting, he pushed me on to my back, raised my buttocks up, and penetrated my anus. I was screaming, whimpering in the sand as he damaged my body with his huge lingam. He slapped me several times, his face a calculated stare.

Without a backward glance, he stood, zipped up his flies, and began the long walk back to the prom.

I lay stunned for a few minutes, and then I staggered to my feet, suddenly, desperately, angry. I felt the madness shouting from my inner being. I threw on my clothes and began to run, following his bobbing shadow that stood between me and the long, loose chain of the house lights along the prom. I caught him, pulled his shoulder, screaming out my rage and anger. I did not see his face as he felled me with a huge blow. I lay on the ground, my jaw in agony, weeping. For a while he stood over me. Then he bent down, his face entirely hidden in shadow.

"Nothing. All that was nothing. I warn it now. I did to your body a few simple penetrations. You're too damned uptight. The body's nothing; nothing and you're nothing. Learn it now. There's a seeping darkness about you, all around. What I did was a fucking favour to what comes next; believe me. We're in so much trouble I could puke."

Incredibly, his face revealed nothing of any sexual intent. He had been uninterested in me physically. Worse, he was uninterested in power. I could tell by his grim visage that he had done something he felt horribly necessary. He had done it the way a research assistant might cut open the belly of a living toad, without malice, without concern.

I threw up on the sand and lay whimpering for a long time.

Keran did nothing. He stared out to the sea.

And then, as I lay weeping, he began to talk. He talked of the stars. I had a peripheral interest in the stars, memories of a year spent under Walters at the institute, who had instructed me in some of the esoteric patterns of Greek cults and their relationship to cosmogony. But my knowledge was like that of a child's when set aside that of Keran. I realised then that this was all a demonstration. Even through the pain and humiliation, Keran's voice penetrated my being. He began to draw vast astrological charts in the skies, relating a stupendous variety of differing systems together, weaving immense patterns from the cosmos. His left hand would point this way and that, until my mind was bewildered with information. It carried on for hours, his eyes reflecting the moonlight like two pale jellyfish. His hand motioning, his body otherwise still. And then the sun was coming up over the sea, and there was only silence and emptiness.

After another hour, when the sun's light had utterly gone, Keran got to his feet.

"It's time to go," he said.

He looked down at me, as if I had appeared for the first moment in the long night.

"Manchester," he said. "Now we go back and retrace the steps. Manchester."

"You raped me," I said.

"Yes."

"Why?"

"You know why."

"Just tell me why."

"Things like that can't be told. They can't be spelled out like some kids' alphabet."

I dried my eyes slowly on my blouse.

"Think," he said.

"Think of what you said to me earlier."

I thought I knew then. "What I saw, the house."

"Yes," he said.

"In the window, I saw someone, something."

"Yes." he said. "You saw a woman. An old woman."

I shuddered.

"And she scared you shitless."

I began to cry, tears wrenching out of my body.

Keran put his arms around me.

"I was terrified. I can't explain it."

"I can. Despite all the ordeals you have endured, this was the most abysmally terrifying thing you have ever experienced, going even beyond your experience in the room while I was with Rodin."

I nodded.

"Look," said Keran. "I don't have time to train you. The kinds of things that are necessary take literally years, some say centuries. The sexual assault: Believe me, it meant nothing to me, but I hope that it might make a significant difference for you."

I sighed. My mind was oscillating between sanity and madness. The physical pain, the feeling of disgust. They were nothing to the vision of that old woman, seen only briefly, because I couldn't look any more, in the window of the crumbling house. Yes, I had watched as the house began to melt, unsure whether it was a confusion of my perception or an objective fact. I had seen the old woman stare with an implacable stare as behind crowded a host of shambling faceless figures, huddled together, framed like some medieval painting of hell in the simple terraced house of an urban estate.

I got to my feet.

"How did you know about the woman?" I said to Keran.

For the first time, he looked uneasy, lacking entirely in confidence. He said quite simply.

"I see her too."

Chapter 11
Killing

WE DECIDED to hitch hike separately. Keran insisted that for the moment we would be better alone. He suggested that we deliberately head in opposite directions - He felt that we must to some extent unravel the spiritual connection we had formed, or we would be too obvious. I didn't question his judgement. I already knew he was beyond my understanding. I purchased an old coat from the cancer shop in Stockbridge, made my way to South Queensferry, and waited for two hours before getting my first lift. It was a long day. The lifts were all short, a few miles down the road. I was pleased, because it gave me a chance to test my disguise as an old tramp. There was never any problem with this. People seemed to see what they wanted to see. Perhaps I had got better at being someone else.

I had elected to head back towards Aviemore

Despite what Keran had said about the rape, I felt I could never face him again; the intimacy of a car journey, the thought of his unpredictable reactions. I felt violated, mentally and physically. I was also disturbed by his last message to me as we had parted in a bar in the Southside, overlooked by Arthur's seat.
"When you get the lifts, try to seduce the drivers."
I wasn't sure if I wanted to see Keran again. But then I wasn't sure if I wanted to live. When I considered as deeply as I could (most things I kept at a superficial level in my mind) I realised that I didn't commit suicide because I felt like small child frightened of the dark cupboard at the foot of the bed. The thought of the final abyss looming up before me also imparted a framed picture of the eyes of the old woman leering over the

top. Her eyes had an ambiguous feel, as though you stared at the dead eyes of a fish head on a plate, or a pig in a pen, and suddenly without any warning a glint appeared, a trace of consciousness. I couldn't kill myself, because whenever I died the eyes of that woman would follow me down. I hadn't considered in any real fashion whether or not I was religious. I didn't even really know if I was an agnostic. I had found out very late in life that you can have rational arguments for the existence of God, for Heaven for Hell, but they meant nothing until you were confronted with the emotional reality of death. Try Pascal's wager: It's better to believe in God, because if you don't, and if he does exist, you trade a few brief moments of joy for the eternity of Hell. Descartes: if God exists, the alternative is some malicious demon creating a dream state. Anselm: Only a fool would believe that the reality of God is less than the conception of him. You can conceive of Him as the greatest being, therefore there must be a greater being in reality. They were all flawed, all defeated by the gut feelings inside.

I didn't want to live, and I didn't want to die. I was stuck, like a lot of people, in the grey limbo of existence, trying not to be seen by a significant predator.

A lorry driver gave me a lift to Preston. He was Turkish, tired. He'd been on the road for seven days and taken a wrong turning because he couldn't speak English. The wrong turning had taken him 200 miles out of his way. He talked to me in a foreign, lilting accent, using Turkish and sign language. I could understand nothing of what he said. The only points of contact came when he gestured and pulled a photo out of his pocket. It was a picture of two bright-eyed children who looked almost feral in their bright wedding costumes. Some traditional dress - happy children in a happy other life.

The only word we seemed to share in any language was pantaloons. He carried a cargo of trousers. He showed me them, wrapped neatly in the back of his lorry in scruffy boxes. He made no attempt to seduce me. The thought of seducing him made me almost vomit.

We stopped in Bolton where I didn't have the heart to tell him that the English storekeepers were throwing out his gear as damaged because of some private angst with the bosses. I thought of the wasted journey as I left him waving and smiling innocently, a simple honest man. I envied him.

Manchester was cold and grey. The last phase of hitching was the usual nightmare. It's always easier to hitch a thousand miles instead of two. No one stopped except for a bunch of youths who waited until I got near the car and then threw a bottle at me before they drove off with a nasty toot of their horn. It was getting dark when a salesman stopped. He was bald, thin, and mistook me for a man. I noticed the mirrors placed at convenient angles all around his car. We had gone seven or eight miles before he had his prick out and was asking me if I wanted to make myself more comfortable. I stared out the window as he beat himself into a husky desperate orgasm. He let me out, without a word, some miles from where I wanted to go. I threw up on the pavement.

I walked on until it was dark, and for an hour I waited for a night bus in the dark deserted Manchester street. I got off about three miles from the centre of town and immediately found a phone. I tried to get through to Jamie, but there was no response. I looked around at the dark night; the ill-lit streets vaguely yellow in the artificial lights. The dim bus stop. As a kid I used to pass a bus stop in the country and there was always someone standing there, morning and night. It was a dark bus stop, which meant that you couldn't see the person, just be aware of his shadow. In time I began to wonder about that lonely bus stop. How it might be a haunted silent place, the waiting figure may have been trapped or incapacitated. They may have waited years for that bus, perhaps a bus that didn't exist, a number they'd forgotten to delete from the sign. One day, I thought I would get off at the stop and find the person there dead a long, long time, a corpse, a skull, a muffled dark cloak. It was strange how these childhood horrors had become in my mind like some simple comforting game. Paradoxically, and against all intuition, I found the horrors of adulthood unexpected and more terrifying than anything a child might conjure.

I sat on the seat of the bus stop, and then tried to find a comfortable position to sleep for the remainder of the night.

Dawn came, bringing aching limbs and a dull hunger. The streets were empty. No traffic, no people. My sleep had been full of unpleasant dreams. If I had been an adept, I would have tried to meditate, but any sense of discipline was gone utterly, and with it any sense of hope. I was an aching vessel, empty even of bitterness. Even my feet hurt with a still pain. I clutched my knees and held on to myself, for fear that I would unravel like a string.

I missed the first bus because I had slowed down and the world had speeded up. When the second bus came, I had my change ready. I fell asleep on the bus and went past the stop. I walked past my flat. The Lenas street beggar was there. He gave me a conspiratorial look. He did not recognise me. I stood for a while across the road looking to see if there was anything different. All I got was a feeling of despair; a clammy sensation in the pit of my stomach, a sense of evil. But superficially nothing had changed. Keran had told me to take as few risks as possible, to trust my instincts. I walked past the window of the flat, round the corner, and a little way down the street to the Salvation Army shop. I bought some clothes: A pair of jeans and a sweatshirt with a hooded balaclava, and a pair of trainers, a small coat with zip pockets. From there, I took a taxi to the auction at Belmont. The cars were going cheap, and I soon had an old Vauxhall Cavalier. I drove out towards Knutsford. Parked the car by the old fisherman's flash and began to jog, so weak I had to stop at various points and walk. The trees shrouded the walkway around the back of the caravan site that led to the back entrance. I jogged through the trees and came to the part of the site where the touring caravans were stored. It was like a cemetery of large white stones. Green moss-covered caravans of obsolete design, and beside these tombs of happy holidays, the odd new gypsy caravan. I walked through this section until I came to the residential site. I was near to where Bower's caravan lay, but it was not my immediate destination. On the far side, the holidaymaker caravans lay, the Southside where I found the caravan I sought, new in that morning. I knocked at the door. It opened, and I walked in, shouting a "hello". Keran ushered me in and left the door deliberately opened.

"This is the lion's den." he said tonelessly. "In the books they say this is the last place where they will look. I hope it's true. In the evening, we're going to see Bower. We won't be hanging about."

Keran looked tired, but we didn't talk about his journey. We sat listlessly for a while staring at the walls, each other, the window. Keran's face, although haggard, was at least animated. For a while, I stared at the man who had brutally raped me, the giant of a man who had been better off without a past, a shambling wreck of humanity. "I love you." I said.

He glanced up. A dark emotion played across his face but he said nothing. We waited hours, ostensibly playing cards. In reality, listening to the sound of outside. The evening fell, and the stars came out crisply like pearl buttons on a dark evening suit. Somewhere an owl roosted, preparing to lift into the evening sky in search of a timid mouse. Looking from the window, it was easy to conceive of dark shapes peopling the fringes of the woods around the caravan site. Somewhere, a dog barked. Keran had been at the table for the better part of an hour, preparing what he had described as a network of magical protection. He claimed it had to be 'low key' because he did not want anyone or anything to become attracted to us. He had become taciturn, silent. After a bit he looked up. "Time to go," he said.

The night air was cold, brisk, the trees surrounding the site waved in a light, suspicious wind. As we approached the forty-five foot caravan, it seemed like we walked in a vast graveyard, the slabs turned on their sides. At various points, small car lights lit up the caravan site signs for the toilet and the entrance. But basically we were in the dark. Keran exposed the ground before us with a torch and, as we neared the battered porch, he stopped for some twenty minutes, checking the ground here and before the door. After some time he gently bent at the foot of the door, and with tweezers lifted something, and then again on the top of the door. It would be hair used to seal the place and for other occult purposes that I could only hazard.

After a few more minutes examining the lock, Keran sighed and then simply pushed the door. The creaking was only marginally louder than the creaking of the rotting porch wood. It was dark inside, and smelt terrible: oppressive; damp imbued with another sickly odour of something gone bad. Keran's fitful little torch picked out the boiler; it had burst open, and the contents, the coal and the fire-bricks, swooned out of the openings like the slag from a tiny dead volcano, or the intestines of some black beast. The tiny hall was empty of anything but the smell. I followed behind Keran as we entered the living quarters. Inside we traced the author of the smell.

I could only assume it was Bower. It was difficult to tell. The body literally decorated the room. Every single part was smashed, broken and cast around, almost as though he had exploded, blowing apart like a burst balloon. The walls and the sagging sack-like curtains were stained a dark red where his living blood had sprayed them. A few body parts, fingers, jaw bone, some grisly blonde hair were discernible amidst the blood.

Amidst all this I could see familiar objects remembered from my last visit: The mattress on the floor. The sad, cheap furniture, and now, painted by his blood, the books: The Koran, The Prophet and the Bhagavad-Gita still lying on the floor. Glittering scarabs and Maasai beads scattered like little tears, unhappy stars in a red night. The drawers where the Golden Buddha had once sat were tumbled on the floor. A few papers moved uneasily in the draught. As I paused, dumbstruck in a calm bewildered suspension, I was vaguely aware that the Catholic sacred heart had remained somehow untouched by blood. The Crucifix, in contrast, had blood congealing from it like a macabre candle. It was the one object in the room that seemed in my memory to have been touched. Some humorist had placed it firmly on the wall, upside down.

I had covered my mouth. Keran held me, his face impassive, his twitching nostrils the only betrayal that he was perturbed. He had gripped my arm immediately to prevent my progress. "Are the cups moved in any way?" I was almost startled by the utter calm of his voice. I had not noticed the cups, hidden as they were beside the votive tray, and now I did. After staring for some few moments I was able to shake my head. The cups that I had drunk from so many months before were in exactly the same position in which we, Bower and I, had left them.

Keran smiled a weary kind of smile. He stepped gingerly into the room and picked something up from beside the drawers, looked at it with the torch, and then stepped back. He looked at me and then began to edge back out of the room.

We got to the door.

Lights blazed all around in our faces. I heard a voice shout. There were three dark figures. At first I was utterly confused, vaguely aware of Keran's immense form blocking one of the shadows. There was an instant of sheer terror. An instant in which the three figures seemed like a window of darkness, as though I could see through each of the figures as into a pitch black night beyond night. As Keran's body enveloped the first, I felt a wave of shock run through me. It was as though these three beings were the ultimate evil. It was a feeling that rose in my brain, my mental operations, but not in my intuition. I watched, incredulous, as Keran struggled for an instant with the first figure. There was a tremendous sound, a crack as though a fissure had opened in the mountain of night; it was a man's neck being broken. Then I heard the screaming, the pleading for God. Keran had jumped forward crashing against and breaking the porch. The figure on the left had started to back away. In the light of a torch I caught a brief glimpse of a terrified face. I could see that he was a young man, nearly a boy. The figure on his left had not moved. I caught a brief image of a hand movement. Keran leapt forward and gripped the boy by the head. Even as the second snap ricocheted off the caravans around us I had leapt to the ground before the third figure. It was a woman; young, terrified into stupefaction. Her hand clutched her mouth. I saw the red shawl around her shoulders, the fine blonde hair. Keran said quietly. "Kill her."

   I did.

Chapter 12
Kennedy

LATER, ON THE BUS up to Manchester, Keran talked in a low empty voice.

"You probably feel that things can get no worse. In fact, you probably don't feel at all. There'll be an empty space where your heart is; there'll be an impending sense that you are going to weep more tears than history or never weep again. I want you to understand that there are worse things than..."

"...than killing innocent people?"

"They were in the way."

I got up quickly only to be restrained by Keran's iron grip. He pulled me down slowly with an irresistible force. And then he hissed in my ear. "They were in the way *deliberately*."

I looked him square in the eyes. "They were innocents."

"I know," he said finally.

"Nothing, no aura, no witchcraft, just people." I felt the darkness rise out of the emptiness in my body.

His eyes turned towards the rain-dashed window of the bus. In profile his face looked slightly haggard.

"They're better off dead."

"I'm fucking sick of hearing that, Keran."

"But believe me, it's true."

"But I don't believe you."

He turned again, his eyes fixing me like a maggot on a pin. "Don't you believe me?"

It was too much. I felt things crawl over my body. Unbelievable irritations as though I was covered with some crawling plague. "Can't you leave me alone?" I said, "What if they were put there deliberately? They were human. What was the point in killing them?"

"The point was that they were witnesses to our presence in

the caravan; they were the best link to the police it could be possible to imagine. When they walked in and found us, we would have been indelibly associated with the crime. The police would hunt us down like a pack of hounds after a hare."

"And they won't now?"

"Of course they'll hunt us down, but do you think they will find it more difficult without a description."

"But…"

"Without a description, someone was killed, that's all."

"But…"

"No "buts", damn you. Use some sense. You find a body sprayed around a room. You see two people running away. You tell the police. Don't you think that we may have been caught? We had to kill them. If they were still alive, we would be in a police cell in a few months, and do you really want to know what that would mean?"

I stared out of the window at the redbrick buildings and the lights of all-night grocery stores.

"What did you do with them?"

He stared again. "Do you really want to know?"

"Yes, things are bad enough…"

"Are they?"

"I want to know"

"You want to know? I waited about twenty minutes while you went off to the caravan, and then I slashed the bodies up as best as I could without messing myself, and I cut them up as much as was possible and threw the bits around the room as much as I was able, and then I strolled back to you and we went off. Satisfied?"

I looked at him in disbelief. "That's what you did. It really is, isn't it?"

"Yes," he said. "And do you want to know why I did that?" He waited. "It's quite simple, really. The police will come to have a look, and they don't know what the fuck is going on, and they'll never believe it wasn't a single maniac gone berserk. Not two people who walked in and walked away as calm as priests. I want you to understand that this is not some silly game."

"A game, mincing people up…"

"It's not a game, a social game, a game with rules. Every rule you knew is now gone as though it never existed. There's nothing. You can't trust anything or anybody. Not even me." He shook his head. "Well, at least you can trust me up to a point, but beyond that, you've only yourself. You're a soul. Don't you see? You're nothing but a soul. The body, the shape the form, the eyes, the nose, the mouth, the cunt. They're nothing. They're all worth nothing, and you better forget them as quickly as possible."

"I don't understand." My voice trembled on the brink.

"Damn it. I thought amidst your many talents that you were a professor of the occult. Don't you see? The body, the same river twice. Heraclites, Buddha, Crowley, Steiner. You name them, and they'll tell you. Every great master says that the body is worth nothing, and it's worth nothing because it's subject to change. We're transient, we're temporary. We don't really exist. I cannot teach you this. I can only demonstrate it."

I began to weep. Slow, dreadful tears pissing out of some sewer in my frame. "But the soul…"

Keran was merciless. That was the one thing I had learned he was very good at. He continued in a low-level tone. "The body changes. It grows. It comes to fruit. It withers and it dies. It's like the blossom on a tree that grows into an apple and then the apple falls. It's like every lesson you learned in nursery school. The body changes, and if you went to certain schools, they taught you that you also had a soul. Now you might have listened to that all day and you might have intellectualised it in your heart but at some point you've got to realise it's true. That what all these painful demonstrations are about."

"You kill people to demonstrate?"

"No, of course not. They were there."

"But, for God's sake, if you have a soul, then your mind comes into it somewhere, making decisions. You don't just kill people without affecting your soul too."

"That may be part of the problem," said Keran, beating the front of the bus. "This sect brings something new to the heavenly equation."

"And rape? Raping me was part of the equation?"

"I told you it was a lesson."

"For god's sake, I'm a human being."

"Yes, yes," He punched his fist through the plastic cover of the seat. "And I'm human, and look what they did to me."

I saw then that first picture. The witless giant brought to me by Kennedy. What was he then? A giant clad in a shabby grey suit, plastic shoes, no socks and a cheap nylon shirt. Even his hat had been ridiculous, like a Charlie Chaplin tramp. What had he seemed like; a busker in an old grey jacket, hopelessly misplaced in the city. Or maybe only in the city could something as absurd have existed; maybe only in anonymous places could a man have become nothing, anyone. And what was I then? Confident assured, immaculate, elegant. I could throw adjectives around like a thesaurus that would have me marked down as good quality antique furniture, well made, crafted and enduring the call of the centuries. Now I was glad I couldn't see myself well enough in the reflection from the bus window. I could smell myself, stinking in the shabby clothes I wore, smelling of fear and hurt and death.

I had reached something approaching the state to which Keran had fallen.

I looked again at him by my side, barely squeezing into the plastic clad bus seat. His figure was intense, carrying more power than his body frame seemed to fill. He was huge, towering above me like a monolith. I would have been scared of him had there been any real terror left in me but then the world in its totality was the most frightening thing I had ever encountered.

I shuddered inside, felt vomit creep up from my empty stomach, and then something utterly unexpected happened. I turned to the next seat and there was Kennedy starting to sit down. She smiled across at me and said "Hi".

In that moment, something happened that was quite unique in my experience. I felt a twisting of my deep intestines as though I was being slowly turned inside out. I could not speak. The bus seemed for a second like a ghost-train bound through the night, and us, carnival figures heading for the darkness. Keran looked at Kennedy and she looked at him. I was intensely aware of her green eyes piercing his, examining, weighing up assessing him - and of him assessing her. There was some bond between them that I recognised. Not the bond I had, but the one I personally wanted to create, between Keran and me. In a second I knew that she had grown up a little, had become a young woman, and, despite the absurdity of it all - the biker's jacket, the rope around her waist, the baggy jeans - he was attracted to her in an intense sort of way. I looked again at him edging me out of the seat, massive, profound masculine. He was overheating in the contact with her, and Kennedy was responding.

Despite the feelings crushing me, I took the chance of her presence, that I felt had to be some sort of lucky omen. "Kennedy we need help; can you find us somewhere?"

"Sure," she said and she smiled, looking again at Keran.

The room was small, and bare of furniture except for a double mattress laid out on a linoleum floor. There was a sheet for a curtain that covered a view to high rise flats across a sward of green, littered with discarded fridges, cookers and rubbish bags. On the way to the 12th storey flat we had seen small children wreck a burning car. Their whoops of delight and high unnatural voices could still be heard some distance away, filling the night with a weird transient edge.

Having seen where we were to sleep, I walked back into the main room. Kennedy was at the open kitchen, talking and making coffee. Three sombre individuals sat on the couch. They stared at the television, apparently oblivious of our presence, fixed on a chat show on the television. One of them was a long-haired hippie with dark Buddy Holly glasses, a short bloke with strong looking physical frame going slightly to fat. The second was a thin, nervy man with short, neatly cut hair, and the third, a swarthy faced man of around thirty with a pock marked skin and some physical problems with his left arm. I found myself looking from them to the object of their interest: The television. With them I began to stare with fascination at its bright glow. I hadn't seen one for a long while, and the inane figure selling some game show to his audience seemed to personally pick on me as his next victim. I had to shake myself away from the vision being presented.

The swarthy faced man put his feet up on the small coffee table, and the thin one mumbled something I couldn't catch. The hippie began to roll a joint on a large book kept especially for the purpose. I watched him carefully and methodically preparing the joint: His nimble fingers, craftsman-like, spliced and gummed the papers.

Keran was at the kitchen. He leant against a washing machine, filling the window with his big frame. He looked relaxed, almost confident. I sat down on the floor next to the settee. In a corner of the room, a cockroach began to sidle from somewhere. It took a few tentative steps forward, and there was a sudden sharp "pang". The cockroach disappeared, leaving a black splotch on the skirting board. There was a chorus of laughter. The hippie on the couch held up an elastic band contraption that he clearly used as a catapult for insects. I became aware that the pattern on the lower walls and skirting boards that looked like a Jackson Pollock design was in reality something of an abattoir for insect life. I got off the floor and sat gingerly on the only other chair.

Kennedy laughed behind me. I heard Keran laughing too; the first time I had ever heard him laugh. I could not help turning to watch him smile. I knew then that, despite everything, I loved him deeply. He could have done anything to me that he wanted. In fact he had already done everything that he might want. I was entirely under his spell, a willing slave, broken, empty, and prepared to die for him. I wanted to die for him.

Kennedy brought some coffee. She sat down on the floor and Keran got on the edge of the couch. There had been no introductions, there was an understanding here that parties met and parted, that people talked or did not talk. We were in a waiting room once again, where acceptance and tolerance of almost any form of behaviour was a simple rule. Kennedy took the joint from the last man on the couch, smoked a few tentative puffs, grimaced and handed the joint to Keran. He shook his head. She offered it to me, and I took it tentatively and toked on it a little, watching the puff of the smoke. I took another toke and handed it back to Kennedy. She got up, and walked with a new grace to the nervy bloke on the other side of the couch and handed him the joint. Keran watched her all the way there and all the way back, with a look in his eyes that he'd never given to me. He then looked back at me with a searching stare and an expression of puzzlement. I felt the bitter, heavy taste of the nicotine in my mouth, and a sensation of sinking deeper into the chair. I felt suddenly sick. I took another sip of the coffee, and then I got up slowly and went to bed.

In the night I awoke, alone. The moon shone through holes in the ragged window covering. I heard the sound of distant voices and saw glistering lights on the edge of my vision. There was a musty, close smell around me, and a light draught played across my face. An eerie sensation clambered in my guts. I thought irrationally that the children we had seen earlier were burning another car in the room beyond the door. I got to my feet and walked out into the empty living room.

The low voices were those of Keran and Kennedy. The flickering lights candles in the room. Kennedy, stoned and naked, knelt on the couch, licking and sucking Keran's erect penis. Her eyes stared up at him in a mockery of delight. He was handling her naked tiny breasts and staring down at her with open-eyed intensity. He turned for a second, seeing my shadow in the door, and then Kennedy saw me. She took his member out of her red mouth and sat back on the couch and opened her waif like legs. Keran's towering frame hovered above her. He got down on his knees level with her opening groins. She pulled his head down and he was about to bury his face between her loins, but she held him there for a second, grinning, her eyes wide with expectation. She looked across at me. I watched, mesmerised, as she tugged him playfully by the ears then guided him, as an expert rider teases a passive horse with bit and bridle, into the gap between her thighs.

Chapter 13
Snow

FOR THREE HOURS I lay on the mattress in the room and watched the moonbeams slanting through the ragged holes in the curtain sheet. Around me the cockroaches travelled on esoteric journeys, decorating the skirting board with their journeys like a moving miniature Bayeux tapestry. As I lay in despair the external sounds of the night were extinguished like a guttering candle; the smell of the room, musty and pervasive, began to explore my body as though my nose and mouth were weak points in a fortification and obnoxious enemies had breached them.

For the first hour or so I was entirely numb, inactive, paralysed by fear and empty despair. I was aware of hurt, of injury, but I also felt distanced from it, as though I observed someone else's body and mind. Later, as the silence began to surround the room like a gloved hand, I felt myself trapped within it. I was vaguely conscious of my body being wrapped and packaged, almost snug, as though a spider in command of silence had poisoned me and now cocooned me as a preparation for the banquet of my body. In this horrific cocoon my mind lay like a dormant Ferris wheel, the thoughts static, not circling in any form. I could see the outlines of past events almost as though the ideas themselves had been petrified into grotesque sculptural shapes. I watched this tableau with my inner mind for a while longer, and then it shattered. Unwilling, for the first time in memory, I was drawn into my psychic garden.

Winter. Snow, and a cold still air. All beside me the crisp snow crackled in the brittle air. To the distances the snow stretched white and unbroken. Utter silence prevailed. I saw the eruption where the white cupola of the flowerpot must presumably rest. My bench was a lozenge of snow. On my left the fuchsia bush rose up, stripped of foliage. Behind it the tall hedges, topped with an icing of snow, seemed darker and more impenetrable than I remembered.

Slowly, I followed the circuit of the trees to where a declivity in the snow showed the place where the small stone steps must lead into the garden itself.

Now that I was here, I felt relaxed again. Although the journey had been taken against my will, just the sight, the smell, the taste of the cool air was enough to reassure me that I was in a safe haven. It struck me that I must have needed this return at some deeper psychic level, and that perhaps it was I myself who had willed it.

The hedges reared up around me like frozen giants ushering the path towards the fountain. It stood in crystallised glory shining in the whitened air. I approached slowly, observing the minute cascades and frozen waterfalls. It seemed as though the water had looked on Medusa and simply stalled. I walked around the circumference of the fountain and scrutinised the surface. Every kink in the dark surface of its basin, every trace of light, every suspect suspended object. I remembered only too well what lay beneath.

It was then that I saw the footsteps. They were on the far side of the fountain, heading Dream North. They trailed into a section of the maze some twenty feet away, smallish prints, almost but not quite those of a child. And there, at the extreme circumference of the fountain, there was an eruption of frozen spray, as though a great object had been dashed into the pool from a height and the waters had exploded for an instant to be caught, cold and frozen. As though an object had been frozen or, as now became clear, as though something had burst forth from the pool, defying all the laws of common sense, leaving the pool on the instant it had frozen, to walk towards the maze of towering hedges in the near distance.

For a long, long while, I stared at that dark place of exit from the pool, the twisted glittering cavern that obscured my passage. But I knew that I was going down even as I stared in fear.

The gap was large. The outward explosion had pushed back more of the frame of the creature that had left it and, although the expansion of the frozen water had fallen back in making the space smaller, there was enough for me to make the descent.

The room was much as I remembered it: Black, deeply back, the stone circular table in the centre of the room now incredibly broken, cleft in two great halves. The draperies torn in places and splattered with dark stains, and the black floor cold and unyielding beneath my feet, but the same room with the same pervasive chill beyond mere cold. I saw now behind the draperies the outline of door frames, all shut thankfully. Above the doors through the rags I became aware of esoteric writing and symbols beyond my knowledge. As I walked around the table I searched for the book, but it was gone. All that remained was a sense of catastrophe, of violent disaster, as though the world had been captured in this tiny spot - captured and then blown apart with unimaginable force. In here it was cold, colder than anywhere outside but it was also heavy, not light and still, but heavy and thick with ice, cold and incredible weight. The place had no smell, and left only a metallic taste in the mouth as though one tasted one's own body and nothing else.

I noticed now that I had touched nothing in the room because my body refused to perform the act. It knew better than any rational extension of mind what this place was - an abhorrent vacuum. I shuddered deeply; felt the cold weight spread up my legs. The doors seemed impassively large in their great sweep around me, as though they were bursting with something. There was no sense of anyone or anything trying to make an entrance, they simply swelled with some sort of lifeless energy, something incompatible even with itself. I felt the torpor spread upwards through my lower limbs and I walked slowly, with care, back towards the avenue of escape.

Now I knew where winter was born in my dreamscape. It started in this room, or perhaps more accurately it seeped in through the doors spread around me in their gaunt circle. I was reminded of Stonehenge and other Celtic stone circles, but only in terms of power. This room was serving no human purpose; it was an awful place beyond anything materially horrific, and I now knew that I would never return to it, regardless of any light of knowledge it might shed on my life.

I walked upwards to the icy eruption that represented the only avenue of escape. The room doors seemed to watch me all the way. Slowly, I ascend, all the time feeling that I might be dragged back. The cold in my legs now spread through me. As I reached the top I saw the bright light out of the white skies above. Around the myriad reflections from the twisted ice everything seemed about to snap in the terrific cold, even my body.

When I stood on the edge of the basin I was able to see the full circumference around me; the south, the east, the west of the dreamscape, the towering hedges, the distant trees and the bushes and hedgerows near me; my old bench beside the flower pot entirely covered in snow. Even as I watched, there was a harsh staccato snap, and I saw a crack appear in the bench, as though an invisible hand had simply tightened an inexorable grip. I shuddered to the core of my being. And then I traced with my eye the small, child-like foot prints that headed north towards the northern maze and beyond as I could see now faintly in the distance. I knew they headed for the mountains, and I knew I would follow them.

There was a moment where the tableau seemed fixed like a mosaic pattern. The mosaic fragmented, and then, slowly, its colours faded. The world of taste and touch was only a few footsteps away. I took them.

The first glimmerings of false dawn broke around me. I was back.

I got to my feet and pushed open the door of the small room. On the floor the supine bodies of Keran and Kennedy lay naked on the cushions taken from the couch. Keran looked like some sleeping buried knight, his great limbs strewn around his body in total relaxation. Kennedy lay on top of him, her face towards me, like an elf in charge of a giant. I walked slowly, quietly, towards them. I think my intention was to kill Kennedy first. A simple snap of the neck would be enough, but as I walked forward, I became aware that she had not been asleep. She was staring directly at me.

I stopped; we exchanged looks for some minutes, and then quite deliberately she allowed her exposed hand to wander to Keran's private parts. With a swift, expert motion she began to draw him into erection. All the while, she stared at me in the soft light, with an intense look of pleasure. I smiled at her woodenly as Keran began to whimper in the limbo between sleep and waking. Softly, I left the room.

As I walked down the damp concrete steps of the tower block, I heard a magnified whisper that by some trick of acoustics appeared to emerge from within my ears.

"Mine."

It was Kennedy's voice

Chapter 14
Ghosts

AROUND ME, the tower blocks rose in series, as though I was surrounded by giant tombstones in varying states of decay. The concrete pavements were littered with debris; from crisp packets to burnt-out cars. The few green hedges were festooned with toilet paper, condoms and spent needles. The streets were empty of living souls, as though I had entered some dreary ante-hell where I was the only thing existent. More so, I felt, in myself, that I was almost less than existent, a tiny guttering candle in a sweep of darkness; a candle on the verge of snuffing out. My mind was defunct, and my limbs seemed to keep up a walking pace, because to stand still would be to contemplate, and I could no longer contemplate anything but the automatic levels of the body. I suppose I was in a state of shock. But then again, that would imply some consciousness of feeling; even of feeling nothing. I saw my feet, walking, walking, the old trainers stubbing along the road like two worn parts of a single tired machine.

Someone knocked me down. The concrete hit me on the ribs. I lay winded. There may have been two of them rifling through my pockets. One kicked me to ensure that I didn't get up. I gagged on my own vomit as they ran off, shouting curses. For maybe an hour I lay on the street, until I could force myself to rise. Around me, the first commuters had emerged, ignoring me as only commuters can do.

I searched my coat. Somehow, beyond any reasoning, they had failed to find the thousands of pounds tucked in my inside pocket. I almost laughed, but the laughter would have emerged from a hollow soul, a skull laughing without flesh. Forcing myself onwards, I hardly had the mental strength to ascertain my reasons for existence. It seemed that some part of me was being pulled like a puppet from one dance routine to the next, as though my destiny was somehow determined.

I had never believed in determinism, never believed that the path one might take was not one that had at least an element of choice. Now, in the bitter cold of my being, I pondered the possibility. Of course, there were other possibilities. I genuinely contemplated the chance that I might be in Hell. Perhaps the cycle of events was some form of eternal torture; the pain, the endless suffering of the here-and-now reaching a trough from which there was no rising up. But then something in me, something faint and far away, rebelled against this. Perhaps the rebel was my thinking mind, which had always supported me in the past. I was a logical thinker, capable of mental operations in excess of those of my contemporaries. Now, even though this faculty had deserted me, in terms of its ability to provide me with answers to problems, the framework, the reasoning process, my ability itself, kept me onwards, onwards, walking through the daylight hell.

It had become a busy road. A little further along, traffic yelled around me like phantasms of an unlikely present. People circled around me as they swept past. They sensed I was somehow inhuman, repellent. I was confronted by school children. A whole party passed, accompanied by their teacher, doubtless. But now, in their sweeping line, like a troop of miniature soldiers, they took unwitting turns in mockery. They made faces, and some pelted me with spittle and other things. Their teacher suddenly appeared, looking incredulous and dismayed. He seemed impotent to stop them, as though they were simply an expression of his secret will. Then they were gone, and the street somehow less busy.

I kept walking and walking. Unconsciously, I directed my steps away from people, until the crowds seemed to be more or less gone. I paused, breathing, noticing my breath for the first time, and then held my head, felt the pain, the tightness of my scalp constricting in the sun. I was leaning against a bricked up doorway. A little to my left, I could see the large brick face wall of some builders yard. Barbed wire fencing like a thorny crown over the top of the wall, some slogans of past love affairs and football team comments. At the foot of the wall, broken bottles, and beside it some end-terraced house, boarded up and obviously vacant.

The street itself was deserted. I suppose it must have been mid morning. I became aware that I had walked for hours, like some martyring pilgrim. My feet ached. It was the first sensation of any kind, the first emotional experience I could testify to since I had observed Keran and Kennedy.

I looked around. Everywhere "for sale" signs, like the flags of beaten armies, rose amidst the derelict buildings. One or two souls had striven to maintain dignity. There was every sign that the street had once housed people with some pride and sense of community. Now it was all gone except for a few die-hards. People doubtless too old, too poor, or too crushed by their own customary habits to move. I walked round to the back of the bricked up house and, as I suspected, I found that I could enter one of the houses by crawling under an inadequately boarded up gate.

I was in a wild garden. Fridges, cookers, old bicycles and strewn papers were in it with me. There had been a rabbit hutch or chicken coop to one side, and the old wire netting that had been its cover now gave the appearance of some web made by cat sized spiders. This netting was decorated with ribbons of paper and plastic bags; it had enveloped a large part of the place. The back door was open, and underneath, a festoon of ivy and brambles, archaeological evidence of a long dead garden, I saw the dark opening that was going to be my new home.

When I entered the place, I was aware mostly of the gloom, the cat piss and the damp. Someone had been there before.

There was a bed raised up off the ground; only a blanket with an old mattress, but it would do. There was evidence that a fire had been lit in one corner; plenty of wood to support that. Old newspapers would help as a bed. The kitchen was gutted. There was a hole in the roof, but there was a sink. Unbelievably, it was still operational. It wasn't clean, but I could clean it. I had water to drink if I wanted to live.

I walked through to the front reception room. It was dark, only a chink of light where the boards did not meet at the top. I walked a little further up the dodgy stairs. The rooms upstairs were all empty. Those at the front of the house were clearly in a dangerous condition, but the bathroom at the back and the back bedroom could be lived in if you could manage to clean them out. It was enough for me to know that the rest of the house was uninhabitable. I could not face the prospect of an army of junkies. I looked out of the back window. There was more space here and, incredibly, I could see the backs of the train station where my office was. I was shocked, but then, somehow, I suppose, my feet had travelled paths that I had unconsciously recognised. I knew this street. I had been here before, getting something; getting papers, from a printer that Jamie and I had used for years. The printer was perhaps a hundred metres away around the bend. It was a short cut, little used. I think very rarely used by anyone, and certainly no one would walk this route unless they lived here. Few people lived here, so I could presume myself reasonably safe.

Downstairs again, I tried to tidy a little. It was surprising, raking through the stuff. As I became more used to the place, I became more and more aware that it was recently settled. Like some preternatural animal, I was conscious of the recent presence of another animal. But this consciousness seemed thwarted by events.

For three days I lay in the place, on the mattress. I slept little, ate nothing. I drank from the sink and, although weakened physically, in a sense, I began to recover something of a personal force. I was able to think again; not able to ponder past events, because they were too painful, but at least I had sensations of pain, I was capable of feeling. Beyond this, I began to function in some sort of sentient capacity. At the end of three days, I was able to go to the shops in the late afternoon when darkness fell, and there, along a busy main thoroughfare, buy some fruit and nuts, a bagful to last three or four days. I also bought a tin opener, a knife and several candles, some orange juice, vitamin pills, string and a whole host of necessities. I struggled back to the house. The bags weighed me down. I felt like a weary old woman as I dragged the bag backwards through the gap in the fence and entered the house. After a small meal of oranges and kiwi-fruit, with a few nuts and orange juice, I spent the day constructing a kind of human flap in the doorway, so that I could disguise the entrance. Exhausted, I fell asleep for a full day. I woke in the dusk, from nightmares too awful to even remember.

I lay on my back, sweating, aware that a fever was coming on me, aware that I should go to a hospital or to the police, or to any establishment that could safely house me. But I realised that any sign of myself in an official establishment would lead to my discovery by those people who Keran had met. I remembered him, the witless giant, and I thought that, even with my mind broken and beaten and my spirit on the floor, I had still a conscious identification with self, with my existence. I did not want to end like Keran's witless giant. I wanted, at the very least, to exist. Even an act of suicide would be a personal decision, an assertion of identity. I was alive, maybe not well, but alive.

I lay on the bed for a while longer trying to recall my dream. All I could remember were a pair of green eyes. Kennedy had green eyes. The thought made me wince. I got up and mounted the stairs, intending to reason out a new plan of accommodation. In the upper room facing the street, I thought there may be a possibility of clearing the rubbish out and getting the fire going. I spent an hour clearing out tins of paint and debris, pushing them into the back room. After an hour, I was exhausted, so I ate another meal of fruit with some nuts and juice. Then I fell asleep.

For three days – or at least in the hours of dusk - like a waking vampire, I set about the room making it habitable. I found the floorboards at the end of the third day, and after several hours there was space upstairs to move the mattress and the bed. I tidied everything out except for a dining chair and a full-length mirror.

I could not bear to look at the mirror. Instead, I put it in the corner of the room beside the window and avoided its surface, not liking what I might see. I dumped all the things that wouldn't burn in the room next door. By the time the stars were fully out, the fireplace was unblocked and, with some wood and endless amounts of paper, I felt ready to enliven the evening with warmth. It would be safe at night, when the smoke would be concealed in the darkness. It was then that I remembered that you needed matches to start a fire.

In the dark and the cold, I went out to the garage at the end of the road. Back upstairs in the dank house, I finally crouched before the fireplace with a whole box of matches. After several futile attempts, I managed to set the paper alight. At first, I thought the fire was not going to take. I actually felt tears coming into my eyes when, on my seventh attempt, the paper caught, and with it some of the splinters of wood. At first, a damp smoke seemed to occupy the room, but, after a few moments, it seemed that the fireplace coughed, and the fire took well. The orange glow filled the room, slowly suffusing light and warmth. I watched my hands stretch out to the fire like a supplicant. I saw the pink orange glow of my chapped fingers, the dark and chipped fingernails. For the first time, I saw the cuts and the bruises. Pulling my sleeves up towards me, I saw my hands riddled with cuts, as though I had been dragged around by a cat. I felt the tears drip from my face, and the pain creep up inside my belly. But I was warming; warming in the light of the fire. The mirror sent the light flickering around the room like a sixties wax lamp, decorating the shabby walls with a new mobile wallpaper. I pulled the chair up close to the fire and sat in its arms, letting the weight fall from my tired feet. I felt like a new age witch hurtled back through time into an age of end terraced houses in a redbrick world.

In a claustrophobia of womb-like space, I fell slowly into a dreamless sleep.

Chapter 15
The Indian Spell

AT NIGHT the sound of the distant cars, like whales surfing an unseen ocean, spumed me into troubled sleep. My dreams were like ghosts of dead fish. They flickered on the edge of my consciousness. Their piscine fins touched my back, their gills my neck; but nothing was ever seen. Or at least seen rarely. Then vague shapes and vague symbolic terrors would form, and sometimes the things I saw would be so terrible that I would thankfully forget them; at other times, the things would be only glimpsed for a second; hazy, uncalculated memories, from which I awoke sweating in the small room in the dark, or even sometimes, which was worse, in the light of day. Worse because this was no warming light.

The room even, when full of sunlight, was only a room full of over-bright things, of objects that appeared to occupy more space than their dimensions, colours that seemed to fill a space but have no substance behind them - as though they were parts of some absurd animation. Sometimes I would awake to an overpowering smell of something rotting. Of course in the cesspit where I slept it was hardly pleasant, but this was a stench beyond imagining, and no amount of searching could trace its author. Worse, sometimes it seemed to be my body that produced the smell; a rank festering odour that made me retch.

During the night when I awoke with my blankets steeped in sweat, the darkness would be almost comforting. The shapes of my imagination were less intimidating than the reality that surrounded me during the daylight hours. My own thoughts and reveries were of things I owned; these other intrusions seemed alien to me, and more threatening. In the relative comfort of the darkness I was plagued by an awful silence. It was as though the room itself created the silence, or as though I was being mummified by a vacuum, enclosed in a silent noiseless space, entombed in utter quiet, while all around there must be noise, noise, waterfalls of cacophony in every part of the universe; the only exception my room. And the silence itself was terrible, eerie as though it were a created thing, as though some huge and anonymous arm cupped me in its palm and the grip was about to strengthen.

In the waking hours, I blundered on as best I could. I had no resources but my memory. I could remember certain skills, basically good habits from my youth when I had studied esoteric religions and practices and dabbled in Buddhism. I knew the theories and I also had certain other knowledge; homeopathic skills, skills as a martial artist, a mathematician. I took these, now hollow ritualistic things, as a starting point. It was not that I had any reserves. There was nothing kept back of will, spirit, energy or the like. I simply could remember things that I once did. It was as though someone had previously trained as a first aid ambulance man on dummies alone. My past life and activities were the dummies, empty and inanimate. I could blow breath into the mouths of the dummies but it would not make them living beings. Now, I could do certain activities, but it would not impel me into being alive. Perhaps, at best, it could allow me to exist as a stain exists on a wall. Of course, people remove stains, and there was a little part of me which, while not wanting to exist, did not want to be removed.

I don't know why, but I retained in my head an image that the philosopher Descartes used: God, infinite and incredible, lay on one side, on the other was the black abyss. In the middle, almost like a tight rope walker, was Descartes, the living conscious entity suspended between the absolute and nothingness. This image, for reasons I could not clearly define, seemed to apply to myself. I used it to sustain some concept of existence.

So, I bought some herbal teas, some St John's Wort, some little known homeopathic remedies that I had gleaned from various esoteric sources, and I began to take the first mental steps towards physical discipline. This consisted in convincing myself that I would do something tomorrow. I swore I would do some physical discipline. The very act of commitment was a beginning.

I knew I could hardly face my martial art, so I searched for something gentler. I had once been an adept in Iyengar Yoga. Now I took it up again, forcing myself to do a few asanas. However, my body was a wreck; beaten, raped, buggered, arthritic, cut, broken in places, my skin like a pizza, my lips cracked and my body covered in bruises and lacerations. I felt the mirror itself might shrink away from me if I dared to look in it.

I started at dawn with "child's pose", kneeling down, hands outstretched before me. Even this was too much, and I simply attempted "the corpse" pose. Lying on my back, I shut my eyes and began to relax. This was really a form of low level meditation, the start of the whole practice, but I felt that, if I could only start, I might resurrect something. I lay for a few minutes and tried to observe the carousel of ideas. The intention was to observe and then slowly dismiss them. It was while I fidgeted in this position that I had my first intimation that the practice would for the moment go no further. There was something terrible blocking it. That feeling of suppression, of suffocation, the grip of the invisible hand, now seemed stronger than ever.

I opened my eyes. The reason was in a place that I had not even considered.

Above my head, on the ceiling, written so boldly that I could scarcely believe that I had never seen it, were these words:

Listen!
Now I come to step over your soul
I know your clan
I know your name
I have stolen your spit and buried it under the earth
I inter your soul under the earth
I cover you with black rock
I cover you with black slabs
You disappear forever
Your way leads to the black coffin in the hills of the darkening land
So let it be for you
The hills of clay cover you
The black mud of the darkening land
Your soul fades away
It becomes the colour of despair, blue

When darkness comes your spirit shivers and decays to disappear forever
Listen!

For fully an hour I lay staring at the writing. I knew it was a spell, and I knew that it was meant for me alone. I lay fighting back the waves of a tidal front that destroyed my very being. The silence around me thickened. With every moment, I felt its deep hush as the noise drained out of the world. The smell grew, the rancid awful smell and the metallic taste in my mouth became the taste of rotting blood. I was in agony. My bowels released and I felt my water spill out around me. It was as though I was personally melting. Something in me fought. I battled with the spell, drew something out of my intellect, the only thing left to me in defence against this thing. My mind laboured with the how of it. How had I missed it? And then, after a time, I realised amidst the agony that this was unimportant. I had no need to question the author of the original incantation, or how they had anticipated my being there; I simply had to find out the name of the spell.

I lay pinned to the floor for longer than I thought possible. My mind constructed vast libraries and explored them like a rat looking for food. Eventually I had it. It came in a flash of inspiration as I saw once gain the serious face of Keran's Uncle Rodin standing in his modern kitchen. He had told me there would be an empty room and an Indian spell. It was a North American spell, an Indian spell for the removal of life. Somehow, with that knowledge, I could fight. My mind reeled, searching for a reply, until from somewhere a voice that seemed to be disconnected from my own vocal apparatus said:

Day rises from sleep
Day wakes with the light of dawn
I must also rise
I must also awake
Together with the day which comes

With this uttered, I had the strength to rise slightly. I got to my hands and knees, finally shielding my burning eyes from the spell. This helped a little. I was able to crawl away like some beast that sought its death lair. But then something compelled me to return.

As I reached the top of the stairs it came to me that to run was not the solution. Slowly, I turned from the stairwell and crawled to the centre of the room. It was far easier to return than it was to leave, but the sensation was that of a masochist reluctantly seeking further damaging pain. I paused, thinking desperately: I had been buried somewhere by the author of the spell and I must use every single part of my being to find out where. I had to rely on my intuition alone, and I had little of that left. I tried my intellect on the words. "Buried"? Someone had done something with my spit maybe, the garden outside.

How did one find spit in a disused garden? I laughed. It was a horrible laugh, but it made me feel slightly better. A needle in a haystack was a likelier prospect. There must be another way.

The only thing I could think of was to construct some magic circle around myself to defend against the spell. I would have simply to defend myself using the only real weapon, attack. Now, at the extremity of my position, when there was literally nothing left of my personal being except some automatic will to survive, now I would become a magician, a witch, a magus, and fight for the protection of the thing that was I.

I knew the techniques. I had studied them academically for years, and was aware of the pitfalls for the unwary. I knew the mental problems they could create, I knew the spiritual abyss they could throw open, and I knew that the path to this type of knowledge was more dangerous than any other path; but then what was there left to do?

Under the auspices of the spell, I cut my hand. It was risky, as it was a further incursion on my material, and, by correlation, spiritual being, but then I could hardly move and this needed to be done immediately by my own artifice with the things most personal to me. Living blood was the best I had.

Slowly and painstakingly, with my bloody hand, I drew a unicursal Hexagram and sat within it. I then erected to a seated posture in the half lotus position (I could not make the full lotus because of the stiffness of my body). I fought back the overpowering desire to faint. It hit me in waves. Then, from this position between life and death, I began to meditate on my breath. I counted each out-breath and then each in-breath, and then I left myself to the breathing. With each breath, I erected a mystical barrier around me, reinforcing the area around the hexagram.

It seemed like hours; certainly the lights had gone and the dusk sky peeped in through the windows, but I began to feel some little power return to me. It was more, I suppose, that the sickening weight and silence of the air was slightly removed. I had, by effort of my will, created a pocket of breathable air around my body.

All night I kept the vigil. My body seemed to be somewhere else, my intellect fuelling the meditational stance. In the small hours of the night I began to chant "aum mani padme hum". I felt the wheel of my personal mantra spin and my thoughts flew off it. I was responding to the challenge, beginning to feel stronger.

Far away, beyond the bubble, I heard a voice singing. It was a voice I recognised. I couldn't quite place it, but I knew it was someone I knew intimately. It kept intruding on the mantra and it took all my force to keep it out. I felt suddenly fatigued, the strain pushed me down. I lifted my head blinked, and then again I felt the deep cold shock of horror as my meditational trance was broken by a single penetrating vision. This vision seemed to be able to attack the bubble of force I had constructed. In fact it did not seem to have to try in any real sense of the word, so strong was it against my own will.

The vision was a face, an incredibly old face, and the green eyes in the face stared at me with an intense and calculating detestation. It was as though they had stepped on excrement and wanted to wipe it off. I was the thing that these eyes wanted removed. I opened my own eyes as though the presence was real, not something intruding into my meditation. The voice had gone and, as I stared upwards, I saw with some horror that the spell was slowly detaching itself from the ceiling. The words themselves were beginning to circle my hexagram, doubtless seeking an entrance. Then, as I shut my eyes again, from the backdrop of blackness, the green eyes stared at me from the old, old face. I saw that this vision was smiling in an unpleasant way, but the thin lips and the baggy, raddled skin were like an abstraction in contrast to the eyes. These eyes, eyes that had seen everything it was possible to see, now looked again at me, and there was no longer detestation.

There was simply a sense that I was nothing. I screamed, the force of my breath rushing out from me. For a second, I thought my breath was going to continue out of my body like an ethereal rope, and that I was going to be sucked and pulled with it, into the black.

My eyes opened with the shock, and I saw that the spell swirled around me like a wraith of Chinese writing. There were silver strings coiling out of my head. I knew then that I witnessed the dispersal of my soul, that this was the beginning of death.

I began to weep. Guttering, sweeping sobs, wrenched from my body. A fear drove through me like a series of inflicted stab wounds. The hexagram was shrivelling up, turning in on itself like a curling leaf in a brazier fire.

I watched my hands outstretch before me and then I uttered the thing that I knew deep down was the only defence. I uttered it. The word; the forbidden word.

In a second, the room was utterly quiet. The surroundings were completely still. The pressure had gone, and the air was the normal air of a damp room.

I fell over.

As I lay staring at the ceiling, I saw that the spell had disappeared.

Chapter 16
Old Friends

I MUST HAVE SLEPT for three or four days. It was a dreamless sleep, a sleep that must be akin to the death described by Ahonita of the Cherkonese. He describes death as the "floating, waking". That is what I did. I floated and I waited - all through the nights and days like a soul in purgatory. When I woke, I was vaguely aware of this. The sensation was like nothing I had ever experienced before; as though I had been effectively dead, or, at the very least, entirely passive in sleep. There were no dreams, and yet there was a sensation of being. Perhaps it could be compared to the "awareness" of parts of a robot on a conveyor belt that await construction prior to the insertion of some artificial mind.

In any case I awoke on the floor, steeped in human smells and tastes - earthy and in my body - my head at rest from wanderings, my limbs aching with pains. As I lay in the dusk, the wounded animal that had crawled away to die, I saw that the ceiling was still bare. However, when I shifted my head, it was apparent that everything in the room had been scattered far and wide by the force of the things going on. The only piece of furniture left standing was the mirror. Even the fire itself seemed to have blown back up the chimney in some final explosion.

I lay on, incapable of movement, waiting for something to happen.

And it did. Far away down the street, I heard a rough familiar voice singing. It was a familiar voice and the song itself was familiar to me.

"...I pray thee speak to me, give me my faith and troth..."

I felt an urgent whisper growling in my throat.

"...thy faith and troth thou'll never get..."

The singing voice, slightly drunk, came closer and closer up the street. The whisper grew in my throat until it spewed out, but my voice was cracked and broken, the vocal chords imploded and finished. I tried again but nothing happened.

"And should I kiss they rosy lips the days will not be long..." My body painfully stretched outwards, but there was nothing of effort left in me to expend on movement. I could not proceed beyond the hexagram, and now the singing voice was beneath my window.

"...my bones are buried in a kirkyard far beyond..."

"Jamie," it was a whisper but it grew. "Jamie."

The voice moved on like the sound of a sailor on a ship easing softly through fog.

"...and a' the live long winter the dead corpse followed she."

He was moving away. I made a despairing final effort. "Jamie."

"...my coffin is made..."

The voice silenced. I tried to call. Only a low moan came from me, the vowel sounds articulating through my throat like wind through a ruined castle keep. In the long silence that followed, I kept moaning in a low whisper.

And then I heard footsteps ascend the stair; they were tentative, fearful. For a long, long time, the presence waited, and then I saw his shadow fill the head of the stairwell.

"Professor?" The voice was querulous and thick with emotion.

I moaned. He walked into the room, a gaunt scarecrow, red faced, clothed in rags, ill, emaciated and with wounds festering visibly through holes in his sleeves.

But it was Jamie.

His eyes looked around the room in terror, and then flicked back to me, speculating. He seemed about to run. Again I tried. "Jamie. It's me."

He sunk to his knees, weeping and sobbing, apparently unable to progress further into the room.

"It *is* me."

Jamie raised his head.

"Help," I said, and blacked out.

It was a long recovery. Jamie sat at the side of my bed on a pile of old leather suitcases. He tended to me, mopped my brow continually with tissues and fed me sporadically with plain, bland fruit juices. He crushed up vitamin pills and herbal substances, and kept singing to me in a low crooning voice - highland melodies with no apparent structure. Sometimes he talked in a low whisper; soothing sentences half English, half Gaelic, full of words of comfort.

At times I thought he was trying to heal himself through his care of me; his ruddy face, covered in sores, and his pale green eyes stared at me with a look of childish fascination. There were ugly times in the night when he seemed to have left me, and I was terrified. Occasionally, I would see his dark shadow leaning against the wall like a mummified body. There were worse moments, when he pulled back the blankets and leered at my naked body with wet eyes, or I would catch him bent over me with a vacant yet incredulous look. It was a look like that of Keran when he had been a shambling idiot saying "Ka, Ka, Ka", or perhaps, more accurately, when he had been on the verge of returning from or receding to insanity.

There came a time when I could sit up. Jamie had found some pillows from somewhere. He fed me like a six month baby: mashed bananas and potatoes and mushy peas. I had lost count of the days in which I recuperated. Now, when I pulled back the blankets, I could see that my wasted body was beginning to come back. I felt slightly, but only slightly, attached to it, as though life had hung by a slender thread that might at any moment snap.

I sipped at the St. Johns Wort tea that Jamie had brewed, and I found that, for the first time since the night of the hexagram, I had some desire left. It was simply a desire; hardly the desire of a living creature battling for survival or revelling in power, but it was a desire: Curiosity.

I looked Jamie up and down. I could imagine that his experience might have been something akin to mine. I wondered if he was sane, or at least if there was enough rationality left to handle talking.

Jamie now looked at me, mirroring my intent. I realised that neither of us had really spoken since our encounter. Yes, he had crooned words of comfort, snatches of old songs, but he had said nothing. We had been like two soldiers of enemy countries incarcerated in a single field hospital recovering from wounds, unwilling or unable to communicate except at the lowest of intellectual levels. Now changes were coming through; changes for us both. I put down my tea.

"Shall I start...Jamie?"

He shook his head suddenly. His face terrified with a fear that I recognised, because it lived within me now always.

"I don't want to...talk about...it...at all," he said in a voice changed beyond all recognition. The confident bluff Scotsman had disappeared forever, leaving in his place some tortured nervous half-man who would never stride into a room or wave an expansive arm or indeed do anything without the bearing of a hunted man. It was over for Jamie too, and the best we could hope to do was perhaps to do nothing at all. To hope that the world would ignore us as people in motorway bound cars ignore ants on the slip road slopes. To hope that we would not walk to a place where we would be annihilated. It became my personal ambition in that moment to become no-one and even then, faced with the horror of being recognised, I began in my head to cast around for an identity less conspicuous than a tramp.

Jamie spoke. He had somehow sensed what was in my head. I think that even then our personal spirit was so shallow, so thin like thin air, that we could almost read each other's thoughts.

"It's no good though. We'll have to face it all sometime."

"We can hide?"

"Maybe not."

"Think of how this room was. They knew you would at least come here. They knew."

"And how did you know, Jamie?"

The cold question hung in the damp air.

He shook his head, his pale eyes wincing in distrust of himself. Then he spoke in a flat urgent whisper.

"I've been wandering all around Manchester for days and nights, singing. It's you English," he almost laughed. "Richard Lion Heart and his minstrel. I kept singing because I knew that you would be somewhere, and that you'd be hidden. But the best way to find someone is always to show yourself," He coughed, his chest briefly racked with some unseen agony. After a time he began again. "I don't know why, but I just knew I would find you. You see, every beast returns to its lair when it's about to die." His eyes grew cold, empty, and then kindled again. "What they…did to me. When they broke me down to… this… I knew that they'd be getting you as well. You still have it you see." He looked with a disturbing awe at the amulet that still burned around my neck. "I knew," he continued after a space, "that you would not be dead."

"They don't seem to kill you quickly."

"No," he nodded thoughtfully. "No, you don't physically die. It's something else they are after. You were always better than me with words, professor, but I think, by most people's standards of erudition, it would be easiest to say that they want your soul."

I shuddered. The trite word, said so easily like some cheap trash-novel speak, was uncomfortably close to the mark. I thought through the incidents. The people at the spiritualist church, the reactions of spiritualists, the empty young things who had chased us in the car. Keran himself, drained of everything. Then the roads up in the north of Scotland. All those people and places haunted by a force that was not in itself intrinsically evil. It was something even further beyond the pale than simple evil.

I had met people in the past who played with power; I have seen people killed, and people return from physical and mental torture. I have seen innocents abused and small things destroyed for fun, but all the incidents and people and things that I had encountered bore no resemblance to this. It was not evil; it was more objective and clinical than evil; and yet in this sense it was not the evil of the holocaust or that of a single chilling man whose purposes were cloaked in surgical clinicality.

This was somehow different. I kept getting images in my head of a woman in an alchemist's haven simply draining bottles of chemicals - rows upon rows of bottles with rows upon rows of different but similar chemicals draining into a great beaker. I pushed the thought away because it felt to close to the edge, to the thing-in-itself. But the expression I could see on her face was one of utter indifference. This was the horror I felt inside. It was the indifference, the utter and complete lack of concern for my humanity.

I picked up my tea. Jamie had gone into a reverie. His face appeared like a mask stuck on top of his skull by playgroup children. I felt an overwhelming pity for him. It was a small and cheap emotion inside of me but it was there, struggling like a toddler to get up and out.

I pulled the covers back exposing my breasts. Slowly, gently I pulled Jamie towards me. His cracked and broken lips played over my right breast, and in a few moments he was suckling like a newborn baby. There was no milk to offer him; there was nothing of nutrition, only faded warmth, and a softness that I offered as a gift to a man who would never know them again.

Chapter 17
The Maze

IT WAS my first dream since the night of the hexagram.

In the half fallen dusk, I began to meditate. I lay prone on the bed, with Jamie at my side for warmth. He had fallen asleep with my breast in his mouth. It was with some difficulty that I released him, his face still like a caricature mask, but now softened to some extent in slumber.

For some time, I had stared at the ravages of pain that marked his face. I knew that they were echoed in mine, but I had to put that behind me. I needed to try to recover, and the recovery began with meditation. I had risen, only to slump against the bed. It was as far as I could get.

Here I began. First, I concentrated my awareness in my feet, feeling the coarse blanket tickle my toes. I moved up my calves and then through to my thighs and hips. Gradually I rested my attention on my stomach. There were a few tensions created by releasing toxins in my head, so I allowed my breath to ride through these. The tensions began to resolve. I let my attention rest back on the slow heave and descent of my diaphragm. Slowly, patiently, with returning psychic energy, I began to focus upon the slow rhythm of my breath.

After a time, I began to formulate the garden, but since my destruction it was not easy. For some time I struggled with the effort and eventually found myself giving up. I retreated like Jamie into mindless reverie. Then I drifted into sleep. It was strange, but every single recent sleep had been dreamless, a vacuum of spirit, and now I was struck almost as by a physical force with the reality of my dream. And quite forcibly, without meditation, I had found the garden. Or rather, it had found me.

I knew with an absolute conviction that I had entered the garden in the exact second of my last entrance. This was contrary to any known dream walking but I knew it to be a fact. The very staccato noise told me; the splitting before my eyes of the wrought iron bench, as the extreme cold broke the iron as though an invisible heavyweight had sat on it. The after echo of the noise rang on through the still, birdless air like a percussive music. It was a lonely sound, and the landscape before me was lonely. The towering privet hedges seemed bereft of life; beyond them the mountains, blue, cold and distant. At my feet, the naked footprints were crisping over, the tracery of snow flakes making innumerable unique patterns on the earth. Everywhere was white, white, white, and endlessly white - the only exception the underside of the towering hedges that were a sombre dark brown. This served only to deepen the contrast with the snow.

Through this lifeless land I began to walk. As the maze approached me I had a decision to make. My instinct told me to avoid the footprints. To simply escape, but then another part of me wanted to confront this thing, whatever it was. I had known before that I would follow the footsteps. It was somehow predetermined, but I felt that I had the choice of following willing or unwilling. I decided to follow, because I wanted to follow them. I wanted, despite the suffering, to face the demon.

I walked past the rose bushes, the rose flowers long gone and the tracery of thorns somehow more cruel in their stark nudity. The stems were almost white, and all deeply frozen. Even as I walked past the rose bushes, my soft footsteps shattered some of them, like small stones hitting a mirror. I took one last look at my fuchsia bush, its forlorn weight of snow like a raggedy hat; I even reached my hands towards it, but the movement fought with the still air and sent a frozen zephyr to flutter through the creaking stems of the bush. If I moved any closer I knew it would break, so I turned from it and walked into the shrouded hedgerows.

The footprints before me were spaced evenly, but heavy on the heel. The creature, human or half-human, had clearly walked slowly and then had increased its stride as it moved through the maze. When I entered the maze proper, I observed that at times the steps took false routes and then came back to the original spot. I could see where, for some unknown delicacy, the creature had avoided its own footprints and come back always on the left hand side of the other prints, leaving twin but opposite prints. I spent some time nearly kneeling, half-crouching, as I stared at the sets of prints to ensure that they were of one creature and one creature alone.

As far as I could tell, they were. At one time, I followed them, and they came to a dead end. For many minutes I stood trying to assess where they had gone. It was as though some giant had stuck a hand out from the sky and snatched the creature quickly from the earth. It took me a long while to see that the designer of the maze, myself of course, had made a little trick. The hedge before me only came to the knees, and there was another hedge placed behind, with a space between of about three or four feet. To a quick superficial observation, it was one hedge. This appearance was more marked in the cold with the air changed and the eyes hurting and smarting. It was clearly intended to be a deception to those who would turn the corner and see only the distant hedge. Up close, it was more obvious, and would be obvious to anyone who had chosen to go that close. The creature had leapt here and it seemed, by the way the footprints went, the toe being heavier and the stride longer, that it had known this deception. If it had not, I reasoned that there would have been a shuffling about of footprints.

I took a running jump and leapt the low hedge, landing with a dull thump, and here the footprints stretched to my left. I was no longer able to tell whether this was West or South, North or East. I was utterly lost.

I walked a little further. The footprints stretched out before me along a long narrow way. There was no sound except my own harsh breath, my heart beating in my ear, and the crisp thump of my footprints; no smell, because my nose was frozen, and likewise with taste. Everywhere was white, white, white, except under the hedges.

The Eskimos have sixty words for snow, and I contemplated adapting my vocabulary to the dreamscape in this respect when I turned a corner and came upon a bridge. The bridge had a low arch and doubtless was covered in moss, now powdered with snow. Its walls were a cool and startling grey. At the far end there was a small pillar. At least I thought it was a pillar, but as I approached, I realised that it was a short plinth with a sculpture of some sort mounted on its crown. It was on the left-hand corner of the far side of the bridge. I walked over the bridge, felt its mass beneath my feet, aware vaguely that a small stream must run under it to emerge from beneath a hedge on my left only to disappear under the hedge on the right. These hedges created a kind of avenue which, after the bridge, led to a low sunken garden just visible under the arch of two twisted giant oaks that overhung the bridge at its far end.

As I walked forwards, more of the sunken garden came to my view. The dwindling perspective revealed a series of laid-out symmetrical paths that doubtless had flowers on either side, now buried under the snow. The footprints lay over the bridge, but with the obscuring shadows of oaks, elms and horse chestnut trees, and the various features of ornamentation, it was unclear where they led through the garden.

I reached the column that came up to my belly and tentatively blew on it. Like a dandelion sending its seed to the wind the light powdered snow blew off and outwards .

I was stared at by the head of a bird. A raven I assumed, from the beak, almost perfect in its execution so that at first I was not sure whether it was simply a frozen bird or a statue. I blew again and more snow, light and airy and unreal, floated into the crisp air, exposing one of the wings that was caught in the act of lifting slightly as though the bird was about to fly. I stared for a little while at the cold black sculpted eye of the raven, but it produced no feelings in me, and I left it behind and began to advance again under the overarching trees, down towards the sunken garden, following the footsteps.

From here I could again see the tops of the mountains on the right hand side, possibly due north. So I assumed this part of the garden maze was on a slight hillock. The air was still and quiet, and nothing moved. I walked into the garden and saw that the footsteps led straight through; disappearing in an arch that was the mirror of the one I had left behind. This sunken section was clearly a herb garden, surrounded by small shrubs that looked now like buried heads and hands waiting to appear from beneath the earth. The footsteps here took the middle lane of the small path that traversed the centre of the garden.

There was no corresponding bridge on the far side of the garden, and the trees were bare. The hedgerows sheared up above me as a blank facing wall but I had the intuition that the maze was nearly ended and that the footsteps that disappeared to the left would soon lead me out.

It was then that I heard the first sound since the echoes of the cracking bench. It was the brief and incisive caw of a raven. The sound came from behind me, and when I turned to look, the pillar remained and nothing seemed to have moved. I could still see the silhouette of the bird that I had partially revealed. Perhaps it was my imagination but it seemed that there was less snow around its neck, that some had been displaced.

From an air of neutrality, as though the cold had numbed the evil, the whole maze became for me a place of malice and danger. I turned my back on the garden and felt the slow birth of fear stir in my guts. I walked quickly following the footsteps until they came to the end of the long broadway. Here the maze opened out slightly, and when I crouched and stared through the thicket at the foot of the hedges I could see that I had come to some outer wall of hedge. The footsteps now stretched unmistakably forward down the broader avenue. In the distance I could see something flutter like a lotus flower against a small wall of stone that seemed to emerge from the side of the hedge. I ran a little way, panting out my breath in the chill air and then as I came close to the outcrop I slowed down. There on a little shelf was a white sheet of paper, crumpled and age-yellow in various parts.

With fingers trembling not just with the cold but with fear, I reached out my hands. The paper seemed to be caught by wind but there was none. It was perhaps a trick of my eye but the paper seemed animated as if it wanted to escape. But I caught it and then tried to decipher the few words on it. This is what remained undamaged

"Divine knowledge, the wisdom of the gods is not the wisdom of God but that possessed by the gods"

There was more but it was in ancient Greek and some Aramaic, all of it blotted out or corrupted beyond translation. Then, as I lifted the paper closer, it seemed to jerk as though someone else had taken my own hands and a giant puppet master tugged quickly on my sinews. The paper leapt and danced around the corner of the stone.

I jumped towards it, feeling that I was getting closer to some truth, and then was nearly blinded by a sharp, all pervasive light.

Now I could see here, just beyond the wall, an exit that was filled like a rectangular lamp with a blinding intensity of light. My eyes hurt with a deep pain as I looked outward from the wall to see the paper, caught and cast upwards into the out-flung branches of a towering oak on the edge of the hedgerow. This tree was twinned with another giant, and marked the entrance or exit from the northern side of the maze to the shattering plains that led to the foot of mountains beyond. Here the footprints stretched out as far as my aching eyes could see.

They were heading for the mountains.

Chapter 18
The Karmic Wheel

"...shapes of all sorts and sizes great and small
That stood along the floor and by the wall
and some loquacious vessels were; and some
Listen'd perhaps, but never talked at all."

The voice had talked for some time, and I had ignored it.

I came up through the lower levels of meditation, gradually finding my bearings, feeling enervated. Then I saw Jamie was up, him talking in a sing song voice as he made coffee. He had woken doubtless earlier and found himself in the bed next to me, warm and comforted perhaps for the first time in a while.

"Omar Khayyam?" I said

He nodded, turning, and flashed me a sheepish smile. "You were in deep?"

"Very deep." I never talked to Jamie about meditation as it was a private thing, but I wondered now how much he had developed personally; whether some of the insights he had recently received had changed him in any spiritual sense.

"How are you feeling?" I said.

"Better." He brought over some black coffee. We did not trust the milk in the house, despite all efforts to clean the place up.

It seemed for a few moments in that commonplace banter that we were back in Jamie's house; back in time to better days, happier innocent times. For a few moments we could forget the squalid surroundings, forget the awful, recent past and simply talk about nothing. The rich dark coffee stirred my senses and a beautiful light shuttered in through the room and played on the dust motes, like suspended spears of veil silk.

Jamie sat down the suitcase beside the bed, his ruddy face

mottled in the sunlight, at times in dark, at times bright, as he shifted his posture slightly. I watched him, assessing, and then said, "Why Omar Khayyam?"

"It was always my philosophy," he replied.

"The philosophy of the drinking man."

"Yes." He flashed me a smile. "I was always good at that."

"Philosophy?"

"Hardly," he said sipping his coffee.

We sat in silence. It must have been mid afternoon and the streets were quiet.

"What now?" said Jamie finally.

"We lie down and die?"

He nodded. "That's what I was thinking."

"But will it work."

"No, it won't work." His eyes dimmed; the little light of normality disappearing to be replaced by the intense fear. "I've thought about suicide but…"

"…it wouldn't escape them."

"No, that's it. I never used to believe in an afterlife."

"This wouldn't quite be one of those tinsel heavens."

"No." He gulped inwardly and looked nauseous, the obvious pain in his face a reminder of my own buried feelings.

"We have to fight back somehow." I had said the words. They sounded ugly and harsh in the small room.

"I can't."

"But you will, Jamie. You have to."

He looked at me as people down the ages have looked at the lover who is about to betray them, or the deserting friend, with a faint hope and a shuddering totality of disgust, mixed with a peculiar reverence. He knew he was going to help, me whether he liked it or not.

"Are you able to get to my office?"

He shook his head in disbelief. "You cannot possibly be serious," he said finally.

"No, I suppose not."

It pained me to say the name, but I knew I would have to try. Eventually it came out.

"Keran." His name hurt me. "Keran. I have to get back to Keran."

"Keran?"

I realised then that between Jamie and I so much had passed us both by. We had both been thrown in differing emotional cesspits and we both had a differing but equally contemptible recent history. Jamie knew nothing of the facts of mine and I knew nothing of the facts of his, beyond their obvious adverse effects on us personally. I tried to explain as much as possible in a few words.

"Keran Westwood, professor of Philosophy. You knew him better as Ka, the witless giant."

Jamie sneered, his face an ugly mask "The big bloke you found. How can he help?"

"Keran was on to something. He knows the group... or the thing. Whatever it is that's got to us. They or it broke him completely but he felt there was a possibility of fighting back." I cast around for an explanation of events. How do you tell a man who loves you like a child that you have been brutally raped, deceived by the man you love, suffered attacks at levels beyond the physical by things beyond understanding, that you have witnessed brutal death and murdered innocent people - in a few words. I looked at Jamie and realised that there was no need to explain anything. His face was a mirror to mine; he had suffered. What he had suffered I didn't want to know, and it was not necessary for him to know my suffering. Jamie would simply follow where I led him. That was it.

"We're going to stand up to these people?" said Jamie. His voice was hollow.

"Not quite. Keran is, and we are going to help him."

Jamie winced. "He must be a pretty brave fellow."

"Possibly, or possibly, like us, just very desperate."

Jamie stood up and walked over to the window. He looked out through a hole in the coverings on to the street below.

"Have you ever wondered what happened to us?" he said.

"What do you mean?"

"You know the law of karma?"

"The ultimate law of the universe."

"I read a bit since we last met. I read that if you wave your hand or think an ill thought or destroy a sun with the force of a million nuclear warheads it all comes down to the same thing. It is all simply cause and effect. Every action is accountable to some greater principle; every action you make, however small, has an effect."

"Karma."

"But where does that leave me, Professor?" Jamie turned from the window. "What did I do in a past life that left me with this legacy? Was I so bad?" His tortured face gaped at me like an animated gargoyle. "Were you?"

"Karma is an objective thing. Simply a law. If we have been bad in a past life, it should play out in our lives now. The implication of our current position is that we have been pretty bad."

"So bad that our spirits have to be cleansed to the bone, that we have to be crushed, and spat out like unwanted gristle?"

I knew in myself that it did not seem to weigh with my vision of me or Jamie. Thinking through my own life, I could see nothing of any great note. A bit of arrogance and self conceit; I'd done a bit of shoplifting as a kid. In all, I'd tried quite hard to help people. Jamie was one of the most innocent, unassuming characters you could meet. Apart from a drink problem, he was hardly spawn of Satan. I searched around a little in my memory to see if there could be anything in the workings of an absolute universe that would give us a clue.

"According to karmic law, our former actions bring us to this point. They created the personalities we have. They were the conditions we had already set in motion through our past lives."

"Yes," said Jamie. "And do you really feel that we were so bad? Or do you feel, as I do, that something somewhere went badly wrong with the karmic wheel?"

I thought about it. Jamie had latched on to something. There was a new aspect of his character here and I suppose, like me, he had been galvanised to action on my departure, doubtless beset by the same incalculable forces of evil that had intruded on me. We had both changed.

"Do you think something happened?"

He rubbed his eyes, returning again into the familiar buffoon. "I don't know. It seems that something happened outside our control. Like you wake up and overnight the whole world has changed. I suppose it might be like the people who live near a volcano. Some day you wake up and the town has disappeared."

"Well, according to karmic law we simply have to accept our conditions and try to perform good actions." I found myself remembering the face of the innocent girl who had died at my hand. I tried to brush aside the picture. "We have to put the past behind us completely. We have to try and live in the here and now. We have to accomplish good things, even if it means only being pleasant to each other."

Jamie turned to look out of the window. "You know I love you." The words were soft, but unhesitant. I only just heard them. I said nothing in reply.

I got up, and dressed in my old clothes. Jamie turned for a second, as though he still expected a reply, saw me dressing and turned again to face the window. He looked shabby and small; his grey clothes ill matched and dirty. Mine were little better. At some point I wanted to discard the clothes and wear something clean, but that would take time and effort. Now I just wanted to get out of the house.

Perhaps it was a misplaced confidence; it was only a small thing, a little bird of hope, but it was something. Maybe the two of us, Jamie and I, could stand together and face the world. It would begin by walking out of the door. Maybe we could go a little further.

Jamie came back from the window. He picked up his old coat from the floor and shook it.

"Let's go," he said.

Chapter 19
Lifted

WE WAITED at the bus stop outside the block of flats where Kennedy lived. We sat with bottles of cider, mine full of water, Jamie's already half drunk, staring at the old people who walked from the building or unlocked the security gates of the car pound. They were all shabby types, some only a little better dressed than Jamie and me. Occasionally, somebody younger and fitter would walk out of the doors and head for a newer car. Once, a drug dealer hung around on the phone. Under his arm I could see the bulge of an illegal pistol, in his hands packets of cocaine. A couple of kids walked by. They looked scruffy, and older than their years.

I sat down on the dingy bus shelter seat, watching up towards the tiny distant windows of the twelfth floor. I recognised the flat by the curtains. As I looked, I thought I saw something flicker, a weird insubstantial light, but it could have been an illusion. The distance made observation difficult. I settled down and tried to get as comfortable as possible.

For all the long day we hung around. At one point, Jamie left, and came back with chips and curry. Even as a decrepit and starving tramp, I found it difficult to eat the stale white chips with their sticky sweet sauce. I forced it down for sustenance and threw the papers down beside their paper and tin friends littering the kerb. Jamie stood around, obviously in a stupor from visiting a pub on the way back. He looked as burned-out as the cars on the littered brown space behind us.

The sun began to descend, and its light struck the windows of the tower block. For a few minutes of that glorious sunset, it transformed the dingy apartment block windows into a magical, sequined coat of orange lights and blinding, golden colours. Then as I turned my eyes from the sheer overwhelming intensity of the reflected light, I saw a huge figure of a man emerge from the glass doorway, like some bewildering black angel. There was only one man who could fill the frame of a large door and make it look small.

I could not help myself. All the carefully laid plans to observe and to wait were thrown aside at my first glimpse of the man I loved.

"Keran, Keran!"

I started to run across towards him, vaguely conscious of Jamie staggering behind me. He growled something incomprehensible, but my attention was firmly fixed on Keran. He hesitated and then, seeing me, strode purposefully across the intervening space. I flung myself into his arms, feeling the terrific weight of his powerful frame, the all encompassing strength of him, as though I was a child throwing myself at an adult.

Jamie must have backed off slightly, prevented from coming near by the aura that surrounded the big man. Keran must have been staring at him.

Jamie croaked something that I vaguely heard behind me; words of greeting or deference.

"Who are you?" said Keran finally.

I drew myself back. There were echoes in his voice of the old empty monster, Ka, but then looking at the grim outline of his jaw and the purposeful strength in the eyes, I realised that this was a different man.

"It's Jamie, my assistant."

"Assistant what?"

"Researcher. He can help us Keran..."

Keran stared at Jamie in much the same way as a doorman stares at a teenager wearing clothes that are possibly casual.

In a single harsh estimate, he pulled something from his pocket. At first, when I caught the gleam of light, I thought it was a knife, but then there was a jingling, tinny sound as coins hit the pavement. In that instant I realised that he had thrown some change at Jamie. "Take this to keep you occupied and wait here until we come back."

He took my arm, turned his back on Jamie, and escorted me back through the glass doors. I took one look at Jamie in his bedraggled grey suit. For that split second, it looked as though he might say something, but then I was pulled away. Walking up the steps, I could see his reflection in the windows of the door way. His frail body bent as he scraped the change from the ground.

As the doors closed and we waited for the lift I rounded on Keran. "There was no need for that humiliation." Keran did not turn around. He stared at the stairwell for a second, watching it attentively, as though he expected an intrusion. It seemed he had not heard me so I repeated it. "Jamie is a human being."

He looked at me as though he had seen me for the first time. "Him," he said contemptuously. "Human? You're sure?"

I could not establish whether this comment was meant to be taken seriously or not. "There was no need to treat him like that."

"I don't trust him. What did Castaneda call people like that: 'Allies'? That was it, 'allies'."

"The magician's ally. They play an ambiguous role in his writings."

"You can summon allies, like Crowley's little gods and demons. They'll help you, that's for sure, but if your will is weak."

"They destroy you."

"That's the feeling I get from him. He'll eat you alive if you give him the chance."

The lift doors opened with a mechanical shriek. Except for the smell of urine, and an old woman dressed in an old fashioned black smock, the lift was empty. We walked into it. Keran pressed the button for the twelfth floor.

"Unlike you?" I said.

"What do you mean?"

"Did you consider how I felt?"

The lift stopped on the first floor but when the doors opened there was no one there. We waited a little and then looked at the old woman. "Up." She said, pointing. She opened her old mouth to reveal yellow teeth.

Keran looked back at me and gave a non-committal shrug. "You're here and you're okay. Why did you leave?"

"Because I love you."

Keran nodded as the lift doors stopped on the third floor.

A tall youth dressed in the clothes of a Goth with a sweeping black cape and dark kohled eyes got in. He gave Keran a look up and down. Keran stared back until he looked away. The youth pulled out a cigarette and lit up. Without a word, Keran crushed the cigarette in his hands and dropped it on the floor. "Don't smoke near me," he said. The youth backed away a little. The lift resumed progress upwards.

Keran seemed to have gained a powerful confidence from somewhere. It might be due to the pleasure that Kennedy afforded him, but even as my mind touched the shores of these thoughts, I could visualise again their naked flesh in the heated glow of the small hours. I pushed the thoughts back; it must be a fad that would pass. She, a young girl, could not hold the attentions of a mature man for long; could not hold him and keep him for herself. At some point I would get him back.

There must be other reasons for his confidence.

"Have you found out anything?"

He gave me a non-committal look that changed as the lift doors opened on floor eleven.

Again the lift doors opened with a creak as of something mechanical dying, and a small child of about five hurried into the lift, with a pregnant mother behind him. The mother stood beside me. I could smell her heavy pregnant smell. The little kid, for one instant, stared upwards at me with big black eyes, and then disappeared somewhere within the mother's clothes.

"I have some clues," Keran said as if to the air. "Things are taking shape. I find this Kennedy girl intriguing."

I stared ahead, unwilling to look at Keran. The grey doors of the lift slid apart.

Standing in the doorway were three men of about Keran's age. They were clad in motor cyclist gear. The two on the left and middle were big men; the one on the right was slightly smaller. In that fractional pause before they entered the lift, the entire atmosphere changed around us. Keran tensed, his stiffened muscles were felt next to mine, and then the warmth of his arm left mine. I knew he was taking on a fighting stance, and I knew I was doing the same thing. The men, on the contrary, seemed totally uninterested in us. None of them even looked our way as their bodies moved in that first step towards the lift door.

Time seemed to collapse in on itself. It was as though two actions took place at the same time. On the one hand, I was aware of the forward movement of the men; on the other hand, I also became suddenly aware that, all the while as we had ascended in the lift, those people who had joined us had been chanting under their breath in slowly increasing volumes. The chant had now penetrated the level of audibility. I could physically hear it. I was also aware that it had been going on subliminally, and beneath my auditory capacity, from the moment that they had entered. At the same time they had closed around Keran and me like participants in some barbaric and surreal country dance. I was instantly cognisant that the three men who had just entered the lift would complete the circle, and equally aware that this would precipitate some psychic catastrophe.

The old woman was directly behind us, the young man to Keran's left, and the mother and child to my right.

Keran had doubtless been there a step earlier than me, but it seemed that he was momentarily at a loss. I threw my body slightly forward, adjusted the weight on my feet and presented myself in a position to defend myself. Two factors hit me with an all-encompassing certainty. I was already weakened, both physically and mentally, and whatever the chant was, the force of its compelling envelope had entirely disturbed my energy forces and left me virtually helpless. My motions forward seemed incomprehensibly slow. It was not simply a lethargic response, it was more that I moved on a much reduced time-scale to my protagonists. I also felt smaller. It seemed that they had grown, not in stature or obvious physical dimensions, but in the sense that they were hugely powerful. This seemed to translate itself into an almost physical perception that they were larger than me. I had become like a child, a very frightened child, in a room full of strange and menacing adults.

I moved my leg forward, about to kick, but the movement was so slow that effectively it never began. Slowly, but yet quicker than I could deliver a karate kick, with unbounded menace, the three men walked into the lift.

I noticed then that Keran shaped a circle around himself in the air. His movements were even slower than I could believe; as though a frozen statue was being moved by the time-bound element of wind over a period of centuries. Yet I knew he was making a circle. I cannot explain how I did, but I knew. I intuited it was some form of protection. The whole episode seemed to be going on at levels of time, disconnected and yet synchronous, as though we operated in some form of parallel, overlapping universes. Even as I watched, the lift doors closed behind, and the lift itself became a metal coffin. The entire atmosphere had transformed to one of intensely depressive, if not evil, brooding.

Around Keran and me the circle of our enemy slowly began to form. Their bodies did not touch, but the individuals came closer and closer, like circling vampires. I felt I was going to snap; there was unbearable inner tension, and a supernatural heat. The lift, in going upwards, seemed to rush uncontrollably, impelled by a force beyond explanation. I felt as though we rushed downwards, upside down, as though the entire world had been reversed, with the exception of the box car of the lift. The chant increased in pitch, in time with the upward rush - the words were just out of reach of recognition, but the hollow voices sounded increasingly less human.

I lost the use of my body, as though I had become entirely possessed, like a zombie, deprived of independent movement. There was one sense in which I had fallen into a faint and should be dropping insensible to the ground. In another sense, I was totally and hyper-sensitively aware. My head remained thinking, my body collapsed, yet I remained standing, still attempting to kick forward. In all, an image came to me as of a murdered woman, waxed over, and imprisoned in a macabre waxwork display from which it was impossible to move. I would remain sentient, but horribly aware of my fate.

I was vaguely conscious that Keran had formed his defensive circle. I did not know whether he was trying simply to save himself. I never knew.

Then, as though a glass had broken and its contents had dropped to the sward of a summer lawn, everything simply exploded and then sank away into the ground: the shrieking of the lift, the chant, the black-clad people and the intense atmosphere of brooding menace; it all simply sank away, disappearing before my eyes like a melted witch.

After some time, I was aware only of the clank of the lift, of Keran's heavy breath and sweating body beside me, my own internal organs labouring, my heart pounding in my head.

It was over, and the lift was empty. Keran staggered, overcome with superhuman effort. He looked as though he had lost weight, his body spindly and weak in the harsh, unnatural light, his face drawn and pained. For a second, his shifting glance wandered around the lift in a daze. He turned towards me; pierced me with blue desperate eyes.

"My God," he said, "Kennedy?"

Chapter 20
The Black Room

THE LIFT DOORS opened on floor twelve.

The small empty hallway stood before us, offering a deep unnatural silence. The small space, about two metres in breadth and four metres wide had two exits one on either side. They led to the apartments, one visible behind the closed fire-doors. This space we entered, Keran visibly distressed and drained, me for some reason exhilarated and strengthened.

Thoughts struck me; thoughts insidious and welcoming; thoughts that Keran was someone less than he had been before and now I might be able to have him; he was within my reach, he needed my help and I could offer him something. I also felt relief at the escape from something that had been dreadful. However, the feelings were tempered by the sense of vacuous stillness around.

Even as we walked forward, into that small space between the apartments, it felt as though we were aliens breaking through from a fish tank. There was a sense of weight and enclosure, of strained and pressurised air. It was as though the space around us had been blasted by some incredible force, and that our entrance to it was the entrance of a foreign body. It was as though we were breaking into ground that we did not own, and that at any minute something terrible would hit us. For a second, Keran held himself upright in the space and then, with a sudden and totally unexpected motion, he dropped forward and to the left. He struck the glass door on the left-hand side. His body weight cracked the glass as he fell. He then slid down the door into a half crouch, holding himself up vaguely with his right arm. It pressed against the shattered glass as his left dropped in collapse. His legs leaned partly on the wall and partly on the glass.

He made a gurgling noise in his throat. As I walked slowly to his side, I felt a drop of pressure in the air around me, I saw that a black fluid escaped from his mouth and slid down his chin. It dripped on to his neck. When the drops hit the floor, they hissed and bubbled. He looked deeply sick, drawn, white, and in his eyes... I had seen emptiness in them and it was horrible enough, but now there was a desperate fear that filled the emptiness with a new and shocking cold. He croaked out in a harsh laboured tone. "Get Kennedy."

I knew speech would be useless, so I walked through the hallway. Kennedy's flat faced me. On my right, I saw that the door of the other flat, which stood at right angles to Kennedy's, was wide open. I risked a quick glance to my left. The large balcony window beside the rubbish chute had been smashed, as though a body had been thrown with some weight in the direct centre of the window. A spider web tracery of the impact remained, and wind lightly whistled through the cracks. Outside, the last glow of the sunset made a filigree of the cracked window and the sun's last rays caught the underside of the cracks, lit them briefly as though the rays threaded the artificial web. Then the magic lights went out, and the sky dulled to a subtle bronze. I was left with the wind and the slowly opening and shutting door. I felt cold, unbelievably cold. I could see Keran's tortured face pressing against the glass of the fire-doors behind. He looked like some caged waxwork tableau. The intrinsic evil of the opening and shutting door prevented me from going any further. I walked back though the glass fire-door.

"I can't go." I said.

"You must." said Keran. He slumped a little further. "I can't go any further... that manifestation..." He shook his head, his mouth twitching. I shuddered inwardly myself. The utter repellence of the things we had seen (they were not in any way human) had unhinged me completely, and they seemed to have left a disgusting aftermath almost like a deeply offensive smell, even though there was no smell; instead there was the absence of nearly all sensual elements, except for a weakened and flat sense of sound, and the feel of cold. Taste seemed metallic, as though everything was hollow; hollow and empty.

Around us, the room seemed to pull outwards from its space. The sensation of being creatures in a fish tank became more pronounced and I began to feel more conscious of my beating heart, its fragility, and the sense of openness around us that was now even more threatening than the previous sensations of claustrophobia in the lift.

"I can't go through there, Keran. There's an open door swinging in the wind and it looks as though someone has jumped. I get a feeling that the door…"

"You have to go on. I need… Kennedy." He looked at me with pleading eyes.

Inside myself, I felt a mix of antithetical emotions. I had him in my power. I could do anything I pleased. Then I noticed the feeling in my groin, the feeling I had managed to shake off; an intense and deep sexual desire, a desire that could never be gratified, but one that gave a brief and terrible power. I felt my hips unconsciously gyrate. My liver, my heart, my lungs became fragile tendrils of a new set of senses. I felt a gleam come into my eyes, as though the moist surface of them was icing over. They were becoming the eyes of a pig or a cow; no sentience, no awareness, only a cold dead sense of external motivation. I was being led by lower automatic levels of my being. I realised that this sensation had hinted its way through my body since the morning or, to be more precise, since I had waited outside the tower block. As I had come into the lift, it had risen slowly like a malignant fever. Now, with my sudden awareness, it burst out like a sudden sweat on the brow, unexpected, but brutally overwhelming. I had no psychic reserve to prevent it.

Keran remained slumped against the glass door. His head bowed. He did not see me slowly lift my skirt.

Once, in a hospice for the dying, I had watched an old woman, crippled and wheelchair-bound, drop a handkerchief in front of a visiting man. As he bent to pick it up, she opened her legs and exposed herself. The look on that young man's face was the same look that appeared on that of Keran's as he raised his tortured head and looked up to see my skirt ruck above my thighs. His mouth opened again as though he was choking. Surprise, fear and revulsion stared back from his mask of pain. I slowly pulled down my knickers until they dropped to the floor. He tried to speak. I simply waited for a moment and then, with a rush of joy, pushed my groins into his face.

Throughout all this an inner voice sang to me, far away. It was a sweet melody, faintly recognisable. The lift door roared into life and slowly shut. Then the lift began to descend. As it descended, I could see from the corner of my eyes (although this was an impossible action) the black clad manifestations that Keran had managed to dispel. They grinned from the little window in the lift door, their white faces like those of satanic cherubs squeezing in to see some baroque mock-miracle play.

Keran's face was turning blue. I smelt the ugly unwashed smell from my private parts and his dripping mouth; I heard my own voice grunting; animal-like, low, bestial and overpowering. Keran seemed to shrink, sucked in by my sex, as though my vagina deflated him as a vacuum pump might collapse a balloon of air. My hips thrust into his face, my hands tore at his head; at times thrashing out, at others locking him down. His huge arms feebly wrapped around me as he tried to break my hold, but he had little strength and the rational part of me knew that he was fading fast. His face turned ashen, then blue-grey. His hands feebly twitched. I felt the rise of orgasm deep in me. I saw it like one sees a train coming down a long Spanish tunnel. It was a roaring like a submerged river breaking through deep dark tunnels. I knew that it was going to blow out like an explosion in a wall. I would be drenched by its strength and depth. And I knew that its climax would be the cusp of Keran's death throes. All this I knew, but the knowledge was only in a small part of me, in the small singing voice in my head far away. The rest of me was a writhing automaton, strong and purposeful, yet uncontrolled.

Keran's face was blue; his whole body jerked with tiny movements.

And then the lift door opened. Time seemed to return like a little happy go lucky friend. I was suddenly pushed away and fell backwards to the far wall: Jamie, red faced, breathing hard. He looked stunned and clown like, staring at me with a range of emotions on his battered face. Then, with a huge effort of will, he knelt by Keran. For an age, we all sat locked in our positions, almost as though an artist had simply paused in the composition of our scenario. The only movement was that of Jamie. Small but expert motions, checking Keran's breathing and touching his face and heart; the only sounds, our breathing, and in the near distance, through glass doors, the light pull of wind and the slow but repetitive slamming of a door.

Time waited while Keran recovered. I felt the absurd feelings dying in me, picked up my knickers, and put them back on. There were tiny drops of blood splattered everywhere; blood on my clothes, Keran's face and the floor and the walls. With the drops of black bile on the floor, the space had become some nihilistic art form. We sat like three clowns caught out of the circus until Keran's face went back to a light grey. It was apparent that we all laboured under the artificiality of this place. Unless we could move soon, we would all cease to be. It was not even that we would die; there was a sense that death was impossible here; there was only some inferior limbo state where one would continue but never become.

Eventually Keran croaked out a whisper.

"Get Kennedy...both of you."

After a few moments, Jamie pulled himself up and then helped me to my feet. We both pushed open the fire-door and entered the wind blasted area beyond. I averted my eyes; I could see Jamie looking with a mesmerised, open-eyed disbelief at the opening door to the left. I pulled him "Don't look." I managed to say, but he seemed not to hear. I looked at room seventy, Kennedy's room. The door was apparently shut. It was ridiculous. After all the things we had done and achieved, to be beaten by a shut door seemed painfully stupid. The Jamie put his hand on the door and pushed. It opened easily, and the dim hall was before us. We staggered in together.

Once inside, the atmosphere subtly changed. In a sense, it became heavier, as though the room were full of invisible smoke. My eyes could hardly see, yet there was a dim light everywhere. The corridor seemed longer than it should. On either side there were doors. I remembered the toilet on my right and two other vague rooms to the side. The living room cum kitchen was straight ahead, its door slightly ajar. I don't know why but it didn't occur to me to shout for Kennedy. Instead, I whispered to Jamie. "Try the doors." Slowly, he pushed the one on the left. It was a small room, entirely empty. We walked a little further. On the left was a larger bedroom. There was a double bed and a pile of old black clothes in the corner. Neither Jamie nor I could bear to walk any further, and the pile of old clothes looked sinister. I backed off and, almost unthinking, pushed the toilet door open.

Inside, a man, I couldn't recognise which man, had been forced down the bowl. His legs were sticking out and the floor was awash with blood. I shut the door and threw up. Jamie looked at me with a tranced expression, as though his mind had shut down. I wasn't sure if he had seen inside. Maybe it was the smell. I gathered myself again, and walked slowly along the corridor to the door.

The living room door was slightly ajar. There seemed to be what I can only describe as an absence of light in the rectangle of space that should have revealed the interior of the room. As I walked forward, the walls of the corridor seemed to breathe, a slight motion as though we traversed the capillaries of a sleeping giant, as though the whole tower block was a living entity only just becoming aware of our intrusion. My mouth dried up, and I felt my whole body and nervous system teeter into the first stages of shock. My head was now beating as with a barrelful of toxins pumping through my blood stream. My eyes were occluding and some neural pains were striking my left eye. Somehow, I gathered the strength to walk forward. I could sense Jamie crouching behind me like a mad scientist's helper and for a second, as I reached the door, I had a striking fear that he would betray me and that, even now, he held a weapon against my undefended back. I couldn't look around because I was too afraid. Instead, I gave the door a light push.

Like a universe spiralling, the room came to my view. It was entirely black, as black as a witch's hat. The contents were exactly as I remembered them, down to the cups on the coffee table and the cutlery in the sink, but now they were all black. Even the windows were black, the floors, the walls, the ceilings the light fittings and the fluorescent light in the kitchen. It was all black.

I turned around. Jamie had gone.

I turned back. The door before me was now wide open. The black room waited, in quiet and awful stillness. I stepped into the room. My shoes seemed to stick on the ground. There was a moment of suction as I raised each foot.

I reached the centre of the room and saw the body on the sofa. I hadn't remarked on it before because it too was entirely black, effectively camouflaged on the black sofa like a tar doll on a tar road. My eyes had become accustomed to the insufficient light. Now, although this light was still relatively indistinct, I could see that the body was sat upright on my left, beside the arm of the sofa. I heard the sound of my own sharp breath intake, and then in the distance I heard a whimper. It was hard to locate. I assume, in my attenuated state, that the little sobbing, whimpering sound came from behind the sofa; in fact, from almost directly behind the seated black figure.

It was such a small noise I might not have traced it in another environment. It sounded like a girl crying. I was terribly scared. I couldn't walk forward to investigate. My soles stuck to the floor. For a second I felt that I was going to melt, that in a matter of instants, my knees were going to go bubbling down like wax and my body was going to sink and sink and disappear into the black pool of the floor. With an effort, I forced up my right foot. I could not go forward, but I could go sideways. I saw from the corner of my eyes the door to my bedroom, the room from which I had watched Kennedy and Keran fucking. I edged towards it, the final room, keeping an eye on the seated figure on the couch and another on the room to my right hand side. When I reached the door I made a quick movement, cast the door open and jumped diagonally backwards.

Like a rain drop falling, a single infant shoe fell from the top of the large pile. It dropped to the ground, its vivid red contrasted obscenely with the black floor. That was my first impression, one difficult to forget. The shoe dropped like a tear of blood and landed with a light thud. Then I saw the mountain of shoes, all children's, towering and bulging from the room. As though a storm broke, in ones and twos the pile began to slowly collapse inwards to the room. There must have been a thousand pairs; a room full, stuffed to the ceiling. They were slowly falling out: different coloured children's shoes, in pairs and singly, in styles ancient, modern, some leather, some plastic. I backed away. The whimpering noise like tinnitus in my left ear. My eyes felt as though they were being dragged one way and then the other by an exterior force. I was being pulled like the victim of Roman amphitheatre between the ropes of the two overpowering terrors on either side of me. The whimpering noise had died and was almost inaudible.

I had explored every room. The only places Kennedy could be were under a pile of children's shoes or clothes in the other room, or behind the sofa. And on the sofa was the blackened body. I crept over to the sofa, all the time glancing back to the children's shoes and then again to the sofa, watching the black face of the body at every other moment. I reached the end of the sofa farthest away from him, and slowly pulled the sofa outwards. It took a lot of my failing strength and, when I lifted my hands to wipe the sweat from my forehead, I saw that they were black. It was apparent then that the room had been painted recently. As I pushed the sofa the body across from me rocked a little. The head lolled slightly.

Behind me, the shoes began to fall again.

I looked to the back of the sofa. There was nothing there, but the exposed floor was yellow linoleum, and it became clear that the painting of the room was incomplete. I stood up. The faint whimper was still somewhere, but where? My mind played with me now. I could hardly focus, my reason was failing. I stepped back a few paces and pulled at the shoes. They tumbled everywhere. Then I saw that the room where I had slept those nights ago had effectively disappeared. There was only a black wall now, and the shoes did not fill an entire room, only a cupboard. I backed away from the room, the blackened corpse, the blackened window, the multi-coloured shoes. As I turned around, I saw a figure slumped in the hallway. It was Jamie. He looked up at me, his face stricken with tears.

"I couldn't stay," he said. I nodded.

"It was you crying, then." He said nothing. It was obvious it was him. Somehow his weakness gave me strength, or perhaps it was the now-fading terror of the black room, and the knowledge that he was the author of the tears; whatever, I could now stride into the large bedroom almost fearlessly. I kicked at the clothes. No demons jumped out; there was no sign of Kennedy. I felt a small and sneaky feeling of pleasure. She was gone; they had taken her, and she wouldn't be coming back. Without looking at Jamie, I walked out of the door and saw that Keran was now standing. He held on to the glass frame with one hand, but his face was no longer grey. He looked pale, wan, but he was definitely recovering. The whistling wind had died down, and the door to my left had almost closed to.

I opened the glass fire-door. "She's not there."

Keran wiped his mouth. A look of pitiful resolve came over him. He shook himself. "I have to see." I helped him through the doors. Jamie was still slumped in the hallway. At first he looked asleep, but then as we walked over him I could see he was almost in a catatonic state of pure fear. I was about to stop and help, but Keran shook his head. We walked past him through the apartment. Keran observed the body in the toilet in silence. When he saw the figure on the sofa, he looked a little pained.

"Kennedy's friends." he said. "Simple innocents; nice people."

It was the most demonstrative I had seen him. He looked at the children's shoes.

"That was my room," I said. "But it's gone."

"I have a very bad feeling about this," he said. "These shoes, I think maybe some kind of absurd ritual protection, but it's the most perverse and tangential ritual magic - out of my experience." For a few moments he looked at the wall. "Get Jamie in here."

"He can hardly move."

A spasm of anger hit Keran's face. He walked back into the corridor. "Get up, Jamie."

Like a zombie, Jamie stood to his feet. He followed Keran back into the living room. Keran pointed at the black cupboard.

"Run at it," he said.

Jamie, without hesitation, shambled towards the cupboard and, like some burlesque actor, his whole body punched through what had been an artificial wall. He sprawled out on a floor as black as the painted room. The room itself, from an angle obscured by the fragments of the false wall, seemed utterly empty. It had also been painted black. There was an uneasy calm. Nothing moved; Keran waited, grim-faced. I watched Jamie lying on the floor shivering and then I heard a faint buzz and became almost at once aware of a rancid smell. I saw that the floor seemed to move. I was about to shout. I felt the words rise in my throat but they didn't come. The moving floor began to dissect and disassemble itself. There were areas of darkness within the darkness; small forms rising and falling all around Jamie's shivering body. Flies, flies everywhere, pulling into motion like tiny helicopters rising from a massive, nigh infinite, landing field. The flies seemed somehow temporally unhinged; as if the room itself was immersed in some kind of slow water and the flies swam rather than flew. They hovered only in the bottom third of the room, about waist height to me. Even this movement was almost indiscernible in the blackness of the room.

Then I saw it, just as Keran's eyes lit up with the knowledge. On the ceiling of the room, there was an unpainted area. I walked a little closer. In a silver underlay, the figure of a man was portrayed. He held in two hands a smaller effigy. The effigy itself contained a circle of sorts, and a serpent, eating its tail. Inside, a Tau, the Egyptian symbol of resurrection; a swastika, symbolic interlaced triangles, the seal of Solomon and the sign of Aum, beneath it, the message I remembered only too well.

"There is no religion."

The flies began to buzz in an ominous undercurrent. Keran stared in a black, desperate grimace. "I've lost her," he said, and his voice was as empty as the contents of a vacuum pump. He seemed about to collapse again. I heard him whisper something under his breath. Even as Jamie crawled to his feet and began to back out of the fly-stricken room, I heard Keran repeat the words I had failed to catch. There was something about them that made my body jerk like a puppet, as though I had been shot through the torso by an explosive bullet. Even as we began the screaming, I heard them. And I heard them as we ran from the painted black rooms, through screaming hallways and doorways, down endless screaming concrete stairs and out into the foyer of the tower block.

"The Death Tableau."

Chapter 21
Butterflies

WE REACHED THE FOYER in a desperate state. As we spilled out of the stair well, clinging together like some distorted Hansel and Gretel, the sounds of our own screams rang on in the air. In the undercurrent behind our screams, the dreadful screaming of others, unseen, unknown and invisible, sounded through the thin and cold avenues and spaces of the tower block. As we stared breathless out of the glass front of the building I think we all simultaneously became aware of the white faces that leered back at us like reflections from some circus hall of mirrors. Through the dense black fog, swirling outside in the night, their triangle noses pressed against the misted glass, ugly lips crushed and distorted by the glass. Vacant, impossible eyes fixed on us like the eyes of pale sirens or gorgons. There was something terrifying in their silence and stillness. No movement, only a sense that they were about to break the glass, and when that happened, as we knew it would, all the slowness would vanish. The pace of their attack would defy all reason and logic, like the onrush of a tidal wave.

None of us could speak. Our breath condensed in front of us in panting clouds. A cold sweat dripped from our brows and trickled under our arms; you could almost hear our individual hearts pump like failing machines. When I turned, aghast, to search for something like hope, towards Jamie's face, I saw nothing but exhaustion and fear. His eyes were the eyes of an utterly broken man. Keran himself had a look of virtual hopelessness; he was played out. I knew he would not go without a fight, but I could see he was nearing the end of his physical strength. He had been sucked dry by events contained within an hour of objective time. But more than this, something had changed again in his face. No longer was he arrogant; no longer was he empty. This time there was a look of weariness, of sickening knowledge.

I knew as he had shouted the words and repeated them as we had staggered screaming down the stairs, that he had had some revelation or epiphany in the fly room, and that the revelation was something deep, shocking and unwanted. "The Death Tableau": He had endlessly repeated this phrase even as we limped and staggered down the stairwell. What did it mean? Was this it: These manifestations of evil beyond the insane, peeking out of the swirling mists and the blackness, waiting to do something unnameable? Or was there something worse? Could there be something worse?

Pale hands appeared, palm forward on the vast glass surfaces before us. There seemed to come a heaving sigh. It enveloped the foyer. The hands seemed to press and sink into the glass as though the things pushed through polythene, but the glass did not give. Keran staggered forward. Dropped to his knees and began to pull salt from his pocket. He swept a great half circle in front of the glass. I sensed then that he simply delayed the inevitable, working in an automatic way to protect himself to the last.

"Can I do anything?" I said. He shook his head, staggering back to his feet when he had finished. "It might hold them if you have some kind of…faith."

"Faith in what?" It was the wrong thing to say. Keran only had faith in himself, and that was leaking out of his soul as water from a holed bucket.

"Love," he said, and I knew that I had been wrong, that he did have faith, but it was a faith based on experiences I could not share with him. It was Kennedy. He had lost her, and he knew he was unlikely to get her back. It meant more than his life or his soul, whatever that four letter word meant, and now he was trying this last little defence in the same manner in which a guttering candle immutably holds to light. He sat back on his haunches and looked at the faces on the outside, almost with the weary eye of a man who has watched too much dull television and who knows he should have gone to bed hours before. "We can wait here or we can fight it higher up," he said. "Either way we will lose. It depends on how much you value this last little bit of this particular life."

"Enough to fight." I looked at Jamie. He was in a trance. He stood like a scarecrow with his arms drooping and his mouth open. "Jamie, we're going up again."

He turned around in silence and started to walk towards the lift.

Keran and I backed away from the glass front. There was an undercurrent of low moaning. Now I could hear that faraway chant just on the periphery of my auditory range. The whole wall of glass seemed move inwards like packing-foam bubbles, pressed by flat white hands and flat white faces.

We were metres from the lift when Mr Jarvis walked down the last of the stairs. He wore a shabby tweed suit and carried a leather brief case under his arm. There was an absurd moment. We caught our breath as he walked past us, unheeding, except for one quizzical glance towards me. There was no time even to think of warning him or saying anything. As he glanced and walked purposefully down the stairs, he seemed to hesitate fractionally in his step and, just half turning to Keran, he said something in a low whisper. As the words struck with a tangible force, Keran fell back against the wall in a kind of paralysis. His hand was outstretched for the lift button. His face grimaced in a strangled pain. And then, with a movement, so quick and utterly impossible that I did not really see it so much as sense its action, Jarvis stretched out his hand and the amulet broke from my neck, jumped the intervening space, and slapped in his palm. He put it in his pocket and, without another glance, walked on, walked out of the building, leaving the door open, and into the black night.

Keran banged the lift button with his gradually relaxing hand. I kept my eyes on him, the lift coming down and the things slowly pushing the glass and the gaping open door.

So they had the amulet, after all my efforts to retain it.

I recalled my moment of inspiration at Glencoe, where I had sensed that only humans could be good or bad, and that the amulet was simply a neutral object, at best a kind of spiritual magnet. Perhaps I should have thrown it away a long time before. But then again I felt no better, no worse. Now I was not sure it was even important to them. I even had the impression that Jarvis took it as a man might pick up his hat in passing a hat stand - for no other reason than that it was his.

"Maybe they have what they want now." I said, but I knew I lied, even to myself.

"What did he say, Keran?"

Keran did not look at me. He seemed to have recovered again.

"He said "Goodbye"," he replied just as the lift doors opened and the glass wall caved in. We walked into the lift and pressed the button. The things, vaguely human in form, seemed to float, as though they were being moved by light beams towards us, as fast as I expected, but they hit the salt line and stopped. Some of them frizzled up like paint burning, writhing in an abject torment as moths in a light rather than sentient creatures. The salt seemed to bubble up. I noticed now that Jarvis had scuffed his foot through one part of the line.

As the lift doors shut, the things found the opening, and as the lift moved, I saw through the glass panel an almost exact mirroring of the previous scenario on floor twelve, the only difference being that we were in the lift going up and they were watching from the outside. Faces, faces on the glass, searching for the next avenue to absorb us completely.

The lift seemed slow down. I didn't have to ask Keran about the goodbye. Jarvis needn't be a high level magician to predict outcomes. Suddenly it seemed ridiculous. I began to laugh. Keran frowned, and then smiled at me. The lift went up a few floors without stopping, and I stopped laughing. "How did you know Jarvis?" I said eventually.

"You knew him?" replied Keran in genuine surprise.

I explained how I had met him at the theosophical meeting.

"Was there a woman with a monocle there as well?" said Keran.

I nodded.

"That's it, then," he said. "That's where it all went wrong for you."

"No, it was finding the amulet."

"Well, maybe, but the amulet simply drew you to them, and once they found you…"

"What's it about Keran? You know it all now don't you?"

"As much as anyone knows. Sadly, I don't think we have the time left for me to unburden the details."

"Who are they?"

"Macdonald, descended from Donald the grandson of Somerled and king of the southern isles." It was Jamie; his pale green eyes stared out at nothing.

Was this an absurd answer to my question? I looked at Keran and then Jamie. Keran shrugged his shoulders. Jamie was back with his ancient people in the land of the fairies.

"They divided the lands between his three sons. Lorn, Mull and Juram to Dugall. Kintyre and Islay went to Reginald. Angus took the rest." The lift rose up a floor like a haunted dumb waiter listening to Jamie's epic tones. "And then Donald of Isla, son of Reginald, gave us our name, which is not to be confused with the Macdonalds of Clanranald, though I wish I too went out with Cherlie and their seven hundreds. Those brave arms gave great honour to the Jacobite cause."

Jamie lapsed into quiet song.

"Prepare yourself to die, Jamie. Fraoch Eilean." Keran patted

Jamie on the shoulder. The Scotsman's eyes lit up with a brief blaze of pride. Then the fire died, and he lapsed into a low chant, the words Keran had used echoing under his breath.

"What does it mean?"

"Battle cry of the Clan. Something about heather and islands. Well, now we're all ready to sell our souls in the conflict."

"I'm not quite ready to die."

"Dying is the easy bit. It's the rest I'm not looking forward to."

"I need to know answers. I deserve that, Keran."

"Well, if I can jam the lift between the floors, we could all listen to a little fairy tale," he said.

"Hansel and Gretel?"

"More Little Red Riding hood, but the old, old version, where the ending is not terribly pleasant. And I have a feeling that we won't even get to the last paragraph before its time to briefly sleep."

The lift stopped on floor nine. We all tensed. When the doors opened, an old lady, dressed in a floral nightgown and wearing a distinctive Celtic cross around her neck, stared at us. We stared back, waiting to die.

"Have you heard the commotion on the stairs?" she said.

I nodded.

"It's the kids. Them and their drugs. I was just going up to Mr Peabody's. You're not safe on your own."

"No," agreed Keran Westwood. "We heard all the commotion and thought we might have a word with Mr Peabody. Nowadays you can't be too careful"

She got on the lift and pressed the button for floor twelve.

Even as she walked on, I saw the brief flickering of the thing coming up the stairwell. It smacked against the glass window of the lift, and stared pointlessly around. The lift shuddered into life, and rose.

"Young people," the old woman continued, "They have too much nowadays. When I was a teenager we didn't have a telly, or a bath, or even a toilet that flushed."

"Yes, that's right," said Keran. "It was the same for me; no wall-to-wall carpets or central heating."

"Is your friend all right?"

"He's Scottish," Keran replied nodding wisely.

The old woman looked sternly at Jamie, and then whispered to Keran in a voice that anyone could hear.

"He's been drinking."

"Yes, but he'll behave himself when ladies are present."

The old woman looked back to me with satisfaction. And then she frowned. "You don't look well, dear?"

"It's been a trying day," I replied.

The lift doors opened on floor twelve. The cold space flaunted out. But now there was no silence, only the vague pressure of the wind on the fire-door, and a low humming noise that I only fully recognised when we stepped out of the lift. Through the glass doors, like a grotesque parody of a summer meadow, its field of flowers awash with bees, black flies drifted, suspended on wind beams through a sickening air.

Without hesitation, Keran opened the door, and he and the old lady walked through the fly-spattered space. Jamie and I followed behind the lady, listening to her complaints. We watched, as she flapped her withered hands across her face. She walked straight to the open door on the right.

"He's a bit deaf," she said. "He sometimes leaves the door open for me at night when he thinks I'll be coming up. These people next door, they live in a pig sty; I think they're all on drugs."

We walked into through the open door. Then we closed the door, and stood in the hallway on an old, worn carpet lightly scattered with leaves blown in by the wind. We smelt the stale air of an old person's flat, the sweat, the urine and the mustiness of old, old days, and another smell, strong, and for the moment unrecognisable.

Keran shut the door behind us all, and began to lay some salt across the door posts. Even as he did so, he stopped, and I too. He was reading the words written and hanging just below the lintel on a piece of coloured paper.

"The creaking door has a spell to riddle, I play a tune without any fiddle."

Garlic festooned the lintel of the door, the source of the strong smell. We turned and walked through a hallway decorated by rosary beads. There were portraits of the Virgin Mary, and Christ crucified on the cross. We passed a room in the right, the toilet on the left and then another room on the left, in exact mimicry of Kennedy's flat. The door before us led to the main living room. It was opened by the old woman. She shouted, in a very loud voice.

"Mr Peabody." There was no answer. She shouted again "Mr Peabody."

"Come in, Mary." The voice was deeper than you might expect.

Sitting on a low elliptical couch was an old man, dressed in a pale green suit, with a matching tie and cardigan. His deep green eyes stared out of an almost childlike face and were accentuated by a ridiculous grey white balaclava. The balaclava covered most of his head. Holes had been cut for his ears, from which depended old-fashioned hearing aids.

He looked a little like a tortoise.

As we all took chairs in a rough circle around him, he placed some cards on the circular coffee table. He had been playing solitaire. Quietly, from an old radiogram, someone sang about remembering April, which I remarked as strange, as the old man could never hear it if he was really deaf. He had a little dog that yapped suddenly. It startled me. And then came from under the table, snuffling and lightly biting.

A dull thump came from the front door outside, and the little dog yapped again, and rushed out into the hallway. There was a second of angry barking, and a moment in which Mr Peabody,

Mary and the dog all seemed to be making a noise. The dog yelped and rushed back through into the living room, its hackles rising. Keran looked at me knowingly, and then he got to his feet and walked towards a cage by the large window. He stood for a while. His shadow reflected from the mirrored surface of the window, shading out the balcony behind. He was so tall I knew he was able to look out of the window and downwards, perhaps not to the immediate ground but certainly to the lower lights of the facing windows in the apartment blocks to the south.

Mr Peabody tinkered with the hearing aids and then smiled at me. "That's better. Now I can hear a little. Make some tea for our guests, Mary. There's a good girl." Mary got up and walked to the kitchen. I realised then that this apartment was not a replica of Kennedy's. There was a kitchen to the side. Mary disappeared into it, and there was a familiar sound of teacups and saucers clinking.

"You're interested in butterflies, Mr..?" Peabody's voice was unusually rich and beguiling.

"… Westwood. Yes, I have a passing fancy. These chrysales, if I am not mistaken are ringlets."

"Aphantopus Hyperantus. They will become ringlet butterflies, almost black."

"Yes, sombre-looking things. When they emerge."

Peabody nodded. Against the front door I heard a low thump, as though a dry hand had gently slapped the door.

"A parallel of life, perhaps?" said Peabody. "They start as eggs, become larvae, become pupae and then imagines or butterflies."

"At each stage, what kind of dream do they dream?" said Keran.

"They don't dream, I think?" said Peabody.

"They only think of being, of eating, of resting, and then of flying?"

"Perhaps." said Peabody "Or perhaps they just eat, rest and fly. Ah, the tea. Thank you ever so much, Mary."

Mary put the tea on a little side table and handed around

saucers. Even Jamie took a cup, but I didn't see him drink anything.

"Caterpillars don't dream of flying, they don't dream at all." continued Peabody, as Keran sat down and picked up his tea, his hand dwarfing the cup.

"I wondered how they ever flew if they didn't dream of it."

"It's a mystery, to be sure," said Peabody, and he sipped on his tea with a benign expression of pleasure.

"It's nice to have guests," said Mary.

"Yes," said Peabody. "A real pleasure."

"There's been some terrible goings on. I couldn't get off to sleep," continued Mary.

"I didn't notice a thing," said Peabody, laughing.

"You never do," replied Mary.

Outside, there was a low pervasive hum. I could hear it now, and it made we wonder why there were no flies in Peabody's house. I could hear the low undercurrent of flies, the oscillations of the wind, a whistling, and somewhere, again below the level of real audibility, a far away chanting. I felt a heat soar up between my thighs; for a second, I vividly imagined Peabody pulling out his member and Mary gripping it in her withered hands. I shut out the thought, shut my eyes, opened them, blinked rapidly. The image fled, and the feeling subsided, but I couldn't help noticing that Peabody's flies were unzipped. I looked away, aware that cold sweat again masked my face. Keran seemed unperturbed.

"Do you mind if I unburden myself a little to you, Mr Peabody?" he said.

"Not at all. I assumed the commotion outside woke a lot of people up. What's the problem?"

"Let me tell it in the form of a story. It might make it more interesting."

"Go on," said Mary. "I like a good story."

Chapter 22
The Fairy Tale

"It all began a long time ago. It began before any one of us was born. It is a fairy tale, and some may find it difficult to believe, but children believe, and I am a child."

"We are all children," said Peabody, and he winked at me.

"Before I tell you the tale, I've got to be clear about something that is quite complex, so I'll explain in a way we can all relate to. It's lucky, Mr Peabody, that you have such fascinating examples to illustrate my little explanation." Keran pointed to the butterflies, and Peabody smiled in a self-satisfied manner. Keran continued:

"Imagine our existence is like that of a butterfly. I asked the question earlier really, but what is a butterfly? Is it an egg, a caterpillar, a pupa or an imago?"

"Imago?" said Mary.

"Technical for the flying butterfly, dear," replied Peabody.

"Perhaps in every waking, or even unwaking moment, we are all the levels that that little Ringlet butterfly exists upon," said Keran

"What do you mean?" said Mary.

"We have four levels," said Peabody. "We're not simply as we seem."

Mary lapsed in to silence. Keran nodded.

"Let's say the egg of the butterfly is quiescent. It does apparently nothing. Let's call it our Lower personal ego. That could be our animal instincts, our passions, our desires. What the Indians call the lower *manas*. It operates within our physical body."

"The gross physical body," said Peabody.

"Yes. Let's say the caterpillar is our higher ego. It is our individuality, our intellect."

"The thing that thinks."

"Yes," replied Keran. "As Descartes said, "the thinking thing" but not quite as he visualised it, not simply existence, but what we would see as our rationalising being."

"The mind, really."

"If you will."

"That leaves us with two more," said Mary. "I remember the mind and body thing from school."

"We're left with the pupa, from the ancient Greek for puppet, I believe, but in this case, the analogy is less than perfect."

"It's not too strong on the other two, either," said Peabody. "The egg doesn't act at all, does it?"

"No," replied Keran, "It doesn't, but neither does the gross physical body, without the action of the mind. Please forgive these rushed examples. It's been a difficult night, and I'm trying to speed things along."

Outside, I heard a dull thud, as though moths hit a light. There was a sense of pressure building in the air. The room had become hot and uncomfortable. Jamie started in his seat. He stood up and shuffled to the door. He opened it. A faint wind stirred the now oppressive air. A disquieting odour wafted into the room.

"That's right, Jamie," said Keran. "*Achean Fohm*. Watch the pass for intruders. We'll keep them out, ye canny wee man."

Jamie walked out, shutting the door behind him.

"More tea?" said Mary.

"There were two other levels," said Peabody

"I am referring to the spiritual ego. In fact, the soul, or bhuddi."

"Presumably this links closely with the mind."

"Of course."

"Then that leaves us with God." said Peabody, his face somehow like an infant in the balaclava.

"Not quite," said Keran. "I think we might not require God."

"Oh, we must have God," said Mary.

"Well, let's say that *you* have God, Mary and we'll leave it at that. For me this is simply the higher self. Like a ray of light coming from light it's difficult to tell which is God and which is the higher self, which is the ray and which the light and which the source of light. Maybe God is in there or maybe not."

"Tush, I'll have to pray for you, young man."

Keran smiled. "Any prayers will be appreciated."

"So, we've lost God in our little analogy?" said Peabody, nodding inanely. "That could be serious."

"Not on the cosmic scale. All we need to think of is a vast karmic wheeling of the universe, a kind of moral absolute. Call it God if you like. It is the ultimate judge of all actions, even if it isn't consciously judging. It judges like any automatic law."

"Ah," said Peabody. "So that is the butterfly. The karmic law - and I always thought the butterfly was the soul. Psyche, that's what the Indians used to say."

"True," said Keran. "I've lost the analogy completely. Suffice it to say that these are the levels of the self; the lower ego or animal instinct, the higher ego or mind, the spiritual ego or soul, and the higher self, where you are kind of soul and God."

"And that's all going on at once," said Mary. "It's all a bit confusing."

"Never mind," said Keran. "My, this tea is good, Mary."

"Yes, it's a special little concoction that I make for Mr Peabody in his kitchen."

"Very invigorating," said Mr Peabody.

"Yes, I feel much better already," said Keran.

"After the commotion," said Mary

"I feel I could face the world," said Keran.

The noise outside became more intense; a spiralling hum that rode in and out of the consciousness. There was a long moment of waiting, the noise hummed on in the periphery of our senses. We were all looking at Keran. He continued:

"So, that's what we are, or at least one way of looking at our existence on this planet." he said finally.

"We're all these things in one then, all at the same time," said Peabody.

"Yes, emphatically we are all these things."

"But how we see life is dependent on our awareness at the time?" said Peabody.

"Yes, we go through these stages all the time, like the life-cycle of a butterfly. Sometimes we are more aware of the stages than others. Sometimes when we are in the higher ego stage we can rationalise our existence, discuss it, argue, but only when we reach the next stage do we see life from the perspective of the spiritual ego, and only when we reach the highest level do we unite with the absolute."

"So, at any one time we must see life from the perspective of the stage we are on. Just like the caterpillar cannot remember the egg, and the butterfly cannot remember the pupa."

"For ordinary people that is the case?"

"And are there people who are not ordinary," said Peabody, bemused.

"Yes, I'm one of them."

"I've heard about that," said Mary with distaste.

"I'm not peculiar, Mary. I am simply trained to appreciate things from different levels. I can see them all. There is only one thing that is denied to me."

We waited in the stifling room as the undercurrent of noise grew more and more frenetic.

"We may have to leave shortly," said Keran, putting his cup down.

"Don't deprive us of your fairy tale," said Peabody. "We were all so much looking forward to it."

"Can I use the toilet first?" I said suddenly. The room stilled as I walked out into the hall. Jamie stood about five foot from the door like a sentinel. The noise in the hall was like the buzzing of inconceivably large flies, an affront to the sense of hearing. I could see an impossible number of hands on the door, in positions where hands could not go. I got a sense through the base fear that Jamie somehow held them all back with some invisible, unconscious power. Before I went to the toilet, I quickly glanced at the other two rooms. They were bare, almost empty of furniture except for a large bed in the main room. They were all decorated in an abundant, incongruous green, and there were leaves all over the floor. On every wall there was a picture of a forest, the same forest. For some reason I found my eyes straying to the pictures, and yet I knew this was not a good idea. I quickly left the rooms.

When I came back, Keran was standing with his back to the large window. "How is Jamie?" he said.

"Fine," I replied.

"We have a little longer, then."

"Time for the fairy tale?" said Mary.

There was a long pause, in which the lights darkened slightly as though a dimmer switched was raised, lowered, raised and then dimmed to just a fraction below the original light. The room became almost stifling in heat momentarily, and then kept fluctuating. After a time, I only heard Keran's voice but, as he spoke, a series of incredible images struck me one after the other, as though part of my awareness saw through differing eyes; through four levels to be precise, like the life cycle of a butterfly viewed all at one time.

"There was a young man once," said Keran "Very brave, very foolish, and he decided he would have the greatest adventures. He wandered far and he wandered near and he found wizards and warlocks and fighting masters and artists and poets and he learned from each one a little thing and then a little thing more. All the time he sought his heart's desire, his holy grail, and though he learned many things, and though he saw many countries, from dark woods full of talking creatures to sandy beaches with only waves to answer his questions, he never found his heart's desire.

So, he settled in a lonely place, a high ruined tower, and he decided to wait until time would give him his heart's desire. When it became dark and the stars were bright, the brightest star spoke to him, and told him that one was coming who would give him all the answers."

"Jesus," said Mary.

Keran smiled, his face only half visible in the deepened shadows. "No, not Jesus. It was my uncle, Rodin. He taught me everything there was to know about magick."

"Aha," said Peabody, "Can you do card tricks?"

"Another time, perhaps."

"So you were the young man?" said Mary

"Handsome too," said Keran. "I left that out because it wasn't relevant."

"Tell us about magick," I said.

"That's the interesting part," said Keran, looking thoughtful. "I was seventeen when my Uncle Rodin introduced me to the occult. I asked to become an initiate. He taught me some of the greatest secrets, things that the profane would simply not believe."

"I can never work out how you saw a woman in half," said Mary.

"Secret of the trade," said Keran. "It's putting her back together again that is the difficult bit." He looked at me in what I thought might be a significant manner.

"So, what did you learn?" I said.

"I won't go into the details, to some extent they would be incomprehensible to anyone but those participating. Suffice it to say, we reached the great work."

"You crossed the abyss?" I said.

"What's that?" said Peabody.

"It's the bridge between life and death, Mr Peabody. One of the great desires of magicians is not to pull a rabbit out of a hat. It is to cross the divide between life and death, and then come back."

"Hmm," said Peabody. "That can't be easy."

"No, on the contrary, it's fraught with perils, the least of which is crossing over and not coming back."

"Ah," said Peabody. "You'd be dead then."

"Exactly," said Keran.

"But you're alive," said Mary, "So, you must have crossed and come back."

"Not quite. I should have crossed, but I couldn't."

"Not easy to cross, I expect." said Peabody.

"No, it is one of the most difficult things imaginable, but I should have done it. My uncle expected me to do it. He was a great magician, and extremely wise. In his eyes and my own I looked, how can I say, destined to do it. It was made for me, and I was made for it. I did everything that was necessary. I was more prepared than virtually anyone you could meet in the history of the world. I should have crossed the bridge."

"What happened?" I said. The room became still. Even the noises from outside seemed to still. Keran's eyes became pained and faraway, remembering vividly his supreme moment of magical triumph, the ruin of it, the majestic failure.

"There was someone in the way."

"What?" said Peabody.

"Just that," said Keran. "There was someone in the way, and I couldn't get past them."

There was a moment of anticlimax. We all stared at Keran.

"How unfortunate," said Peabody.

There was a loud crash in the hall.

"Commotion," said Mary.

Keran went first. I followed, peering round his side. I could see in the hallway, beyond Jamie's shoulders, hands, arms and, behind them, impossible faces. There was a sickening smell of deep rotted things and the air, from being stifling, switched, as though a submarine had suddenly sunk a mile in a second, to freezing cold, cold water. My tongue could almost taste the terror. In an instant , we would be obliterated

And then Keran shouted, in a golden tongue, as though he was calling voices from the long, long past

"*Fraoch Eilean, Fraoch Eilean.*" And Jamie charged into the multitude. Even as we backed away into the hall, I could see a flailing of unintelligible arms and legs. I heard, as we pulled back in to the living room, an unearthly screaming, like a thousand machines grating to a halt, amidst which people died and died again in obscene mashings.

"He's back in the Forty-five killing the Redcoats," said Keran to me, and louder, to Peabody, he said. "May we take some air on the balcony?"

"Certainly," Peabody sat supine in the chair nodding quietly, looking at his butterfly cage. I could hear Mary in the kitchen, making more tea.

"More tea?" said Peabody.

"Another time," said Keran.

We walked out on to the balcony. The cold air seeming less cold than the chill of the hall. The air was fresh, biting, but real air.

"It's a long way down," I said.

"But a short way up." replied Keran

I looked up, craning my neck and then I looked down. It was still a long way down.

Chapter 23
The End of All Tales

"WHAT ABOUT JAMIE," I said. "And the others?"

"Be serious," said Keran. He was craning his neck towards the roof, some three floors up.

"I am."

"Really?" In a moment of sickening vertigo, I watched him jump to the balustrade. The thick metal balusters bent under his great weight, and he appeared almost ludicrous on a rail spanning only the width of my hand. Then, like an expert gymnast dressed in the wrong body, he walked lightly along the rail, the whole structure of the balustrade heaved and bent. He said "Jamie was already dead when I instructed him to defend us at the hallway of Glencoe." He turned to look at me.

I felt a sudden rush of anger. For a second, I visualised jumping forward. I would push Keran off. I could see his body, arms flailing, eyes staring wildly as he dropped the twelve floors on to the concrete paving stones below. Keran watched the look in my eyes and smiled.

"You think I can't fly?" he said, laughing. And then for a single instant, there was a look of deep sorrow.

"Wish I could," he said.

"Peabody and Mary?" I said, with more anger than I really felt, "What about them?"

"I'm not sure about those two," said Keran, "but I know that I'm currently battling with forces beyond even my consummate understanding, I'm standing on a ledge hundreds of metres in the air, and I'm on the point of physical and spiritual destruction. Thoughts of rescuing remote and unusual strangers who may not even need rescuing are not going to help me any, so I'm tossing the thoughts out. Got it?"

The words died on my lips.

For a second, Keran looked almost sympathetic. "Look," he said. "I would guess that, in an attempt to scale this building, we are both going to die. No point in arguing. If we concentrate our collective will on the problem, we might have a chance." He held out his hand.

I hesitated. From behind me, through the blinds, I saw Peabody and Mary, like caged specimens, brightly coloured and over-lit in a museum display; I heard wailing, humming, intense yet distant screams, as though they seeped under the door. I turned and, from this despairing tableau, I looked out at the dark vista of night. The tower blocks stretched out like giant filing cabinets; faraway apartment lights on each block, like tiny bright page leaves in a vast catalogue; to the far south, the bright flames of a burning car and the hoot of fighting youths in a below too frightening to even observe.

I held out my hand and leapt to the balustrade.

It creaked and yawed under our combined weight. I took one unwise look downwards facing out onto what was the whole world. Far below I saw, disappearing into dimness, the black, black ground, the small objects like a child's toy set. The ground seemed to rush to meet me. I felt the vacuous attack of vertigo, the dizziness; the sickening, sickening visions of a body smashed and pulped like a peeled tomato - my body. And then the training took over; the years of martial art discipline and the pleasant hours of Tai chi under a master. I was able to balance my inner self. I was able to raise my eyes, feel the centre of my being, send the awareness to my feet and the strength and activity to my legs. I could stand unfettered. Keran sensed it and let go of my hand. He turned from me, his back to my side, and began exploring the heights. "We could do with a rope," he said after a moment's reflection."

"Maybe a curtain?" I suggested.

"Too late," he replied, and I knew he was right. Even as we poised on the balustrade, there was a long and pitiful scream and a muted explosive cacophony. The lighted room before us seemed to transform to a collage of black lights, of flitting objects; the room itself seemed about to burst, and there was heavy and monotonous drone of flies. At that moment, without warning, Keran seemed to leap out into space. For an instant, in some wild fantasy, I thought he had simply given up and had launched himself into oblivion. I swayed, as though a deep gust of wind had caught me like a yacht sail, and then I saw Keran clinging like a spider to the concrete façade. At that moment, the wind really did catch me with great force and I fought as though with an invisible demon to maintain my balance. Keran was climbing with unbelievable speed. He was above my head and still travelling. Without knowing what he had done, but seeing the room before me turn into a maelstrom like a hellish kaleidoscope, knowing I was about to go one way or the other, I, too, leapt to where he had leapt.

I realised then what it was like to die, because part of me died in the space between the wall and the balustrade; the infinity of space below, above and behind me, the vast nothingness in which my tiny frail body hung poised. There was a sickening smack as my body and particularly my left cheek hit the wall. My hands faithfully and blindly snatched and grasped. My whole being tried to will itself as paper, as light, as airy and insubstantial, as stickiness and gum. I tried to glue myself to the wall. Somehow, my left hand found a grip, a projection. My right hand could not find another in that first instant, but my hands seemed to move faster that the hands of a human. My knee had caught something. A part of my brain told me that my cheek was smashed and my knees were hurting, but I ignored everything but the idea of adhesion. My free hand found something to hold and I was there, stuck on a concrete wall a thousand metres in the air.

Only after it happened was I able to make any kind of mental reflection on the surface of the tower block and how I was still alive. There were some crenellations, a feature of the architecture that could not be observed in the dim light or until close at hand. It appeared as a uniform series of projections rising presumably up this whole section of the building. There was enough for a grip on either hand of about three centimetres' projection. It was enough to hold, to grip, to make ascent possible. And I began to ascend, following quickly the feet of Keran above.

It was not a climb. That would be too dignified a word. There was not even a sense of consideration or care. I had led several expeditions in the past. It might take over an hour to adjust all my gear before descending an apparently simple slope. Keran and I, with no equipment, were taking appalling risks. But then we were not wrestling with the challenge of a daunting task. We fled unspeakable things that at any moment might appear to enact unspeakable things.

Keran had travelled about five metres when he disappeared. I followed desperately. My hand reached the spot where I last saw his feet, and then suddenly it happened. For some reason that I could never explain, I had lost all fear. I was simply climbing, scrambling, grovelling up an artificial cliff. It was simply a thing to do. It was not even in my mind dangerous, so much had I excluded anything but the task in hand. It was in this false security that it happened.

I slipped.

In that instant, I realised that I was plainly about to die a horrible death. I watched incredulous as my hand came away from the projection. The white claw shook and trembled. I noticed, almost in passing, that my fingernails were broken, cut and bleeding. It was my last act. To look at bloodstained fingernails and to reflect how once they had been manicured for a lot of money. I watched the grey white wall behind my hands tip away from me as I fell. My right hand still clung. It held and then did not hold. I was falling backwards. My foot had caught on a lower projection. I fell straight back ,as though I was an old fashioned wooden board puppet who had been sprung up from its board, prevented from the downward drop in that moment by my right foot. Two things happened at once. Keran, who had watched it all and leapt at the same time, caught my leg while hanging on the balustrade of the floor above, and my head banged off the concrete. I watched the entire world swathed below me in a panorama of starlight and black landscape. As my head struck, I saw the creatures crawling up the tower block. Pale white faces and disembodied eyes like dark stars filled with night; crawled and crept with infinite slowness; hundreds of them, issuing from the downstairs window and spreading across the face of the tower block like a vast plague.

I hung, held like a yo-yo, but weeping and whimpering like a baby. I heard Keran grunt with the terrible exertion. I felt my whole body weight being slowly pulled upwards. My back and head banged on the wall. Up I went, at every moment expecting Keran's grip to give out. But it didn't. Another hand grasped me and, like a sack ,I was thrown over the balustrade. Keran pulled himself over with difficulty, breaking one of the balusters as he came, and fell back against the window of the apartment, clutching his right arm in agony.

"Jesus," he said.

"They're coming. There are thousands of the things," I said.

He grimaced in pain. "I can't climb," he said. "My hand's given out."

"Thanks for..." I said.

"For God's sake. It's not time to be polite. Do something."

At that moment, one of the things appeared at the balustrade. I didn't see it. I only knew because Keran pushed himself off the wall and kicked out with his good foot. There was a soft "plop" as though he had kicked a pumpkin. I turned in time to see the pale face hurtle back. The body disappeared into the black. The sound of the wind filled the empty space. Keran sank to his knees with the effort. I jumped over his body and knocked on the apartment window.

The curtains were shut, but they opened quickly enough. An incredulous face stared out with fearful eyes. I didn't see if it was a man or a woman.

"Let us in," I shouted. I suppose that if I had reflected on it a little more, I would have realised that it was a request unlikely to be granted. The occupant shut the curtains, with a terror stricken face. In desperation, I head-butted the window. Even in that moment, I saw the reflection of a pale unholy face appear behind me. I turned as the window cracked and flung out my foot in a roundhouse kick. It clipped the thing on its triangular nose just as it pulled itself over the top of the balustrade. But its hand reached out, pale and thin, gripping my foot, as a black ooze spewed out of the face. Keran's hand came from nowhere and in a movement, quick and profound, caught the thin arm of the creature on his leg, snapping it in half. The body tumbled into space. After a second, the hand relaxed its grip and fell to the balcony floor, oozing a black liquid from severed arteries that burned where it touched.

Without waiting, I simply ran forward and threw myself at the window. The crack enlarged into a spider web of running splinters. I was stuck in the glass like a car crash victim, but the window, like the glass surface of an iced-over pond, would not quite give. Blood threw out from lacerations on my arms and head. Shards of glass were embedded in every exposed part of my body. I screamed in pain, panting with exhaustion at the same time and going berserk. I pulled out, gasping and biting my tongue in agony and then ran forward again. This time I crashed through into the curtains, tearing my legs as I fell. Behind me, I heard Keran shouting something unintelligible, words of power I presume, as he defended himself against more of the things. I felt someone hack and poke me with something from behind the curtains. There was shouting everywhere from the room beyond, from Keran's tortured battle cries. I was shouting myself, but I couldn't hear what I was saying. Somehow I rolled forward towards the centre of the room, and as I did, the curtain gave way, falling on me and protecting me from the worst of the blows; blows that I could now see were being delivered by a woman with a mop handle. Behind her, there was a man, holding a baseball bat.

Keran must have taken this opportunity to jump back into the room. I only saw his feet as the curtain was somehow kicked from my face. I saw in a blur several people standing incredulous and terrified. Clearly they wondered why the world had suddenly become a scene from Dante's Inferno. I saw, I think it was in the reflection of a mirror or television set, an army of the things spewing over the balustrade, for some unaccountable reason, perhaps as dogs are confused by water, waiting on the balcony as though they had not discovered where we had gone.

It must have appeared to the occupants of the room that Keran was some half human angel leading less respectable demons into their room on the way to Hell. They stood in horrified silence.

There was a moment in which I managed to stagger to my feet. The disbelieving occupants of the room, about six in number, tough looking individuals but terrified nonetheless, parted their ranks slightly and backed away.

"Let us out," said Keran. I recognised him investing his entire voice with power; a magician's trick, but clearly he was in no condition to operate in the material world, never mind the spiritual. I reinforced as best as I could.

"Just let us walk out. We won't harm you."

There were five men and one woman. They looked like criminals, drug addicts, and they had being doing something highly illegal. Without waiting for an answer, Keran walked forward, hugging me to him. They parted their ranks a little further. It was obvious that they were in a state of profound shock. As he reached the far door, Keran threw a gesture at the things that had been slowly exploring the window and had now begun to enter the room. He said, "I don't know about them, though." He pulled the door shut. The screaming began.

Through the hallway, terrified, we staggered out of the door into a replica of the floor below. At each moment I expected to see the things, but there was nothing. Not even the low hum of despair, or the shifting of wind. There was only silence. We pushed through the fire-door - on our right the lift, on our left the stairs. Without hesitation, Keran pushed through the next fire-door and on to the stair well. Here the silence was as impressive. I felt the metallic taste of fear as a single fly rose up into the air, like an insect ambassador of evil.

When I saw it, I felt any unlikely glimmer of light extinguish. I wondered why I had done what I had done in the last few minutes. I wondered at its possible purpose, impressed with the absurdity of hope that I had somehow maintained despite everything. Suddenly, I knew it was over.

"I want to die." I said to Keran. "I'm in terrible pain and I'm exhausted. It's over for me. Snap my neck, please." I was begging. I didn't want to live. Life had become a burning, intolerable agony.

Keran looked at me with a monumental sympathy, as close an emotion to love as it was possible for another human being to give without loving. "I would do it," he said carefully. "In fact, I would kill myself too, if it wasn't a useless act." I saw tears form in his blue, blue eyes. When he spoke it was so low I hardly heard. I felt my eyes shut. I felt his arms close around me. I heard him grunt in agony, was aware of him letting go with his useless hand, and felt my body lift as he threw me over his giant shoulders.

As I sank into unconsciousness, I heard his voice faraway in the tunnel of black that spiralled around me.

"Sadly, I know where we are going." he said.

The measured pace of his exhausted steps walked with me into my night.

Chapter 24
Footfalls

THROUGH THE BLINDING GAP of intense light, through and into a landscape of burning ice-cold white, I leapt.

My feet struck the ground and were swallowed to the ankle in a covering of crisp snow. My body fell forward slightly, and my face pressed close to the ground. Here my breath panted out before me in a fine mist that did not disturb the snow. With care, I slowly raised my head to where the footprints could be seen, stretching out into the limitless south. The pale, distant mountains, to which, like a long necklace, these steps seemed to be attached, hung like a canvas. The stillness was embedded in the brisk air; all around there was a feeling of vacuum, of sobriety, of cool emptiness.

I turned around and looked at the garden. Before me, the exit, with its twin giant oaks, rose up like the gates of a giant sepulchre. It seemed as though the space between the trees was enchanted, almost as though it might be impossible to return; an invisible barrier would prevent access. It occurred to me that in jumping out I had felt something like a sharp snapping in me somewhere, an indefinable breaking of links.

I gazed for the last time inside the garden to where the further wall of the visible inside hedge hid the secrets within. Then I resigned it to the past. I looked instead to either side of the exit where the hedgerows spread until they disappeared in dwindling perspectives. The hedgerows were unnaturally high, and close to me their lofty tops disappeared beyond my range of vision.

I felt nothing but a deep fear. The maze that I had left seemed to be a lunatic construct; I could hardly visualise the person who would have made it. It no longer seemed like a safe haven; only something to escape from.

I turned my back with a shudder and began to move off. There was only one possible direction. Like the trackless waste of an empty uncharted desert, the only hope lay in following the steps of others. These steps might have been made in madness. They might lead nowhere, or to a lonely death and bleaching, brittle bones in a valley indistinguishable from a thousand like valleys, but they constituted a direction. I followed them, driven by synchronicity, by coincidence, by serendipity and by the cold that now seeped from the external environment through my skin to the internal environment of my body.

For a timeless period I kept on, never wavering from the footprints; at times it became a children's game, walking beside them, walking around them, jumping over them, jumping in them, walking in them, walking out of them. The game became a chore, the chore became a burden. I walked on. At times my eyes never left the footprints, as though I was afraid that they might suddenly disappear and I would be left in a world white and cold where even my hands and my feet would become white and would disappear into the landscape; I would become the landscape. At other times I allowed my vision to rise and trace the steps ahead where the pale mountains seemed never to come closer. My eyes were painful with a dull ache. I wondered whether there would come a time when I could no longer see. I wondered whether, blinded, I would wake in a world not dark, but eternally white, a burning light of ages, subsuming my existence with its immaculate clarity.

On a sudden, a light wind picked up, an almost imperceptible breeze that sent the lighter snow dancing in clouds across the plain. It felt as though something had changed. The change was only small, but any change was a momentous event in the monotony of this existence. I became aware then that what I had taken to be a level plain was in fact a gradual incline - a low, gentle, undulating slope, going ever upwards.

I stopped, looked ahead, to where the footprints struck on into the distance. Then, for the first time, I looked over my shoulder. Some instinct made me look up to the sky above: Grey-white and cloudless. There was nothing to see. I allowed my vision to spiral all around. I craned my neck, feeling the incipient madness of nothingness. Then I saw it - in that entire world of stillness, the only movement.

A black dot, wheeling high, high above in the endless grey white sky. I knew instantly that I watched the raven from the garden. It dipped and wheeled above like a sentinel. I knew instinctively that it would follow me like a dark watcher for purposes of its own, until I dropped to the ground. I recalled again its stone eye - inanimate, unflinching - dead like the eye of Medusa, and I shuddered deep inside. I turned, but now my walking was haunted by this new menace; by a pitiless vision of doom. I felt the chill seep deeper into my being.

Walking; nothing but walking and cold, my eyes unwavering on the footprints before, and then, I don't know why it hadn't occurred to me before, I turned and I saw far away the garden like a single oxidised coin on a white tablecloth. For the first time I saw it in its entirety.

The garden at the centre, a single unblinking eye, the maze stretching around like an uncoiling serpent. I was made aware that this garden was the only feature of a featureless landscape, this tiny oasis of life. It was therefore an impossibility. More than this I realised, with an impact that nearly brought me to my knees, that my maze was shaped in an all too familiar fashion: The figure of a man holding in two hands a smaller effigy. The effigy itself is holding a serpent eating its tail. Inside, a Tau, the Egyptian symbol of resurrection; a swastika symbolic of the tremendous forces of nature; interlaced triangles, the seal of Solomon, the star of David. And even with the snow draping each far distant bush and tree like a shroud I could see the sign of Aum. The sign that completed the spiritual amulet locked in my own meditation and echoed by the material amulet I had worn for so long: The final proof, if any were required, that the garden had never been mine, and that it had long been a device for my own ensnarement.

For how long had I laboured to construct a familiar and friendly haven for my soul, lacking the knowledge that I was constructing my own prison? For how long had I developed my infantile occult powers under the concealed tutelage of darker adepts, adepts who must have watched and laughed and schemed as I, like an infant child, thought the world was made for me alone?

Down on my knees in the biting cold, I heard a scream ring out over the snowscape. It pierced the air in anguish and terror, evoking pity from the ice itself. It was my voice, my scream, carrying with it every hopeless quest, every vanquished human word. The silence became deep, intense and heightened, as if it had been given a shock. The air was charged. It was as if my scream had vibrated through the ice of the air and that at any moment the entire world would crack; as if I was the author of Ariel storms. The world would become as fragile as single sliver of ice, and my agonised voice would shatter it with the violence of a trained singer.

And then, as I raised my eyes, I heard the answer across the intervening distances. The scream echoed through the vastness of the ice world. It was winging back in the charged air but it had taken on a new tone, a tone of vehemence and menace. At one and the same moment, a tiny figure leapt from the very exit I had left. It was a thing, in human form maybe, the distance was too great to tell and, winging above it, in a great wheeling circle, was the tiny black dot of the raven, answering with a hideous caw. The thing itself ran now, leaving the garden behind. Led by the voice of the raven like some blind, insensate wolf spirit, it followed the only trail it could: the footprints to the mountains.

I turned and at first began to run; but my legs were like numb weights, dragged down into the ground. I felt as though I waded through the snow. Soon, I was simply raising one foot after another, inspired by deep, deep fear alone, not by courage or conviction.

After a time, I could only hear noises, the slap of my feet against the crisp snow; my eyes were blind in a white, white darkness. As I raised my head to turn I saw nothing; only a figure running, following me many miles away. When I looked ahead, I saw nothing, and then I realised that the footsteps were gone.

It was not that I had lost them, there was nothing to lose. They had never been there, because they had always been my own running steps, fleeing from insanity and pain.

Chapter 25
Stairway

FOOTSTEPS, pacing upwards, weary yet indefatigable. At first I thought that they were mine, and that the world was snow. Then my sense of sight began to return. I saw blinding white, greyness, but, as my eyes opened fully, I also saw signs for fire escapes in green and white. Fluorescent lights appeared above my head, and the dark domino shape of outside windows gave out on to the darkness of night. I saw the backs of Keran's heels as he mounted the steps, labouring at each slow lift of the foot. I heard the pad of his soles on the concrete.

"Keran," I tapped his back. He kept on for a few seconds, grunting with the strain, and then suddenly he lurched forward as though my voice had acted like a bullet on the brain of a dinosaur. We collapsed together in a heap at the top of floor fourteen. There we lay, side by side, half on the steps, half on the landing. Eventually, we both struggled to a sitting posture. Keran stared down the steps blankly, but I kept my glance hovering between the steps and the outside windows.

"How long have we got?" I said in a whisper.

At first, Keran didn't speak, and then he shook his head. "I've heard nothing in the last few minutes. I don't know if that's a good sign." His breathing was heavy, his face ashen.

"I can walk, I think."

"Good," he replied after a space. "I need a moment or two."

My body hurt everywhere. I noticed an erratic trail of blood drops on the stairs. It was not arterial blood, and as far as I could tell, nothing important was broken. I could go on.

We waited, and then, surprisingly, Keran spoke in a soft voice, as though he talked to himself: "I've always known there was a spirit; technically a *manas*. We die and we live on. I've always known it. I didn't need to be taught by my uncle. What I did learn from him was what happens to it, and that was very interesting."

"Are you talking about the life-cycle of a butterfly?"

He smiled softly. "It's all I had for immediate analogy, and in a way it's as simple as that."

"We go on, then, after death? I've always wanted to think so."

"I used to want that, too," He grimaced, and after a time went on. "There is a post-mortem period in which the soul continues. You see, this is all illusion, the soul is the only thing that really exists."

"The Gnostic doctrine?"

"Not quite. This is more esoteric. There are aspects to the soul. For example, the bhuddi aspect is impersonal, closer aligned to what some people call God but which I term the absolute. The lower *manas* is our spirit which forms and develops and draws from the higher buddhi. When we die we regain our knowledge of the Buddhi State which recollects previous incarnations. The whole panorama stretches out before us like a wonderful tapestry reaching to the infinite

"And our future lives doubtless going on in the other direction?"

"I don't know," said Keran. "I was denied this knowledge by something…"

"What?"

"Whatever it is, I see it in the creatures that we face now. I see it at night in the eyes of an old woman. Green eyes that look into the soul and weigh and calculate, balance order and then, with cynical and clinical precision, cut and shape the soul. I've seen it. I've seen it and it was…" He clutched his hands to his face.

I put my arm around his huge shoulder, shuddering in myself. I had seen those eyes before, and I remembered again the broken witless giant in my office so many months before, in his battered trilby and plastic shoes.

"Do you know what happens after death?" Keran said finally.

"I believe in reincarnation."

"Yes, we do reincarnate. Our bodies now are the development of a selection of the previous soul. Well, not so much a selection, it's an immutable, unchangeable law. Your actions determine where you go."

"That's a buddhasistic concept. They believe that every action conditions the present moment. If you are bad, you get tangled up in past actions, if good, then your life simplifies."

"It's the same principle. It's the karmic law. You can't stop it. Everything you do shapes your present. You become what your actions lead you to. Karma is the judgement of the universe and it cannot be denied."

"So, we die and are reborn and it goes on, depending on what we do now." I thought of an innocent girl in a caravan park.

"Yes," said Keran, rising slowly to his feet. "But what is forgotten or ignored is that there is a post-mortem state." He turned to me and fixed me with his eyes. "Do you know what happens there?"

A fly drifted up, buzzing loudly in the stairwell, its sluggish body fat with blood. Keran snatched it with a look of disgust and then he opened his blood stained palm. "There is a period that feels like infinity. During it you get your desserts."

"What?" I felt I was losing him. He towered above me, filling the stairwell with his huge presence.

"When you die, it's like a waiting room. You don't just pop into the next body with a cheery goodbye to the last. You wait, and while you wait the entire panorama of your previous life is played out like an infinite picture show. It goes on and on and every action you took is played, and every consequence of that action is shown. You hit Billy in infant school and he hurt; well, now you hurt. You told lies about Anne when you were six and she cried; well, now you cry. You tortured and you teased, you hit and you insulted, you cheated and you lied. It's all there, and you become the tortured, the teased, the cheated. You get it all. And it hurts. God, it hurts so much. You cannot believe how much suffering stems from a single, ill-thought action"

Tears were falling from his eyes. His face was ashen with horror. He was shouting in terror as the past rushed in like a giant avalanche.

"The Christians made that one mistake," he screamed out in a voice bordering on incoherent. "They did not look beyond it, but they knew it for what it was." He turned again to me with eyes like wells of hopeless darkness. "It is the Death Tableau and they called it Hell."

Incredibly, he screamed: A tortured, agonised cry, like some primal beast in the process of being torn apart.

It impacted irrevocably on me then that this was no theoretical treatise. That Keran had been the unwilling recipient of this Death Tableau. It was part of his experience.

His screaming echoed and re-echoed through the stairwell. It transfixed me. And then his hand rose up, and I thought my time had come. I stared at a demon from Hell and I was going to die. I thought his hand was going to rip my head from my body. I shut my eyes and felt in a second as though my heart had been grasped by something made of ice; as though a hand had gone through my skin like a butter knife. I opened my eyes as a loud slap rang through the stairwell. I looked as Keran's hand still above my head clutched the neck of a decapitated body. I looked away to see a vapid head bouncing like a misshapen ball down the steps and then back to see Keran shake the thing in disgust and cast it from him like a rag, black blood boiling and hissing; burning his great hands. He pulled me to my feet. "Run if you can," he whispered.

One glance was enough. The stairwell was a cauldron of unwholesome half-life, and it crept like a simmering broth towards us. On our right, the dark window seemed about to implode with the pressure of innumerable white palms. Blank eyes stared from white faces. I staggered past them, feeling my own silent scream build inside my head.

Keran pulled me along. The stairs were like a mad circus cakewalk. I circled around and around, feet battering off the steps, missing them, stumbling, being dragged. And then, suddenly, we reached the top. Above us a ceiling, beside us a fire-door. Keran stumbled against it. Looked inside, withdrew.

"Apartments," he said. "The final two. There's a skylight. I can lift you to it, but I don't think you can lift me."

I leaned against the wall. "What can I do on the roof alone?"

"In that case, we have no alternative." He turned and I watched, incredulous, as he took the large fire-door in his two great hands. He seemed to be praying. I watched his lips move and his hands strengthen their grip. There was a moment of tension, and then his shoulder bunched, and the arms of his sleeved ripped. With a wrenching shriek the door gave on its hinges. With a wild cry, Keran spun around and heaved the door with one mighty throw. It flew over my head and crashed through the window beyond, sticking for a second in the vacuum of space, before it tottered over into the dark abyss of night. In that second the vacuum, created by the broken window, sucked me forward, and I was pulled out towards the window to watch the door sweep downwards like some moving entrance to another dimension. I felt Keran grab me from behind as I lurched over the partition. "Sorry," he said through gritted teeth. "I don't have many shots left."

I hardly listened. I was watching the ground far, far away and the door, now tiny, still falling. And then my eyes were drawn closer to the things only a few floors below. They crept on impossible hands like vampires towards me. I looked upwards at the few metres to the roof.

I turned to Keran. "What is the point? I can't do it, Keran. I love you. I'd do anything for you, but I can't do this. I've nothing left." He shrugged and looked around at the concrete façade. The crenellations were there, uniform to those on the lower floors. "I don't know if I can either, but it has to be worth a try. Quick." He pulled my arm, and then I realised what he had in mind. We rushed back through the torn door frame and without even waiting he pulled me to his shoulders like a child. In a matter of instants I was balancing on his shoulders. My head was level with the skylight and without hesitation I pushed on it. "It's stuck," I shouted, and below me I felt Keran's body shake. It took me another second to realise why.

He was laughing. I knew in myself why he found it funny. I drew back my shoulder and began to thump upwards with it; each jarring, concussive blow wreaked agony through my body; but it gave. Suddenly, the skylight fell off my upstretched arms. "I've done it, Keran, I've done it!" I pulled myself up, up and through and then I rolled out on to the roof. I lay on my back, panting out cold breath into a night sky jewelled like the coat of a pearly king. The stars were everywhere, lighting the coat of night. I could have laughed with joy.

It was a short-lived joy. There was a sudden shout below, half muffled in pain. I dragged myself to the open skylight frame. Beneath me, Keran was surrounded. At his feet, a broken body lay twitching unnaturally, black blood hissing in the floor where it seeped from the carcass. Keran put his hand in his pocket, made some simple vocal comment and then suddenly flung a circle of salt around him in an arc. The creatures leapt back, as though stung. Keran threw himself towards the fire-door. I saw him disappear from view, pale white arms clutching for his body, and in the silence the sound of droning flies and flapping unnatural feet lifted upwards from the echoing stairwells.

I rolled over on to my back and whimpered, the screaming in my head seemingly about to flower into life.

I was weeping uncontrollably, too afraid to move, transfixed to the ceiling of the world, the stars witness to the end of hope, as they must have been since people hoped. I felt my hands clench and unclench with despair. And then I had to pull myself up. My numbed body fought against the pain and the gusting wind that blew over the surface of the tower block. I rose up somehow; around me the wind seemed to take a tangible form, as though it were the author of shadows. The whole of the city was sprayed around like an incredible firework display frozen in ice. My eyes swept around circling the extremities of the building. Where would they come from first? Which side would see the shadow forms emerge to blot out the lights? Or would they leave when they had Keran? I choked back the sobs. I debated wildly whether I should throw myself down the skylight, die with him. Even as I did, I saw the shadow. In the darkness, my quick observation had passed it over, but now I could see with a terrible clarity, almost like a black hole in space, a standing figure on the north east corner of the roof, some thirty metres from me. I backed away towards the opposite corner, holding my bleeding hands to my mouth. I turned in desperation, and there before me I saw the white of a clutching hand crawl over the roof like a giant spider. Its partner followed; a blood stained hand. I heard a scream, terrifying in its smallness, fighting with the rising wind. I looked back in desperation. The shadow had begun walking towards me. I backed away. Looked to the hands. They were clutching the roof. The screaming had stopped.

And then I ran; not from the shadow, but towards the hands. I threw myself along the ground and held just as they gave way.

"Keran. My God. Keran." Slowly, I began to slip, my hands gripping his left hand. The right hand made a wild grab, and then I was pulled to the edge. Below, I saw the wheeling panorama of the ground fifteen floors down and there, immediately below me, like some ludicrous, topsy turvy, circus balancing-troupe, a virtual posse of the things, clutching below at Keran and spilling out of the window and all around the levels of the building. Keran's eyes stared at mine with a look of anguish, pain beyond the physical. His great frame like some church architecture gone astray, his mouth grim-set, nostrils flaring like a fixed gargoyle.

"Sorry," he whispered, through clenched teeth. And I knew he was dead. The arms began to slip. He was falling. I heard a scream miles away, and I knew it was me. I was shrieking incredible things, as though my head had burst open with too many personalities and they had to come out. And then I did something inconceivable.

My wasted arms stretched over the precipice and, like some vast juggernaut, my frail, wounded body seemed to anchor itself to the roof. I pulled with a force gifted to me from some unthinkable source. Keran's body rose in the air. It was as though all his latent energy and massiveness had crept into my body, as though he, at the height of his vast powers, had simply entered my frame. I lifted him. As I did, his legs shook away the nearest two things. I watched them, taken like paper cards out into the night. Their vapid bodies struck others as they fell and sent a multitude to a rag doll death below. Keran fell over me. It was only a second of relief. My arms could not move and we were both in shock, deeply ill and doubtless dying even as we moved, but move we did. I looked up. Keran's gaze was drawn with mine to the shadow walking towards us. I knew that now it was over. I had nothing. It was the end. I looked at Keran, a tiny flicker of hope extinguished by his ashen, exhausted visage. Even he was simply waiting.

In the starlight, the shadow became less than a shadow.

Keran smiled through the pain.

"Uncle Rodin," he said.

"Hello, Keran. I've been expecting you," replied the magician. He smiled cheerily.

Chapter 26
The Final Conflict

"WHY DIDN'T YOU help earlier?" I said bitterly.

Rodin didn't even look at me. "Do you think either of you would have made it if I had?" He felt my doubt. "Think, woman, would you have got this far if you had even a grain of belief in outside help?" He was already dragging Keran back from the roof. I managed to crawl from the side and far enough away to lean on the skylight window. I saw a white head beginning to appear. Rodin looked at it with curiosity, sent his arm flashing forward, palm outstretched. As though the creature had been physically struck, it flew back into the abyss. Rodin paced forward. "Anyway," he continued "I have been helping. I haven't been idle." He drew some salt from his pocket and I saw him reforming a salt line at the point where Keran had climbed up. I looked and as far as I could see in the dim light this line extended. Doubtless it contained the whole perimeter of the roof.

He seemed satisfied with his work and stood back. Then he took two vials from his pocket. "Drink this," he said, "It will help." Keran and I drank from each of the bottles. It was a sweet heavy liquid and I felt some energy course through my veins. Rodin pulled his cape off and wrapped it round me, all the time checking for damage, his expert hands pulling and pressing. I had dislocated something in my shoulder. He pulled it, and there was a sharp feeling of pain. "That's better," he said and he knelt beside Keran, massaging and working his aching limbs. "We don't have long," he said, putting a thick blanket around Keran.

"They may bring the whole building down. I don't know. I have a feeling we may be too trivial for amateur dramatics. They may not even know we are here. They may have simply left us to their simple conjurations - these awkward looking manifestations that you've already encountered."

Keran nodded. "You saw Jarvis?"

"Rodin shook his head. "I sensed him and I don't think he sensed me. The monocled lady was here as well if you didn't know. I smelt her." Rodin smiled. "I have been waiting here for a week."

"A week?" I blurted it out.

"I saw it; precognition" said Rodin simply, and when I looked incredulous he patted my shoulder. "It's a talent," he said. "Not always entirely accurate. At one time I thought I was the most talented adept in the world. I met Keran and thought he was to succeed me…"

"And then we met our new friends." said Keran.

"Jarvis?" I said, recalling the little man and his nonchalant departure.

"We think Jarvis is the leader," said Rodin "but in the face of the little evidence, we have we can only surmise."

"They've taken a girl." said Keran suddenly. I felt my stomach contract.

"Young?" said Rodin.

Keran nodded. "I have an interest." The words ran through me like the rising ice winds.

Rodin grimaced. "The only interest you have, Keran, is in remaining alive a little longer."

"We must find her," he said.

Rodin laughed. "Is it a joke, Keran?" He pointed around him. "I've had a week to prepare this. Even with that I may be a simple toy, an amusing little by-play for them. Do you rate our chances?"

"I believe in you." replied Keran.

"Yes," said Rodin. "And I believed in you, and look at you now."

I looked at Keran. If I looked even remotely like him, I was closer to death than I imagined.

He grinned. "I've felt better." His teeth flashed in the darkness.

"What will they do to the girl?" I only asked hoping that it was something awful and final.

Rodin sat on his haunches and looked at Keran intently. "Does she know about the Death Tableau?" He indicated me with a short precise nod.

"I started to explain, but things got a bit hectic." said Keran

"It's the karmic law, if I understand rightly" I replied. I was getting a little sick of being the only one who knew nothing.

"That's exactly what it's not," said Rodin.

Keran nodded. "You know."

"I've guessed," replied Rodin. "Perhaps you should tell."

Keran nodded. "I remembered." he said.

At that moment, the wind rushed up like a beast and drove into us. Rodin looked around, faintly disturbed. Keran frowned in pain. All around we watched as the salt began to drift from its place. Lights began to go out over the city in ones and twos. I felt a shuddering fear deep in my bowels. Rodin sighed. "Its beginning, I'm afraid. The wind isn't natural, and there seems to be a big shift of energy forces. Sadly, I don't think they've forgotten about us. I had hoped that we were nothing to them, but like gadflies we must have stung a little." Even as he spoke, pale hands began to clutch at the sides of the roof. Grotesque white faces like rows of misshapen dolls came leering above the roof perimeter. Slowly, with morbid intensity like the final rising of the dead, the things - "conjurations", Rodin had called them - began to form on the edge of the roof on all sides. They crept into postures like some shadow dance troupe in a peculiar midnight show.

Rodin rose to his feet and then, in a graceful movement leapt to his hands, and then into the warrior pose.

"What did you remember?" he said.

"I remembered a pair of green eyes," said Keran.

"And whose eyes were they?" said Rodin.

"They were the eyes of a woman; an old, old woman."

Rodin nodded.

"She was a member of the sect?"

"The sect of the Death Tableau," said Rodin.

"Yes." said Keran. He too rose to his feet, staggering at first, but somehow managing to move into the warrior's pose. I lay watching, my heart beating loudly.

"I saw her too, twice. The first time was at your house, Rodin, and the second time was in a place I had made for myself." Painfully, I got to my haunches. "Who is she?"

"She is, or was, a member of the sect," Said Keran grimly. "She is powerful, but then they all are. I have a particular interest in her because she took an interest in me."

"What do you mean?"

The things began to unite in a slow ritualistic dance. Even at my low level of appreciation, I could see that they were trying to find a weakness in the barrier that Rodin had spent the week setting up.

"You remember the amulet?"

"How could I forget?" I thought again of my dream garden, of Bower's exploded body and Keran when I had first met him sporting a silver amulet.

"They wear the amulet and it is not simply an identifying sign. It is a symbol of their purpose."

"What is their purpose?"

"Remember I said that the human journey was like the life cycle of a butterfly."

"Yes." I rose to my feet, and with agony searing through my body, dropped to the warrior's pose.

"The butterfly has many enemies, not least of which are birds. The image that never fails to move me, though, is the sight of a beautiful butterfly trapped in a web." Keran's voice trembled as though the now violent wind sieved through his body.

"The spider is the true enemy, because it opposes something intrinsically beautiful with something intrinsically ugly, something which takes flight with something that lurks in stillness."

The things were beginning to penetrate Rodin's invisible shield; in ones and twos they made increasing gaps. As they did, their long arms stretched and unfurled. Slowly, those who had entered began to crouch low like giant predatory insects.

"The members of this sect are simply that: Spiders."

Rodin broke in. "They are adepts in the occult and they have occult powers equal to Keran and myself."

"That's why the spiritualist, Pontefract, wouldn't go near me when she saw the amulet." I said.

"She must have known that even its presence would act like a lure to the sect." said Rodin. "And a highly developed spiritualist would be aware of their tangible force. I suspect, though, that she did not know the true horror."

The creatures were all through the perimeter. They had waited and now, as a single unit, they moved slowly forward, feeling their way, seemingly unaffected by the growing wind.

"Which is?" I said.

"You recall that the justice of karma is objective and absolute. If you perform good actions they are balanced out, your Death Tableau is played out like a motion picture and you are reborn at a higher level to meet new challenges and finally achieve Nirvana, the freedom of the soul from all desire."

"Heaven?"

"That's the Christian conception of a much older knowledge," said Rodin.

"Imagine if you like," said Keran, "Ten thousand years of work and labour. The individual striving of a few powerful adepts working out their sorcery on all the levels of human experience. Imagine them dying, being reborn, stepping upwards in their journey through endless reincarnations. At then end of each life facing the Death Tableau and always feeling this perpetual chain of cause and effect, of pain and punishment. Waiting for the absolute justice of the universal law of karma. Then imagine if one discovered a simple trick."

The things mobbed around us, but somehow held back, blinded by Rodin's aura.

"And the trick?" I said.

"Simple," replied Rodin. "You wait until you are about to die and you take another soul with you."

"What?"

"You find an innocent person, a good person with a life untainted by any particular evil actions."

"Difficult?"

"Not difficult if you have amalgamated the intelligence and thaumaturgy of others equally skilled and equally powerful. Not if you have perfected black arts over a series of life times and with a variety of occult experiences. Not if you have been practising every form of wicked desire that humans delight in. Not if your time on earth has been spent doing exactly as you please." I could see Rodin's face from the corner of my eyes, impassive and controlled. He continued after a space. "Anybody with a well formed moral sense will do. Or anyone young enough to have time to change. Anyone like this young girl, or like my nephew, like poor Keran, whose idealism was unique and faultless."

The creatures had begun to claw at the space between us as though they had found an immaterial net, their black eyes staring at us with an abstract intent, their pale faces without expression.

A voice came out of the night and the wind. It was Keran's, but it sounded as though it came from a well of despair in a hole at the bottom of the universe.

"They took me," he said. "It was my curiosity that led me to them. I thought I found them but they took me. It was after the great work. I had to know why I had been stopped, and who had stopped me. I finally found them, and they took me. It was a room, somewhere near the sea; I heard the sea, and I saw it from a bay window. She was resting in reclining couch. I think she was over a hundred years old. She lay there like some grotesque malformed spider in a black dress draped in pearl jewellery, her amulet, I remember it around her neck shining like a hypnotist's pendulum before my eyes. I was made to kneel before her. Then she drew me to her and kissed me. I could not move, and like a vampire she began to suck my spirit from my enslaved body. I was locked to her eyes. Green, green eyes that I can never forget. She was dying, expiring before me and she was gripping me and making me stare into her eyes. Believe me. I saw her soul, a tortured, depraved, writhing thing that should have been rent apart and annihilated by the justice of karmic law, but my soul was there too, drawn from my body. In that single moment I lived a thousand years. I was between her and the absolute, the blasting light of infinite justice searing through me and, can you possibly understand? Shielding her. Shielding her iniquity from eternal law. I was the one who was judged, condemned and punished. She slid through beyond like a thief in the night, as she passed through the portals of death to her next incarnation."

The wind for a moment abated. The creatures themselves seemed stilled. In the silence I heard Keran softly speak.

"While she reincarnated in some other body, innocent and new, I was condemned to pay the penalty for every evil she committed. The Death Tableau is subjective, but if you imagine a thousand years of torment, you will get the sense of it."

I saw it then, the vacant eyes of the shambling giant in my office, the eyes of a man who had been wrongfully imprisoned for a thousand years, who had suffered the torment of the agonies of fellow innocents and paid the penalty for the crimes of another, watched and felt the humiliations, the pain, the desperation and the terror. Lived with madness and eternal despair. It was as though a man had walked through a door and found himself in the wrong room with no key; who listened to the sound of his own voice explaining to the inquisitors that it was all a simple error. And his listeners were deaf.

I felt the tears well up in my eyes. Keran continued:

"As she died, she spat my mangled soul back into my body. Perhaps it gave the others amusement to watch my humiliation. It is the sort of simple vice that a thousand years of absolute power confers on those who have it. Doubtless from time to time it relieves their boredom. The rest you know. I was cast out, wandered God knows where until Kennedy found me and now, if I wasn't about to die, I would try to find her for that one kind action alone."

"And you must." It was Rodin. The things were less than a metre from us. The wind was whipping up again. The temperature dropped like a heavy stone as they brought their own world of ice to us. All around, the lights of Manchester were blacking out as some terrific internal disruptions shuddered through the ether.

"You must understand, Keran, that this was all prepared for you and your friend. I saw it and I know the outcome. It is quite simple. You drop down the skylight. I drew them up here deliberately and I can keep them occupied."

"I can't desert you."

"It is not desertion, my boy. You know as well as I that this life is only a waiting room for the next. I'm sending you on ahead." He turned and flashed a smile, "Nice meeting you again, Professor Peralis. See you next time around."

Keran hesitated for a fraction, and then, without a backward glance, he nodded to me and we leapt for the skylight. As we did, the sky exploded into a violent storm. I was thankful that the sound of the beating rain masked other less pleasant sounds.

Chapter 27
The Bubble Gum Card

JAMIE'S BODY lay on the forecourt of the tower block, pulped by the fall. Whether he had been dragged, or simply fought his way forward through unseen enemies to pitch through the open window, I would never know.

Above us, in the storm driven night, the roof was ablaze with charges of unbelievable energy, as though the whole force of a storm had focused on this single point. Even as we stumbled across the wastelands, I could see crowds of youths begin to gather, drawn by these powerful forces like iron filings to a magnet. We were both weary beyond fear, but Rodin's elixir had kicked us back into the capability of movement.

Some distance from the tower block, but still within sight, we found a burnt out Vauxhall Cavalier. Like two unexpectedly vital crash victims mistakenly replaced in the wrong accident, we crept into the front seat. We wrapped the blankets around ourselves, huddling together for warmth.

For a long while, unable to sleep, we watched the admixture of dawn rise up behind the funereal tower block and the chaotic blazes of energy course along the roof. The storm continued with violence until the smouldering sun cast the ground before us into a long tombstone-like shadow; the courses of bright light electrically lighting the sky were at first humbled, then finally vanquished by the light of the sun. The storm began to abate. As it did the sunlight broke through. The final last flickerings died on the roof.

Before us, a huge crowd had gathered, and the police and fire brigade, bringing their noise and colour, occupied the portico of the building. Parts of the roof were now alight with a low smouldering fire.

When the sun appeared like a God between the tower block

facing us and the one in the far distance, I heard Keran sigh deeply. There was no need for him to say anything; I had felt it too. Rodin had just been killed. His life force was seeping out like the sun's rays into the void. Like the final blow from the fist of the boxer, Rodin's death sent me reeling into limbo of unconsciousness. I fell asleep unsure whether I would ever wake up.

I did wake, unsure if I had slept for hours or days.

Keran had gone, leaving me a note. He felt he had a chance to save Kennedy. He said he loved her; it was not something simply sexual. He knew where she was being taken; he had remembered it all. He left me without saying goodbye, because he did not want me to follow.

I had retained the book dealer's list of coven members. At the time, there was one who had interested me in particular.

The lawyer who answered the door to his urban palace lived alone. My brief explanation of his indiscretions might have resulted in my immediate demise. My assurance that his colleagues would be opening the incriminating photographs on my death ensured his immediate cooperation. Although he was unable to recognise me, I had already recognised him in the photographs retained by the Aberdonian book dealer. He had enjoyed the rape of his victim, who was long dead, by his hand. He probably didn't remember her name. I did. It was my daughter, Kirsty. This act of synchronicity may well have been a triumph for the members of the Death Tableau. It was a testament to their manipulative brutality that I was beyond caring.

I didn't kill him. The prison justice of Strangeways would doubtless do that for me after the letter arrived.

I left instead in his expensive car, clothed in his mistress's dress and carrying most of his money.

I found my way somehow to a hospital where I paid a passing nurse a lot of money to take me to her house and tend to my wounds. I told her some glib lie about a husband who beat me. She believed my story and I kept her quiet with money. Doing things in secret had now become a habit, but the deep-seated fear had left, with Keran. I suppose that because I loved him so much life ceased to have any meaning or reason when he left.

Fear is something you have when you have something to lose.

I recovered enough to move in a matter of weeks. Then I left her house and went back to the office. I didn't care if they still watched it. I would be fleeing in any case, and if I found one of them I intended to use it to my advantage. I had learned a lot. I felt there might be some hope of using their own power against them, and in that way somehow finding Keran again. It was my only reason to live.

When I came to the office, there seemed to be nothing amiss. I pushed open the door and left the huge pile of mail in the hall. A quick search of the rooms revealed that nothing had been touched. The office was empty, and carried the silence of long disuse. The rooms were covered in dust; there were no footprints to say that anyone had been in or out. I recalled Rodin's speculation that we were too trivial to be of any interest to the sect of the Death Tableau. I realised that in all probability Rodin was important enough to be an irritant to them. His superior knowledge of magic had, at the last, occasioned an hour or two of frustration to their plans. Perhaps I, on the other hand, was a meaningless pawn who doubtless could be dealt with and exterminated at their leisure.

I picked up the mail from the hall and began to sift through. Amidst the bills there were letters from institutions requesting assistance, offering posts, asking for evaluations. It was another person's life. I returned to my back room and switched on the answer phone. There were several messages. As I heard the first voice, I was forced to switch off the machine. It was Jamie, weeping, and stumbling out some kind of tale that for the moment I could not face.

For a few moments, I stared around the office trying to recall my previous life. I saw faces, innumerable faces. Kennedy, the flower fairy who I now detested as a robber, Bower the desperate hunted man. I knew him now better than anyone else. I had in part lived his life and suffered. I saw my lost baby, Kirsty, and my husband, Conrad, thankfully both out of their misery. Pontefract was there in her beautiful white dress, her face alight with fearful understanding, Conal the priest, the hitch-hiker, who had probably died in the mountains in Scotland, and Jamie Macdonald. Now, with Jamie's voice ringing in my ears I could picture his handsome Scottish face wreathed in genial smiles. Why did we have to come to this? Innocents suffering for the crimes of others.

I stood up. It was time to go, but I had to hear Jamie's voice for the last time. I replayed the tape from the start. As I listened, I looked through my two-way mirror at the Hepplewhite chair, the little table, the familiar office surroundings. It was incredible, but even as I sat in a world composed of shadows, people passed the window at the front, unconsciously going about their daily business as if the world was an ordinary sort of place.

Jamie was incoherent in the first section of the answering machine tape, and I knew then that this must have been him alone, wondering where I had gone; faithfully researching, faithfully attempting to extricate me from a hole that grew more and more consuming like sucking quicksand - watching his own world collapse and implode with increasing, numbing terror. I realised then that I had hardly spoken with him when he had discovered me; that I had hardly known of the anguish that he had faced.

The last stage of the tape was a series of calls all by Jamie. Each call revealed a mounting desperation as he discovered more and more of the full horror of my situation and then found himself inexorably carried into the penumbra of evil. He talked of the Death Tableau sect, their powers, unravelling the mystery without fully understanding the implications. He had found sections of the book owned by Bower's grandfather, some texts on the history of the amulet in coded ciphers and *grimoires*.

I was hardly listening. I was reflecting on the nightmare of my recent recuperation, the ministering hands of the frightened nurse as she tried to restore something of my broken health. I recalled the vivid dreams, some of a butterfly caught in the beak of a black raven, others too horrific to remember. All bound by the same rigid strictures like the rehearsed section of a play that an actor must endlessly repeat: the running, the falling and the stumbling as I lurched forwards through blinding snow followed by something too awful to face, something that I knew deep in my frozen heart was the author of the entire snowbound landscape; something that inched closer with each moment.

I made plans to leave immediately. There was nothing to keep me in this unfamiliar tomb. And then I heard Jamie's words clearly. I stopped the tape and replayed it from the later sections. I replayed it again and again.

I found Jamie's final discovery deeply interesting. It was a simple feature that I had overlooked, and it made me realise with a cold certainty why Keran had left me behind.

He had been destined to.

Sects recruit their members by a variety of means. Those who are members of the sect of the Death Tableau reincarnate into the sect. For a number of years they live as you and I in ordinary homes and conventional houses, unconscious of anything unusual in their lives, playing as children play, growing as children grow. And then in the years between nine and seventeen, the age of reason where they become aware of their powers, they are drawn back into the embrace of the cult to which they have belonged for thousands of years.

The eyes are the windows to the soul, and Keran had looked again through a window made unfamiliar only by the architecture around it. He had failed to recognise the difference between love and enslavement.

Kennedy had not been taken by the sect.

She had simply returned.

And I knew now the hunter who stalked me through my dreams.

The manuscript on my desk was now almost complete, my reasons for recording the events obscure even to myself. A few more words to write and I was ready to leave the building. I would never return.

In the two-way mirror, I saw the door to my office open, and an old man entered. I walked out to face him. He greeted me with a happy smile. "Professor Peralis? It is, isn't it? You've been closed for months. I've popped back, but you've not been in."

"I'm closing down." I replied.

"You don't recognise me, do you?"

I shook my head, and he stared back with a bewildered, embarrassed smile.

"The bubble gum man. You remember the cards?"

"Oh yes. I remember." His face wreathed in a happy smile.

"I came back to thank you again, you were so nice to me, and look; I found I had a spare card at the bottom of the box, forgotten. I brought it for you. It's no good to me but you might be able to use it. Thanks for everything, Professor Peralis."

I shut the door behind us both. On the streets of Manchester I watched him limp away. In my hand I saw he had placed a golden card. It was Osiris, the many-eyed Judge of the dead and potentate of the kingdom of ghosts.

An old friend.

THE END